# The M

ANTHONY POWELL was born in London in 1905. Son of a soldier, he comes from a family of mostly soldiers or sailors which moved from Wales about a hundred and fifty years ago. He was educated at Eton and Balliol College, Oxford, of which he is now an Honorary Fellow.

From 1926 he worked for about nine years at Duckworths, the publishers, then as scriptwriter for Warner Brothers in England. During the Second World War he served in the Welch Regiment and Intelligence Corps, acting as liaison officer with the Polish, Belgian, Czechoslovak, Free French and Luxembourg forces, and was promoted major.

Before and after the war he wrote reviews and literary columns for various newspapers, including the *Daily Telegraph* and the *Spectator*. From 1948–52 he worked on the *Times Literary Supplement*, and was literary editor of *Punch*, 1952–8.

Between 1931 and 1949, Anthony Powell published five novels, a biography, *John Aubrey and His Friends*, and a selection from Aubrey's works. The first volume of his twelve-volume novel, *A Dance to the Music of Time*, was published in 1951, and the concluding volume, *Hearing Secret Harmonies*, appeared in 1975. In 1976 he published the first volume of his memoirs, *To Keep the Ball Rolling*, under the title *Infants of the Spring*.

In 1934 he married Ladv Violet Pakenham, daughter of the fifth Earl of Longford. They have two sons, and live in Somerset.

*Books by Anthony Powell*

*Novels*
Afternoon Men
Venusberg
From a View to a Death
Agents and Patients
What's Become of Waring
Oh How the Wheel Becomes It

*A Dance to the Music of Time*
A Question of Upbringing
A Buyer's Market
The Acceptance World
At Lady Molly's
Casanova's Chinese Restaurant
The Kindly Ones
The Valley of Bones
The Soldier's Art
The Military Philosophers
Books Do Furnish a Room
Temporary Kings
Hearing Secret Harmonies

*To Keep the Ball Rolling (Memoirs)*
Volume I: Infants of the Spring
Volume II: Messengers of Day
Volume III: Faces in My Time
Volume IV: The Strangers All Are Gone

*General*
John Aubrey and His Friends

*Plays*
The Garden God *and* The Rest I'll Whistle

Anthony Powell

# The Military Philosophers

*A Novel*

Published by Fontana Paperbacks
by agreement with Heinemann

FOR GEORGINA

First published by
William Heinemann Ltd 1968
First issued in Fontana Paperbacks 1971
Sixth impression June 1981

This Flamingo edition first published
in 1983 by Fontana Paperbacks,
8 Grafton Street, London W1X 3LA



Printed and bound in Great Britain by
Richard Clay (The Chaucer Press) Ltd,
Bungay, Suffolk

## CHAPTER ONE

Towards morning the teleprinter's bell sounded. A whole night could pass without a summons of that sort, for here, unlike the formations, was no responsibility to wake at four and take dictation—some brief unidentifiable passage of on the whole undistinguished prose—from the secret radio *Spider*, calling and testing in the small hours. Sleep was perfectly attainable when no raid intervened, though recurrent vibration from one or both machines affirmed next door the same restlessness of spirit that agitated the Duty Officer's room, buzzing all the time with desultory currents of feeling bequeathed by an ever changing tenancy. Endemic as ghouls in an Arabian cemetery, harassed aggressive shades lingered for ever in such cells to impose on each successive inmate their preoccupations and anxieties, crowding him from floor and bed, invading and distorting dreams. Once in a way a teleprinter would break down, suddenly ceasing to belch forth its broad paper shaft, the columns instead crumpling to a stop in mid-air like waters of a frozen cataract. Jammed works might at this moment account for the call. More probably the bell signified an item of news that could demand immediate action. I went through to investigate.

Grey untidy typescript capitals registered the information that small detachments of Poles were crossing the Russian frontier into Iran, just a few men at a time, but enough to suggest some sort of evacuation had begun. This was very much our concern. It had been long awaited. My first thought was to ring Colonel Finn at once at his flat, but, reconsidering matters, day nearly come, a copy of the cable would be on his desk when he arrived in a few hours' time.

Nothing effective could be done until consultations had taken place. Besides, working late the night before—past eleven when last seen heavily descending the stairs with the tread of Regulus returning to Carthage—Finn deserved any repose he could get. I returned to bed. The teleprinters continued to clatter out their incantations, sullen and monotonous, yet not without a threat of suddenly uncontrolled frenzy. However, shattered fragments of sleep were no longer to be reconstituted. After a while attempt had to be abandoned, the day faced. On the way to shave I paused in the room of the Section handling incoming signals. For the tour of duty one came under orders, whatever his rank, of their officer in charge for any given period, on this occasion a near-midget, middle-aged and two-pipped, with long arms and short legs attached to a squat frame, who had exacted regulation rights—waived by the easy-going—to assistance in his postal deliveries the evening before. As he had hurried fretfully down the long dark passages, apportioning hot news to swell the in-trays at break of day, he seemed one of the throng from the Goblin Market. Now, opening the door of their room, identification was more precise. The curtain had obviously just risen on the third drama of *The Ring*—Mime at his forge—the wizened lieutenant revealed in his shirtsleeves, crouched over a table, while he scoured away at some object in an absolute fever of energy.

'Good morning.'

There was no concealing a certain peevishness at interruption of the performance at such a crucial juncture, only a matter of seconds before the burst of guttural tenor notes opened the introductory lament:

> 'Labour unending
> Toil without fruit!

The strongest sword
That ever I forged . . .'

However, he discontinued his thankless task for a brief space, though still clutching the polishing cloth in claw-like fingers. It was not, in fact, Siegfried's sword to which he was devoting so much attention (trading with the enemy, when one came to think of it), but that by now almost universally adopted—possibly Moghul—contribution to military tailoring, the Sam Browne belt, doubtless his own, the unbuckled brace of which waited treatment on another table.

'Can I see the cable about Poles leaving the USSR?'

The distribution marked at the foot would provide a forecast of immediate contacts on the subject. Rather grudgingly producing the night's harvest, he held the sheaf of telegrams close to his chest, like the cards of a cautious poker player, so that, as he thumbed them through, no other eye should violate their security. The required copy was at the bottom of the pile. Recipients noted, we had a further word together on the subject of the building's least uninviting washing place, agreeing in principle that no great diversity of choice was available. Shaking his head despairingly, either at the thought of rows of grubby basins or his own incessant frustration as swordsmith, or rather leather worker, Mime returned to the Sam Browne. The door closed on sempiternal burnishings. Outside in the corridor, diffused in clouds by the brooms of the cleaners' dawn patrol and smarting to the eye like pepper, rose the dust of eld. Messengers in shabby blue uniforms, a race churlish almost to a man, were beginning to shuffle about, yawning and snarling at each other. Theoretically, night duty continued until 9 a.m., but the Nibelung allowing fealty to himself and his clan by now sufficiently discharged,

I dressed, and, not sorry to be released once again from this recurrent nocturnal vassalage, went out to find some breakfast. As well as stimulating teleprinter news, there were things to think over that had happened the previous day.

An unfriendly sky brooded over lines of overcrowded buses lumbering up Whitehall. Singapore had fallen five or six weeks before. Because of official apprehension of a lowering effect on public morale, Japanese excesses there had been soft-pedalled, though those in touch with documents of only relatively restricted circulation knew the sort of thing that had been going on. Withdrawal in Burma was about to take shape. In London the blitz, on the whole abated, would from time to time break out again like an incurable disease. The news about the Poles being at last allowed to leave Russia was good. Something cheering was welcome. The matter had particular bearing on my own changed circumstances.

Nine or ten months before, a posting had come to a small, rather closed community of the General Staff, the Section's establishment—including Finn himself, a lieutenant-colonel—something less than a dozen officers. Gazetted captain, after a brief period of probation, I had been transferred to the Intelligence Corps 'for purposes of administrative convenience'. Like most of those who could claim an earlier military incarnation, I continued to wear the badges, deemed for no particular reason to carry an enhanced prestige, of my former line regiment. Pennistone, for example, recently promoted major, would not even abandon his anonymous lion-and-unicorn under which he had first entered the army. I was Pennistone's assistant in Polish Liaison. The rest of the Section were concerned either with the other original Allies—Belgium, the Netherlands, Luxembourg, Norway, Czechoslovakia—or the Neutrals—some of whom from time to time were metamorphosed into Allies or enemies—

running to nearly twenty in number who boasted a military attaché.

A military attaché was the essential point. He provided the channel through which work was routed for all but three of the Allied forces. Exceptions were the Free French, the Americans, the Russians. Only matters innate to the particular appointment of military attaché as such—routine invitations to exercises and the like—involved Finn with this trio. They were, for their part, dealt with by special missions: Americans and Russians, on account of sheer volume of work involved; Free French, for the good reason they lacked an embassy to which a military attaché could be attached. The Vichy administration, unlike German-established puppet régimes in other occupied countries, was still recognized by Great Britain as the government of France, though naturally unrepresented diplomatically at the Court of St James's. Pennistone had explained much of this when we met a year before at the Free French Mission itself, where Finn, then a major, had interviewed me for a job to which I was not appointed. That interview had in due course brought me to the Section, though whether it would have done so had not Finn himself decided to accept the promotion he had so often in the past refused is another matter. Pennistone might have got me into the Section anyway. There seems no avoiding what has to be.

'Finn's good nature makes him vulnerable,' Pennistone said. 'But he can always fall back on his deafness and his VC.'

Finn was certainly prepared to use either or both these attributes to their fullest advantage when occasion required, but he had other weapons too, and took a lot of bypassing when it came to conflict. Quite why he had changed his mind about accepting promotion, no one knew. If, until that moment, he had preferred to avoid at his age (what that age was remained one of his secrets) too heavy responsibilities, too complex duties, he now found himself assailed by work as various as it was demanding. There was perhaps a parallel with Lance-Corporal Gittins, storeman in my former Battalion, a man of similarly marked character, who, no doubt to the end, preferred a job he liked and knew thoroughly to the uncertainty of rising higher. Possibly a surface picturesqueness about the duties, the people with whom he was now brought in contact, had tempted Finn more than he would have admitted. That would be easy, for Finn admitted to nothing but the deafness and the VC; not even the 'L' of his own initial, though he would smile if the latter question arose, as if he looked forward one day to revealing his first name at the most effective possible moment.

'Finn's extraordinary French is quite famous in Paris,' said Pennistone. 'He has turned it to great advantage.'

Pennistone, capable, even brilliant, at explaining philosophic niceties or the minutiae of official dialectic, was entirely unable to present a clear narrative of his own daily life, past or present, so that it was never discoverable how he and Finn had met in Paris in the first instance. Probably it had been in the days before Pennistone had abandoned commerce for writing a book about Descartes—or possibly Gassendi—and there had been some question of furnishing Finn's office with Pennistone's textiles. In peace or war, Finn was obviously shrewd enough, so he might have ferreted out Pennistone as assistant even had he not been already one of the Section's officers, but, on the contrary, concealed in the innermost recesses of the military machine. He enjoyed a decided prominence in Finn's councils, not by any means only because he spoke several languages with complete fluency.

'Why did Finn leave the City for the cosmetics business?'

'Didn't he inherit some family interest? I don't know.

His daughter is married to a Frenchman serving with the British army—as a few are on account of political disinclinations regarding de Gaulle—but Finn keeps his wife and family hidden away.'

'Why is that?'

Pennistone laughed.

'My theory is because presence of relations, whatever they were like, would prejudice Finn's own operation as a completely uncommitted individual, a kind of ideal figure—anyway to himself in his own particular genre—one to whom such appendages as wives and children could only be an encumbrance. Narcissism, perhaps the best sort of narcissism. I'm not sure he isn't right to do so.'

I saw what Pennistone meant, also why he and Finn got on so well together, at first sight surprising, since Finn had probably never heard of Descartes, still less Gassendi. He was not a great reader, he used to say. Such panache as he felt required by his own chosen persona had immense finish of style, to which even the most critical could hardly take offence. Possibly Mrs Finn had proved the exception in that respect, lack of harmony in domestic life resulting. Heroes are notoriously hard to live with. When Finn conversed about matters other than official ones, he tended on the whole to offer anecdotal experiences of the earlier war, told favourites like the occasion when, during a halt on the line of march, he had persuaded the Medical Officer to pull a troublesome molar. Copious draughts of rum were followed by convulsions as of earthquake. Finn would make appropriate gestures and mimings during the recital, quite horrifying in their way, and undeniably confirming latent abilities as an actor. The climax came almost in a whisper.

'The MO made a balls of it. The tooth was the wrong one.'

Had Finn, in fact, chosen the stage as career, rather than war and commerce, his personal appearance would have restricted him to 'character' parts. Superficial good looks were entirely absent. Short, square, cleanshaven, his head seemed carved out of an elephant's tusk, the whole massive cone of ivory left more or less complete in its original shape, eyes hollowed out deep in the roots, the rest of the protuberance accommodating his other features, terminating in a perfectly colossal nose that stretched directly forward from the totally bald cranium. The nose was preposterous, grotesque, slapstick, a mask from a Goldoni comedy. He had summoned me a day or two before the teleprinter news of the Polish evacuation.

'As David's still in Scotland,' he said. 'I want you to attend a Cabinet Office meeting. Explain to them how one Polish general can be a very different cup of tea to another.'

The Poles were by far the largest of the Allied contingents in the United Kingdom, running to a Corps of some twenty thousand men, stationed in Scotland, where Pennistone was doing a week's tour of duty to see the army on the ground and make contact with the British Liaison Headquarters attached to it. The other Allies in this country mustered only two or three thousand bodies apiece, though some of them held cards just as useful as soldiers, if not more so: the Belgians, for example, still controlling the Congo, the Norwegians a large and serviceable merchant fleet. However, the size of the Polish Corps, and the fact that the Poles who had reached this country showed a high proportion of officers to that of 'other ranks', inclined to emphasize complexities of Polish political opinion. Some of our own official elements were not too well versed in appreciating the importance of this tricky aspect of all Allied relationships. At misunderstanding's worst, most disastrous, the Poles were thought of as a race not unlike the Russians; indeed, by some, scarcely to be distinguished apart. Even branches more at home in this respect than the Censorship—to whom it always came as a complete and chaotic surprise that Poles wrote letters to each other expressing feelings towards the USSR that were less than friendly—were sometimes puzzled by internal Allied conflicts alien to our own, in many respects unusual, ideas about running an army.

'The Poles themselves have a joke about their generals being either social or socialist,' said Finn. 'Only wish it was as easy as that. I expect you've got the necessary stuff, Nicholas. If you feel you want to strengthen it, apply to the Country Section or our ambassador to them. This is one of Widmerpool's committees. Have you heard of Widmerpool?'

'Yes, sir, I—'

'Had dealings with him?'

'Quite often, I—'

'Some people find him . . .'

Finn paused and looked grave. He must have decided to remain imprecise, because he did not finish the sentence.

'Very active is Widmerpool,' he went on. 'Not everyone likes him—I mean where he is. If you've come across him already, you'll know how to handle things. Have all the information at your finger tips. Plenty of notes to fall back on. We want to deliver the goods. Possibly Farebrother will be there. He has certain dealings with the Poles in these secret games that take place. Farebrother's got great charm, I know, but you must resist it, Nicholas. Don't let him entangle us in any of his people's goings-on.'

'No, sir. Of course not. Is it Colonel Widmerpool?'

'He's a half-colonel—Good God, I've been keeping Hlava waiting all this time. He must come up at once. You'd better ring David in Scotland and tell him you're standing in for him at this Cabinet Office meeting. He may have something to add. Make a good impression, Nicholas. Show them we know our business.'

The fact was Finn was rather overawed by the thought of

the Cabinet Offices. I was a little overawed myself. The warning about Farebrother, whose name I had already heard mentioned several times as a lieutenant-colonel in one of the secret organizations, expressed a principle of Finn's, almost an obsession, that his own Section should have as distant relations as possible with any of the undercover centres of warfare. He considered, no doubt with reason, that officers concerned in normal liaison duties, if they swam, even had an occasional dip, in waters tainted by the varied and dubious currents liable to be released, sometimes rather recklessly, from such dark and mysterious sources, risked undermining confidence in themselves *vis-à-vis* the Allies with whom they daily worked. Secret machinations of the most outlandish kind might be demanded by total war; they were all the same to be avoided—from the security point of view and every other—by those doing a different sort of job. That was Finn's view. You could take it or leave it as a theory. For his own staff, it had to be observed. All contact with clandestine bodies could not, of course, be prevented, because, where any given Ally was concerned, common areas of administration were bound to exist between routine duties and exceptional ones; for example, transfer of individual or group in circumstances when the change had to be known to the Liaison Officer. Even so, Finn's Section saw on the whole remarkably little of those tenebrous side-turnings off the main road of military operations, and he himself would always give a glance of the deepest disapproval if he ran across any of their representatives, male or female, in uniform or *en civile*, frequenting our room, which did occasionally happen.

The meeting was to take place in one of the large buildings at the Parliament Square end of Whitehall. I had set off there the previous morning, aware of certain trepidations. After the usual security guards at the entrance, Royal

Marines were on duty, either because the Ministry of Defence had been largely shaped in early days by a marine officer, because their bifarious nature was thought appropriate to inter-service affairs, or simply because a corps organized in small detachments was convenient for London. The blue uniforms and red capbands made me think of Chips Lovell.

'I know it's a tailor's war,' he had said, 'but I can't afford that blue get-up. They'll have to accept me for what I am in khaki.'

I asked for Colonel Widmerpool.

'Aye, aye, sir.'

This old-fashioned naval affirmative, recalling so many adventure stories read as a boy, increased a sensation of going between decks in a ship. I followed the marine down flight after flight of stairs. It was like the lower depths of our own building, though more spacious, less shabby. The marine, who had a streaming cold in his head, showed me into a room in the bowels of the earth, the fittings and decoration of which were also less down-at-heel than the general run of headquarters and government offices. A grave grey-haired civilian, evidently a chief clerk, was arranging papers down each side of a long table. I explained my business.

'Colonel Widmerpool will be here shortly,' he said. 'He is with the Minister.'

He spoke with severity, as if some regulation had already been transgressed by too early arrival, which had made it necessary to reveal Widmerpool's impressive engagement. I hung about. The chief clerk, like a verger distributing service papers in a cathedral before a wedding, set out a further selection of documents, adjusting them in some very exact relation to those already in the table. A naval captain and RAF wing-commander came in together, talking hard.

Ignoring the chief clerk and myself, they sat down at the far end of the long table, produced more papers from briefcases and continued their conversation. They were followed in a minute by a youngish lieutenant-colonel, with the air of a don in uniform, who this time muttered a faint 'good morning' in my direction, then joined the sailor and airman in whatever they were discussing. It was impossible to remain unaware of an atmosphere of exceedingly high pressure in this place, something much more concentrated, more intense, than that with which one was normally surrounded. This was not because work was unplentiful or disregarded in our own building; nor—some of it—lacking in immediacy or drama. However much those characteristics might there obtain, this ethos was something rather different. In this brightly lit dungeon lurked a sense that no one could spare a word, not a syllable, far less gesture, not of direct value in implementing the matter in hand. The power principle could almost be felt here, humming and vibrating like the drummings of the teleprinter. The sensation that resulted was oppressive, even a shade alarming. I was still kicking my heels, trying to rationalize the sense of tension, when the same marine who had escorted myself, blowing his nose hard, ushered in Sunny Farebrother.

Farebrother came through the door looking as quietly distinguished as ever. He was wearing on his threadbare tunic the badge of a parachutist. The qualification was held desirable for those who, in the course of their administrative duties, had to arrange the 'dropping' of others, usually into destinations of excessive danger. Its acquisition was not to be sneezed at for a man in his fifties. It bore out the rumour that Farebrother's DSO in the previous war had been a 'good one'. I was glad to see someone I knew already, but Farebrother's arrival did not in other respects make the atmosphere of the room substantially more cordial; if anything, the reverse. In fact none of the people at the table even looked up. Farebrother himself was obviously on his best behaviour. He addressed himself to the other half-colonel.

'Hullo, Reggie.'

After this ranging shot, he greeted the rest in a manner precisely to indicate appreciation that the sailor was a rung above him, the airman at the same level, both employed in other arms of the Services, therefore unlikely to have immediate bearing on his own interests and promotion. Farebrother's capacity for conveying such subtleties of official relationship was unrivalled. On this occasion, his civilities were scarcely returned. He seemed to expect no more, accepting his status as small fry in the eyes of people such as these. The others continued their discussion. He came across to me.

'So you've had a move up too, Nicholas.'

'Not long after your own, sir.'

'Have you taken David Pennistone's place? I expected him to be your Section's representative here.'

Pennistone regarded himself as rather an authority on Sunny Farebrother, often laughing about that 'charm' against which Finn had warned me.

'Farebrother himself refers to it,' Pennistone said. 'The other day he remarked that some general had "ordered me to use my famous charm". The extraordinary thing is that he has got a way of getting round people, in spite of boasting about it himself. He does put himself over. A remarkable fellow in his way. Ambitious as hell, stops at nothing. I always enjoy his accounts of his own small economies. "Found a place off Baker Street where you can get a three-course luncheon for three-and-six—second helpings, if you ask—a man of my build needs proper nourishment. It's becoming hard to get nowadays, especially at a reasonable price." '

This taste for saving money, usually to be thought of as

a trait threatening to diminish an air of distinction, never seemed to detract from Farebrother's. His blue eyes always smiled out bravely on the world. Parsimony, like the dilapidation of his uniform, the one product of the other, positively enhanced his personality—his 'charm' perhaps—even when you knew he was well off. Indeed, Pennistone, like others before him, took the view that Farebrother was decidedly rich.

'And then when he puts on his holy face and tone of voice,' said Pennistone. 'A sacred subject is mentioned—the Prime Minister, religion, some high decoration—Sunny sucks in his cheeks and drops his eyes.'

Farebrother pointed to the strip lighting with which the underground room was equipped.

'Wish I could afford to install something like that in my peacetime office,' he said. 'What you need, if you're going to get any work done. Can't tell whether it's three o'clock in the morning, or three o'clock in the afternoon. No disturbance from time. I expect you know we're going to meet an old friend here this morning?'

'Kenneth Widmerpool?'

Farebrother laughed. Concealing as a rule his likes and dislikes about most people, he scarcely attempted to hide his hatred of Widmerpool, whom it must have been galling to find once more his equal in rank, after temporarily outstripping him; not to mention the fact that Widmerpool's appointment was of such undeniably superior standing to Farebrother's.

'Oh, Kenneth, of course,' he said. 'No, I didn't mean him. This is certainly Kenneth's bower, a very cosy one, don't you think? No—Peter Templer. I was talking to him yesterday about some matter in which his Ministry was concerned, and he told me the usual man's sick and he himself would be representing Economic Warfare here this morning.'

Templer came into the room at that moment, followed by another civilian. Sir Magnus Donners—who continued to hold his place in the Cabinet, in spite of a concerted attack for several months from certain sections of the Press—had probably had some hand in finding this job for him in MEW. Catching sight of me, Templer nodded and gave a slight smile, but did not come over and speak. Instead, he sat down with the party at the table, where he too began to produce papers. He seemed to know them all.

'I must have a word with Peter,' said Farebrother.

He went across to Templer and said something. At Stourwater, where I had last seen him, I had been struck by a hardness, even brutality of expression that had changed someone I had once known well. That look had seemed new to Templer, perhaps to be attributed to lack of concord with his second wife, Betty, then showing herself an unassimilable member of Sir Magnus's houseparty; indeed, so near the borderline of sanity that it seemed unwise ever to have brought her into those formidable surroundings. Templer had not lost this rather grim appearance. If anything, it had increased. He was thinner, more resembling himself in his younger days in that respect. To go through his papers he had put on spectacles, which I had never before seen him wear. While I was wondering whether I too ought to go and sit at the table, Widmerpool himself entered the room.

'My apologies, gentlemen.'

Holding up a sheaf of documents in both hands, at the same time making peculiar movements with his head and arms in the direction of the small crowd awaiting him, he looked very pleased with himself; like a dog delighted to show ability in carrying a newspaper in his mouth.

'You must excuse me,' he said. 'I was kept by the Minister. He absolutely refused to let me go.'

Grinning at them all through his thick lenses, his tone suggested the Minister's insistence had bordered on sexual importunity.

'Let us be seated.'

Everyone except Farebrother and myself was already sitting down. Widmerpool turned towards me, somewhat abating the geniality of his manner.

'I was not informed by Finn that you were coming here in Pennistone's place, Nicholas. He should have done so.'

'I have the necessary stuff here.'

'I hope you have. Finn is rather slack about such notifications. There are security considerations here of which he may not appreciate the complexity. However, let us begin. This Polish business should not take too long. We must be brisk, as a great many more important matters have to be got through this morning.'

The other civilian, who had entered the room with Templer, turned out to be the Foreign Office representative on this particular committee, a big fat man with a small mouth and petulant manner. He had brought a paper with him which he now read aloud in the tone of one offering up an introductory prayer. There was some general talk, when he had finished, of Pilsudski's *coup d'état* of 1926, from which so many subsequent Polish complications of political relationship had arisen. I consulted my notes.

'The broad outline is that those senior officers who stem from the Carpathian Brigade of Legions tend to be nationalist and relatively right-wing, in contrast with those of the First Brigade—under Pilsudski himself and Sosnokowski—on the whole leftish in outlook.'

'The First Brigade always regarded itself as the *élite*,' said Widmerpool.

He had evidently read the subject up, at least familiarized himself with its salient points. Probably the knowledge was fairly thorough, as his capacity for work was enormous.

'General Sikorski himself was entirely eclipsed after the coup. Henceforth he lived largely abroad. Since taking over, he has shown himself very reasonable, even well disposed, towards most of his former political opponents.'

'Though by no means immune to French flattery,' said Widmerpool.

'Let's hear something about General Anders,' said the sailor.

'He's GOC Polish troops in Russia, I understand. How's he doing at that job?' said Widmerpool.

'Efficiently, it's thought—insomuch as he's allowed to function with a free hand.'

'Where will Anders fit in, if he comes over here? Will there be friction with the present chap?'

'Up to now, Anders has not been a figure of anything like comparable political stature to Sikorski. There seems no reason to suppose he wishes to compete with him at that level. Unlike Sikorski—although he actively opposed Pilsudski in 'twenty-six—Anders never suffered in his career. In fact he was the first colonel to be promoted general after the change of régime.'

'Anders is a totally different type from Sikorski,' said Widmerpool. 'Rather a swashbuckler. A man to be careful of in certain respects. Ran a racing stable. Still, I'm no enemy to a bit of dash. I like it.'

Widmerpool removed his spectacles to emphasize this taste for ardour in living.

'The Russians kept him in close confinement for two years.'

'So we are aware.'

'Sometimes in atrocious conditions.'

'Yes, yes. Now, let's get on to lesser people like their Chief of Staff, Kielkiewicz, and the military attaché, Bobrowski . . .'

Clarification of the personalities of Polish generals continued for about an hour. The various pairs of hands lying on the table formed a pattern of contrasted colours and shapes. Widmerpool's, small, gnarled, with cracked nails, I remembered from school. Farebrother's, clasped together, as if devotionally, to match his expression, were long fingered, the joints immensely knobbly, rather notably clean and well looked after, but not manicured like Templer's. Those of the Foreign Office representative were huge, with great bulbous fingers, almost purple in colour, like lumps of meat that had been chopped in that shape to make into sandwiches or hot-dogs. The soldier and sailor both possessed good useful hands of medium size, very reasonably clean; the airman's, small again, rather in the manner of Widmerpool's, nails pared very close, probably with a knife.

'That seems to be about all we want to know,' said Widmerpool. 'Is that agreed? Let us get on to more urgent matters. The extraneous personnel can go back to their own work.'

Farebrother, apparently anxious to get away quickly, rose, said some goodbyes and left. Templer also wanted to be on his way.

'I was told you wouldn't need me either after the first session, Kenneth,' he said. 'None of the stuff you're moving on to will concern my people directly and we'll get copies of the paper. There's a particular matter back at the office I'd like to liquidate, if I could be excused—and Broadbent will be back tomorrow.'

'It isn't usual,' said Widmerpool.

'Couldn't an exception be made?'

After a minute or two of sparring, Widmerpool assented ungraciously. I suggested to Templer we should walk a short way up the street together.

'All right,' said Templer indifferently.

This exchange between Templer and myself had the

effect of making Widmerpool restive, even irritable. He looked up from the table, round which a further set of papers was being doled out by the chief clerk.

'Do go away, Nicholas. I have some highly secret matters to deal with on the next agenda. I can't begin on them with people like you hanging about the room.'

Templer and I retired. On the first landing of the stairs, the sneezing marine was drying his handkerchief on the air-conditioning plant. We reached the street before Templer spoke. He seemed deeply occupied with his own thoughts.

'What's working at MEW like?'

'Just what you'd imagine.'

His manner was so unforthcoming, so far from recognizing we were old friends who had not met for a long time, that I began to regret suggesting we should have a word together after the meeting.

'Are you often in contact with Sunny Farebrother?'

'Naturally his people are in touch with the Ministry from time to time, though not as a rule with me personally.'

'When I saw him at my former Div HQ he rather indicated his new job might have some bearing on your own career.'

'That was poor security on Sunny's part. Well, you never know. Perhaps it will. I admit I've been looking about for something different. These things take time. The trouble is one's so frightfully old. Kenneth's sitting pretty, isn't he?'

'He thought he'd never get that job. He was in fairly hot water when last seen.'

'Kenneth can winkle his way out of anything,' said Templer. 'God save me from such a grind myself, but, if you like that sort of thing, it's quite a powerful one, properly handled. You can bet Kenneth gets the last ounce out of it.'

'You grade it pretty high?'

'Of course, it's nothing to find yourself working fourteen hours a day at a stretch, even longer than that, night after night into the small hours, and then back again at 9 a.m. If you can stand up to it physically—get the rest of the committee to agree with what you've written down of their discussion over a period of six or seven hours—you, as their secretary, word the papers that may go right up to the Chiefs of Staff—possibly to the PM himself. You've only seen the merest chicken feed, Nick. A Military Assistant Secretary, like Kenneth, can have quite an influence on policy—in a sense on the whole course of the war—if he plays his hand well.'

Templer had dropped his distant manner. The thought of Widmerpool's potential powers evidently excited him.

'It's only a lieutenant-colonel's appointment.'

'They range from majors to brigadiers—there might even be a major-general. I'm not sure. You see there are quite a lot of them. In theory, they rank equal in their own particular work, but of course rank always carries its own prestige. I say, this possibility has just occurred to me. Do you ever come across Prince Theodoric in your racket?'

'I believe my Colonel has seen him once or twice. I've never run across him myself—except for a brief moment years ago before the war.'

'I just wondered,' said Templer. 'I used to have business dealings with his country. Theodoric's position is a trifle delicate here, politically speaking, his brother, the King, not only in such bad health, but more or less in baulk.'

'Musing upon the King his brother's wreck?'

'And the heir to the throne too young to do anything, and anyway in America. Theodoric himself has always been a hundred per cent anti-Nazi. I'm trying to get Kenneth to put up a paper on the subject. That's all by the way. How's your family?'

The abruptness of transition was clearly to mark a deliberate change of subject. I told him Isobel and our child were living near enough to London to be visited once a fortnight; in return enquiring about Betty Templer. Although curious to hear what had happened to her, I had not asked at first because any question about Templer's women, even wives, risked the answer that they had been discarded or had left. His manner at that moment conveyed that revelation forced on him—if anything of the sort were indeed to be revealed—would be answered in a manner calculated to embarrass. There had been times when he liked to unload personal matters; this did not look like one of them. In any case, I hardly knew Betty, at least no more of her than her state of extreme nervous discomfort at Stourwater. However, enquiry was not to be avoided. Templer did not answer at once. Instead, he looked at me with an odd sardonic expression, preparation for news hardly likely to be good.

'You hadn't heard?'

'Heard what?'

'About Betty?'

'Not ill, I hope.'

It occurred to me she might have been killed in a raid. That could happen to acquaintances and remain unknown to one for months.

'She went off her rocker,' he said.

'You mean . . .'

'Just what I say. She's in the bin.'

He spoke roughly. The deliberate brutality of the statement was so complete, so designed to let no one, least of all myself, off any of its implications, that it could only be accepted as concealing an abyss of painful feeling. At least, correctly or not, such downright language had to be given the benefit of the doubt in that respect.

'Rather a peach, isn't she?'

That was what he had said of her, when I had first seen them together at Umfraville's night-club, a stage in their relationship when Templer could not remember whether his future wife's surname was Taylor or Porter. Now, he made no effort to help out the situation. There was nothing whatever to be said in return. I produced a few conventional phrases, none in the least adequate, at the same time feeling rather aggrieved that Templer himself should choose, first, to carry curtness of manner to the point of seeming positively unfriendly; then change to a tone that only long intimacy in the past could justify. Perhaps—thinking over Betty's demeanour staying with Sir Magnus Donners—this ultimate disaster was not altogether surprising. Having such cares on his mind could to some extent explain Templer's earlier unaccommodating manner.

'Just one of those things,' he said.

He spoke this time as if a little to excuse himself for what might look like an earlier show of heartlessness.

'To tell the truth, I'm feeling a shade fed up about marriage, women, my job, in fact the whole bag of tricks,' he said. 'Then this awful business of one's age. You keep on getting back to that. If it isn't one objection, it's another. "You're not young enough, old boy." I'm always being told that nowadays. On top of it all, a bomb hit my flat the other night. I was on Fire Duty at the Ministry. Everybody said what a marvellous piece of luck. Not sure.'

'Did it wreck the place completely?'

Templer shook his head, indicating not so much lack of damage at the flat, as that he could not bring himself to recapitulate further a subject so utterly tedious and unrewarding.

'You haven't any good idea where I might go temporarily? I'm living from hand to mouth at the moment with anyone who will put me up.'

I suggested the Jeavons house in South Kensington. Ted Jeavons, having somehow managed to find a builder to patch up the roof and back wall—an achievement no one but himself would have brought off at that moment—was still in residence. Only the rear part of the structure had been damaged by the bomb, the front remaining almost untouched. Jeavons ran the house more or less as it had been run when Molly was alive, with a shifting population of visitors, some of whom lived there more or less permanently, paying rent. Lots of households of much that kind existed in wartime London, a matter of luck if, homeless like Templer, you knew where to apply. He wrote down the address, at the same time showing characteristic lack of interest in information about Jeavons.

'I might propose myself,' he said. 'If a bomb's already hit the place, with any luck it won't happen again, though I don't know that there's any real reason to suppose that.'

He paused, then suddenly began to talk about himself in a manner that was oddly apologetic, quite unlike his accustomed style as remembered, or the tone he had been using up till now. Until then, I had felt all contact lost between us, that the picture I retained of him when we had been friends years before had become largely imaginary. Now a closer proximity seemed renewed.

'I've given up girls,' he said. 'I thought you'd be interested to know.'

'Charles Stringham said the same when I ran across him in the ranks. Is this for the war?'

Templer laughed.

'I used to think I was rather a success with the ladies,' he said. 'Now one wife's run away and the other is where I indicated, I'm not so sure. At least I can't be regarded as a great hand at marriage. It's lately been made clear to me I'm not so hot extra-matrimonially either. That's why I was beefing about age.'

He made a dismissive gesture.

'I'll ring your friend Jeavons,' he said.

He strolled away. There was always the slight impression of which Stringham used to complain—persisting even into the universal shabbiness of wartime—that Templer was too well dressed. I had never before known him so dejected.

While eating breakfast after Night Duty, I reflected that it would be as well to warn Jeavons that Templer might be getting in touch with him. Without some such notification, knowing them both, nothing was more likely than that they would get at cross purposes with each other. Then I put personal matters from my mind and began to think about the day's work that lay ahead.

'You'll be surprised at the decisions one has to take on one's own here,' Pennistone had said when I first joined the Section. 'You might think that applied to the Operational people more than ourselves, but in fact captains and majors in "I" have to get used to giving snap answers about all sorts of relatively important policy matters.'

When I returned to the building, this time to our own room, Dempster, who looked after the Norwegians and had a passion for fresh air, was trying vainly to open one of the windows, laughing a lot while he did so. He was in the timber business and knew Scandinavia well, spending skiing holidays in Norway when a boy with an aunt who was a remote kinswoman of Ibsen's. Dempster was always full of Ibsen stories. He had won a couple of MCs in '14-'18, the second up at Murmansk during the War of Intervention, an interlude the less inhibited of the Russians would, once in a way, enjoy laughing about, if the subject came up after a lot of drinks at one of their own parties. That did not apply to the Soviet military attaché himself, General Lebedev, who was at all times a stranger to laughter. Dempster was a rather notably accomplished pianist, who had been known to play a duet with Colonel

Hlava, the Czech, also a competent performer, though not quite in Dempster's class.

'No good,' said Dempster.

Holding a long pole with a hook on the end with which he had been trying to open the windows, he looked like an immensely genial troll come south from the fjords to have a good time. Still laughing, he replaced the pole in its corner. This endlessly repeated game of trying to force open the window was always unsuccessful. The sun's rays, when there was any sun, penetrated through small rectangles in otherwise bricked up glass. The room itself, irregular of shape, was on the first floor, situated in an angle of the building, under one of the domed cupolas that ornamented the four corners of the roof. In winter—it was now early spring—life here was not unlike that lived at the earth's extremities, morning and evening only an hour or two apart, the sparse feeble light of day tailing away in early afternoon, until finally swallowed up into impenetrable outer blackness. Within, lamplight glowed dimly through the shadows and nimbus of cigarette smoke, the drone of dictating voices measuring a kind of plain-song against more brief emphatic exchanges made from time to time on one or more of the seven or eight telephones. This telephonic talk was, as often as not, in some language other than English; just as the badges and insignia of visitors tended, as often as not, to diverge from the common run of uniform.

Pennistone, still wearing a blue side-cap, was sitting in his chair, preparing for action by opening the small gold hunter that always lay on the desk in front of him during working hours, a watch that was wound with a key.

'Good morning, Nick.'

'You came down from Scotland last night?'

'Got a sleeper by a bit of luck. I shared it with an

air-commodore who snored. How did the Cabinet Office meeting go?'

'All right—look, I'm just off night duty. What do you think? A message has come through that a few Poles are trickling over the Persian frontier.'

'No?'

'The Russians have released a driblet.'

'This could mean a Second Polish Corps.'

Pennistone had fair hair with a high-bridged nose over which he could look exceeding severe at people who annoyed him, of whom there were likely to be quite a few in the course of a day's business. Without possessing a conventionally military appearance, a kind of personal authority and physical ease of movement carried off in him the incisive demands of uniform. More basically, he could claim an almost uncanny instinctive grasp of what was required from a staff officer. Indeed, after months of dealing with him from day to day, General Bobrowski, when informed Pennistone was not a Regular, had exploded into a Polish ejaculation of utter astonishment, at the same time bursting into loud laughter, while executing in mid-air one of those snatching, clutching gestures of the fingers, so expressive of his own impatience with life. A major-general, Bobrowski, who was military attaché, had been with the Polish contingent in France at the beginning of the war, where, in contravention of the French Chief of Army Staff's order that no Polish troops were to be evacuated to England, he had mounted brens on locomotives and brought the best part of two brigades to a port of embarkation.

'Bobrowski began his military career in a Russian rifle regiment.' Pennistone had told me. 'He was *praporschik*—ensign, as usually translated—at the same time that Kielkiewicz was an aspirant—always a favourite rank of mine—in the Austro-Hungarian cavalry.'

Hanging his cap on one of the hooks by the door, Pennistone went upstairs at once to get orders from Finn about the news from Iran. Polish GHQ must have received the information simultaneously from their own sources—reports almost always comprehensive, if at times highly coloured—because Michalski, one of General Kielkiewicz's ADCs, came through on the telephone just after Pennistone had left the room, seeking to arrange an interview with everyone from the Chief of the Imperial General Staff downwards. He was followed almost immediately on the line by Horaczko, one of Bobrowski's assistants, with the same end in view for his master. We were on easy terms with both Michalski and Horaczko, so temporizing was not too difficult, though clearly fresh and more urgent solicitations would soon be on the way.

Michalski, now in his late thirties, had served like Bobrowski with the Polish contingent in France. Of large size, sceptical about most matters, he belonged to the world of industrial design—statuettes for radiator caps and such decorative items—working latterly in Berlin, which had left some mark on him of its bitter individual humour. In fact Pennistone always said talking to Michalski made him feel he was sitting in the Romanisches Café. His father had been a successful portrait painter, and his grandfather before him, stretching back to a long line of itinerant artists wandering over Poland and Saxony.

'Painting pictures that are now being destroyed as quickly as possible,' Michalski said.

He was accomplished at providing thumbnail sketches of the personalities at the Titian, the former hotel, subdued, Edwardian in tone, where headquarters of the Polish army in exile was established. Uncle Giles had once stayed there in days gone by, a moment when neither the Ufford nor the De Tabley had been able to accommodate him at short notice. 'I'll be bankrupt if I ever do it again,' he had declared afterwards, a financial state all his relations in those days supposed him to be in anyway.

Horaczko had reached England in a different manner from Michalski, and only after a lot of adventures. As an officer of the Reserve, he had begun the Eastern campaign on horseback, cantering about at the head of a troop of lancers, pennons flying, like one of the sequences of *War and Peace*, to intercept the advancing German armour. Executive in a Galician petroleum plant, he was younger than Michalski, having—as Pennistone and I agreed—some of the air of the junior lead in a drawing-room comedy, the young lover perhaps. When Poland was overrun on two fronts, Horaczko had avoided capture and internment, probably death, by escaping through Hungary. Both he and Michalski held the rank of second-lieutenant. While I was still speaking to Horaczko on the telephone, our clerk, Corporal Curtis, brought in a lot more stuff to be dealt with, additional, that is, to the formidable pile lying on the desk when I came in from breakfast.

'Good morning, Curtis.'

'Good morning, sir.'

'How are things?'

Curtis, a studious-looking young man, whose military career had been handicapped by weak eyesight, was a henchman of notable efficiency and wide interests. He had once confessed to Pennistone that he had read through the whole of Grote's *History of Greece*.

'A rather disturbing letter from the Adjutant-General's branch, sir.'

'Oh, Lord.'

'But not so bad as my first premonition on reading it. In fact, sir, I all but perpetrated a schoolboy howler in that connexion.'

'Impossible.'

'On the subject of redundant Polish officers taking commissions in West African units of our own forces—*Accra*, sir—the AG.10 clerk spoke indistinctly, as well as using what I understand to be an incorrect pronunciation, so that, to cut a long story short, sir, the place was first transcribed by me as *Agra*. The error did not take long to be righted, but it was a disturbing misconstruction.'

By the time I had run through the new lot of papers Pennistone had returned. He reported that Finn—after a word with the more sagacious of the two brigadiers—had been told to consult the Major-General in charge of our Directorate. I reported that Michalski and Horaczko had telephoned.

'Ring Horaczko back, otherwise Bobrowski will make him persecute us all day. Tell him we'll let him know the very moment anything comes through that his general should have. Don't worry about Michalski. I'll be seeing him. I'm off to the Titian at once to get Kielkiewicz's reactions.'

'What were the Colonel's?'

'He's in one of his flaps.'

Sudden pressures of this kind always upset Finn, whose temperament unpredictably fused agitation with calm; violent inner antagonism of these warring characteristics having presumably motivated whatever he had done—killed goodness knows how many enemy machine-gunners with a bayonet?—to be awarded his VC. No doubt the comparative lack of precedent for the situation now arisen in Persia, its eccentric deficiency of warning at the diplomatic level, general departure from normal routine—even from official good manners so far as the Soviet was concerned—discomposed Finn, a man both systematic and courteous. Although not a professional soldier, he had, one way and another, seen a good deal of military service, having, like Dempster, stayed on for a while in the army after the Armistice in 1918; then been re-employed in the rank of major as early as 1938. In short, he had enjoyed plenty of opportunity to observe military problems, which on the whole he seemed to prefer to semi-political ones, like the evacuation of the Poles.

'He'll be all right when he's used to the idea,' said Pennistone. 'At first he could consider nothing short of flying out there at once and arranging it all himself.'

He reached for his cap again, unhooking it from the wall with the crook of a walking stick. Then he returned the watch to the breast pocket of his tunic.

'Have a talk with Q (Ops.) Colonel,' he said.

Borrit, who looked after the Netherlands, passed on his way towards the door.

'Borrit . . .'

'Yes, Pennistone?'

'You're not making for the car?'

Borrit's small fair moustache was set in a serious melancholy face, deeply tanned, as if he had spent much of his life under a blazing sun. Perhaps he had. He had come to the Section from employment as one of the Intelligence Officers at Headquarters on the Gold Coast, owing his knowledge of Spanish—at first naturally steering him to duties with the Neutrals—to many years spent on the wholesale side of the fruit trade. Language as usual proving of less consequence than facility for handling an 'opposite number' with tact, he had in due course gravitated to the more responsible job with an Ally. Stebbings, who took Borrit's place with the Spaniards and Latin-Americans, was also, oddly enough, in the fruit business, though on the retail side, where he had a nervous breakdown when his firm went into bankruptcy at the outbreak of war. If addressed sharply, Stebbings's left eyelid twitched, probably in consequence of that collapse. He remained always rather afraid of Finn. All the same, he tackled his duties with judgment. Stebbings was recently married to a Portuguese, a fact that continually worried the Security people. Borrit, on the other hand, was a widower. He must have been forty, perhaps a shade more, because he had seen action in the first war, though only as a result of having falsified his age to the recruiting authorities. During the occasional lulls of work Borrit and Stebbings would talk earnestly of fruit. Pennistone and Borrit had a standing rivalry over the Section's car—a vehicle of inconceivably cramped seating accommodation—for the first use in the morning.

'Wait a moment . . .' said Pennistone.

'I'll drop you,' said Borrit. 'If you're on the way to the Titian.'

Pennistone turned to me again.

'Where was I?'

'Q (Ops.).'

'Ah, yes—the point is there's only the traditional one man and a boy at Meshed.'

'That's the key name?'

'We shall be hearing a lot about Meshed—and resorts like Yangi-yul and Alma Ata. Some sort of a reception centre will have to be rigged up. There may be quite a party to deal with once they start.'

'What am I to say to Q (Ops.)?'

'Just ventilate the question. They may have other ideas to ours.'

'They're presumably prepared for this. They were on the distribution.'

'But will want to be brought up to date from our end—and we'll need their background stuff to tell the London Poles.'

'Do you mind if we go, Pennistone?' said Borrit. 'Otherwise I'll be late for my appointment with Van der Voort.'

Pennistone, never to be hurried, stood in deep thought. He was as likely to be reflecting on Cartesianism as on the best way to approach Q (Ops.). Borrit made another move towards the door.

'What was it? I know—trouble again about Szymanski. You wouldn't think it possible one man could be such a nuisance. There's now doubt whether it's his real name, because a lot of people are called that. MI 5 want a word about him. Try and clear it up. Another good deed would be to extract an answer from Blackhead about the supply of straw for stuffing medical establishment palliasses. They're frantic about it in Scotland.'

'Blackhead's not raised objection to that?'

'He says straw comes under a special restrictive order. He should be alerted about the evacuation too, so that he can think of difficulties.'

Borrit opened the door, allowing a sharp current of air to drive in from the passages. This was done as a challenge. He leant on the handle, looking rather aggrieved. There were some shouts from the others requiring that the door be shut at once. Borrit pointed to Pennistone and myself. He would not venture to leave without Pennistone, but, to humour him, we both made a move towards the corridor.

'Come as far as the staff entrance,' said Pennistone. 'In case I think of other urgent problems.'

We followed Borrit down the back staircase. On the first floor, Intelligence, in its profuse forms, mingled with Staff Duties, a grumpy crowd, most of them, especially the Regulars ('If they were any good, they wouldn't be here,' Pennistone said) and a few Operational sections, on the whole less immediately active ones, the more vital tending to have rooms on the floor above, close to the generals and higher-grade brigadiers. A few civilian *hauts fonctionnaires*, as Pennistone called them, were also located here, provided with a strip of carpet as they rose in rank; at the highest level—so it was rumoured—even a cupboard containing a chamber pot. The Army Council Room was on this floor, where three or four colonels, Finn among them, had also managed to find accommodation. The great double staircase leading from the marble hall of the main entrance (over which the porter, Vavassor, presided in a blue frock coat with scarlet facings and top hat with gold band) led directly to these, as it were, state apartments. On the ground floor, technical branches and those concerned with supply rubbed shoulders with all sorts and conditions, internal security contacts of a more or less secret sort, Public Relations, typing pools, dispatch-riders, Home Guard.

'Kielkiewicz has heard of Kafka,' said Pennistone, as we reached the foot of the stairs.

'You put them all through their literary paces as a matter of routine?'

'He laughed yesterday when I used the term Kafkaesque.'

'Wasn't that rather esoteric?'

'It just slipped out.'

Pennistone laughed at the thought. Though absolutely dedicated to his duties with the Poles, he also liked getting as much amusement out of the job as possible.

'In the course of discussing English sporting prints with Bobrowski,' he said, 'a subject he's rather keen on. It turned out the Empire style in Poland is known as "Duchy of Warsaw". That's nice, isn't it?'

'I don't look forward to this tussle with Blackhead about palliasse straw—by the way, what happened in the war about the Air Cooperation Squadron and which command it came under?'

'One of my notable achievements up there was to settle that. But go and see Q (Ops.). That's the big stuff now. Then have a talk with Finn. Where's the driver?'

Borrit gave a shout. An AT came quickly from behind

the screen that stood on one side of the untidy cramped little hall, crowded with people showing identity cards as they passed into the building. She glanced at us without interest, then went through the door into the street.

'Not bad,' said Borrit. 'I hadn't seen her before.'

Very young, she was one of those girls with a dead white complexion and black hair, the only colouring capable of rising above the boundlessly unbecoming hue of khaki. Instead of the usual ATS tunic imposed by some higher authority anxious that the Corps should look, if not as masculine as possible, at least as Sapphic, she had managed to provide herself, as some did, with soldier's battledress, paradoxically more adapted to the female figure. It had to be admitted that occasional intrusion at 'official level' of an attractive woman was something rather different from, more exciting than, the intermittent pretty secretary or waitress of peacetime, perhaps more subtly captivating from a sense that you and she belonged to the same complicated organism, in this case the Army. At the same time, Borrit's comment was one of routine rather than particular interest, because, according to himself, he lived a rather melancholy emotional life. His wife, a Canadian, had died about ten years before, and, while Borrit marketed fruit in Europe, their children preferred to live with grandparents in Canada. His own relations with the opposite sex took an exclusively commercial form.

'I've never had a free poke in my life,' he said. 'Subject doesn't seem to arise when you're talking to a respectable woman.'

He had confided this remark to the room in general. In spite of existing in this amatory twilight, he presented a reasonably cheerful exterior to the world, largely sustained by such phrases as 'What news on the Rialto?' or 'Bring on the dancing girls'. He and Pennistone followed the driver to where the Section's car was parked outside. I turned away from the staff entrance and made for Q (Ops.).

The new flight of stairs led down into the bowels of the earth, the caves and potholes of the basement and subbasement, an underground kingdom comparable with that inhabited by Widmerpool. It might have been thought that Mime and his fellow Nibelungen haunted these murky subterranean regions, but they were in fact peopled by more important, less easily replaceable beings, many of whom practised mysteries too momentous to be exposed (in a target registering already more than a dozen outers, though as yet no bull's eye) to the comparative uncertainties of life at street level or above. Here, for example, the unsleeping sages of Movement Control spun out their lives, sightless magicians deprived eternally of the light of the sun, while, by their powerful arts, they projected armies or individual over land and sea or through the illimitable wastes of the air. The atmosphere below seemed to demand such highly coloured metaphor, thoughts of magic and necromancy bringing Dr Trelawney to mind, and the rumours in the earlier war that he had been executed in the Tower as a spy. I wondered if the Good Doctor, as Moreland used to call him, were still alive. Indiscreet observance of the rites of his cult, especially where these involved exotic drugs, could bring trouble in this war, though retribution was likely to stop short of the firing squad. Moreland himself, with Mrs Maclintick, had left London months before on some governmentally sponsored musical tour of the provinces.

Like a phantasm in one of Dr Trelawney's own narcotically produced reveries, I flitted down passage after passage, from layer to layer of imperfect air-conditioning, finding the right door at last in an obscure corner. Q (Ops.) Colonel was speaking on the scrambler when I entered the room, so

I made as if to withdraw. He vigorously beckoned me to stay, continuing to talk for a few seconds about some overseas force. Abyssinia might have been a good guess. He hung up. I explained where I came from and put myself at his disposal.

'Ah, yes . . .'

He began to sort out papers, putting some away in a drawer. He gave an immediate impression, not only of knowing what he was about himself, but also of possessing the right sort of determination to use any information available from other sources. Inefficiency was rare in the building, but there was inevitably the occasional boor or temperamental obscurantist.

'Polish evacuation—here we are—these troops held by our Russian Allies since their invasion of our Polish Allies in 1939. They've retained their own units and formations?'

'We understand some in Central Asia have, or at least certain units have already been brigaded after release from prison camps. General Anders is organizing this.'

'The lot are in Central Asia?'

'At least eight or nine thousand Polish officers remain untraced.'

'Rather a large deficiency.'

'That's a minimum, sir. It's been put as high as fifteen thousand.'

'Any idea where they are?'

'Franz Josef Land's been suggested, sir.'

'Within the Arctic Circle?'

'Yes.'

He looked straight in front of him.

'Unlikely they'll be included in this evacuation, whatever its extent?'

'Seems most unlikely, sir.'

'Just the figures I have here?'

He pushed them over.

'So far as we know at present. On the other hand, anything might happen.'

'Let's have a look at the map again . . . Yangi-yul . . . Alma Ata . . . There's been constant pressure for the release of these troops?'

'All the time—also to discover the whereabouts of the missing officers.'

He wrote some notes.

'Lease-Lend . . .'

'Yes, sir?'

'You see the consignment papers?'

'From time to time some minor item is earmarked for the Polish forces in Russia and the papers pass through our hands.'

Once, when one of these interminable lists of weapons and vehicles, *matérial* of war for the Eastern Front, had come to us, Pennistone had compared the diplomatic representations of the moment, directed to obtaining the release of the immobilized Polish army, with a very small powder in a very large spoon of Lease-Lend jam. Now, the Germans penetrating into the country on an extended front, these solicitations seemed at last to have attracted official Soviet attention. This must have been four or five months before the siege of Stalingrad. Q (Ops.) Colonel ran through facts and figures, asked a few additional questions, then shook the papers together and clipped them back into their file.

'Right?'

'Right, sir.'

He took up the green telephone again.

'If the London Poles have anything to add to what I have here already, let me know.'

'We will, sir.'

He 'went over' on the scrambler with whomever he was

talking to, and, as I withdrew, could have been dealing with Icelandic matters. Like Orpheus or Herakles returning from the silent shades of Tartarus, I set off upstairs again, the objective now Finn's room on the second floor.

Outside the Army Council Room, side by side on the passage wall, hung, so far as I knew, the only pictures in the building, a huge pair of subfusc massively framed oil-paintings, subject and technique of which I could rarely pass without re-examination. The murkily stiff treatment of these two unwontedly elongated canvases, although not in fact executed by Horace Isbister RA, recalled his brush-work and treatment, a style that already germinated a kind of low-grade nostalgia on account of its naïve approach and total disregard for any 'modern' development in the painter's art. The merging harmonies—dark brown, dark red, dark blue—depicted incidents in the wartime life of King George V: *Where Belgium greeted Britain*, showing the bearded monarch welcoming Albert, King of the Belgians, on arrival in this country as an exile from his own: *Merville, December 1st, 1914*, in which King George was portrayed chatting with President Poincaré, this time both with beards, the President wearing a hat somewhat resembling the head-dress of an *avocat* in the French lawcourts. Perhaps it was fur, on account of the cold. This time too busy to make a fresh assessment, aesthetic or sartorial, I passed the picture by. Finn's door was locked. He might still be with the General, more probably was himself making a round of branches concerned with the evacuation. There was nothing for it but Blackhead, and restrictions on straw for hospital palliasses.

The stairs above the second floor led up into a rookery of lesser activities, some fairly obscure of definition. On these higher storeys dwelt the Civil branches and their subsidiaries, Finance, Internal Administration, Passive Air Defence, all diminishing in official prestige as the altitude steepened. Finally the explorer converged on attics under the eaves, where crusty hermits lunched frugally from paper bags, amongst crumb-powdered files and documents ineradicably tattooed with the circular brand of the teacup. At these heights, vestiges of hastily snatched meals endured throughout all seasons, eternal as the unmelted upland snows. Here, under the leads, like some unjustly confined prisoner of the Council of Ten, lived Blackhead. It was a part of the building rarely penetrated, for even Blackhead himself preferred on the whole to make forays on others, rather than that his own fastness should be invaded.

'You'll never get that past Blackhead,' Pennistone had said, during my first week with the Section.

'Who's Blackhead?'

'Until you have dealings with Blackhead, the word "bureaucrat" will have conveyed no meaning to you. He is the super-*tchenovnik* of the classical Russian novel. Even this building can boast no one else quite like him. As a special treat you can negotiate with Blackhead this afternoon on the subject of the issue of screwdrivers and other tools to Polish civilian personnel temporarily employed at military technical establishments.'

This suggested caricature, Pennistone's taste for presenting individuals in dramatic form. On the contrary, the picture was, if anything, toned down from reality. At my former Divisional Headquarters, the chief clerk, Warrant Officer Class I Mr Diplock, had seemed a fair performer in the field specified. To transact business even for a few minutes with Blackhead was immediately to grasp how pitifully deficient Diplock had, in fact, often proved himself in evolving a really impregnable system of obstruction and preclusion; awareness of such falling short of perfection perhaps telling on his nerves and finally causing him to embezzle and desert.

'Blackhead is a man apart,' said Pennistone. 'Even his

colleagues are aware of that. His minutes have the abstract quality of pure extension.'

It was true. Closely 'in touch' with the Finance branch, he was, for some reason, not precisely categorized as one of them. Indeed, all precision was lacking where the branch to which Blackhead belonged was in question, even the house telephone directory, usually unequivocal, becoming all at once vague, even shifty. The phrase 'inspection and collation of governmental civil and economic administration in relation to Allied military liaison' had once been used by a member of one of the Finance branches themselves, then hastily withdrawn as if too explicit, something dangerous for security reasons to express so openly. Such prevarication hinted at the possibility that even his fellows by now could not exactly determine—anyway define to a layman—exactly what Blackhead really did. His rank, too, usually so manifest in every civil servant, seemed in Blackhead's case to have become blurred by time and attrition. To whom was he responsible? Whom—if anyone—did he transcend? Obviously in the last resort he was subservient to the Permanent Under-Secretary of State for War, and Blackhead himself would speak of Assistant Under Secretaries—even of Principals—as if their ranks represented unthinkable heights of official attainment. On the other hand, none of these people seemed to have the will, even the power, to control him. It was as if Blackhead, relatively humble though his grading might be, had become an anonymous immanence of all their kind, a fetish, the Voodoo deity of the whole Civil Service to be venerated and placated, even if better—safer—hidden away out of sight: the mystic holy essence incarnate of arguing, encumbering, delaying, hair-splitting, all for the best of reasons.

Blackhead might be a lone wolf, a one-man band, but he was a force that had to be reckoned with, from whom there was no court of appeal, until once in a way Operations would cut the Gordian knot, brutally disregarding Blackhead himself, overriding his objections, as it were snapping asunder the skinny arm he had slipped through the bolt-sockets of whatever administrative door he was attempting to hold against all comers. Operations would, as I say, sometimes thrust Blackhead aside, and continue to wage war unimpeded by him against the Axis. However, such a confrontation took place only when delay had become desperate. There was no doubt he would make himself felt by delaying tactics when the evacuation got under way, until something of that drastic sort took place.

'Of course I'm not an officer,' he had once remarked bitterly to Pennistone when a humiliation of just that kind had been visited on him, 'I'm only Mr Blackhead.'

Some years after the war was over—by chance attending a gathering of semi-official character, possibly a *soirée* organized for a fund or charity—I enquired Blackhead's story from a former colleague of his who happened to be present. This personage (even in war days of distinguished rank, one of the *hauts fonctionnaires* on the second floor) would at first do no more than laugh, loudly though a shade uncomfortably. He seemed anxious to evade the question. In fact, all at length recoverable from his answers, such as they were, became reduced to the hypothesis that Blackhead had been deliberately relegated to an appointment peculiar to himself—that in which our Section had dealings with him—chiefly in order to keep him out of the way of more important people. As unique occupant of his individual branch, even if he did not promote the war effort, he did not greatly impede it—so, at least, my informant insisted—while duties almost anywhere else might prove less innocuous. This highly successful person nodded several times when he admitted that. Self-esteem made the reply a little unacceptable to me. Did we matter so little? I argued the point. Why could not Blackhead be eradicated entirely? No such machinery existed. That was definite. Blackhead's former colleague showed himself as nearly apologetic about the fact as anyone of his calling had it in him. He fiddled with the decoration round his neck.

'The process was known afterwards as doing a Blackhead,' he allowed. 'Alternatively, having a Blackhead done on you. The public may think we're a staid crowd, but we have our professional jokes like everyone else. I say, what are your views on liquid refreshment? Would it be acceptable? I wouldn't say no myself. Don't I see a buffet over there? Let's make tracks.'

This subsequent conversation explained why Pennistone and the rest of us, like Jacob and the Angel, had to wrestle with Blackhead until the coming of day, or nearly that. Such was the biblical comparison that sprang to mind as I climbed the stairs leading to Blackhead's room, the moral exile to which his own kind had banished him emphasized not only by its smallness, but also by the fact that he lived there alone, isolation rare for one of his putatively low degree—if, indeed, his degree was low. I opened the door a crack, but further enlargement of entry was blocked by sheer stowage of paper, the files thickly banked about the floor like wholesale goods awaiting allotment to retailers, or, more credibly, the residue of a totally unsaleable commodity stored up here out of everyone's way. Blackhead himself was writing. He jumped up for a second and fiercely kicked a great cliff of files aside so that I could squeeze into the room. Then he returned to whatever he was at, his right hand moving feverishly across the paper, while his left thumb and forefinger, both stained with ink, rested on the handle of a saucerless cup.

'I'll attend to you in a minute, Jenkins.'

Not only was Blackhead, so to speak, beyond rank, he was also beyond age; beyond or outside Time. He might have been a worn—terribly worn—thirty-five; on the other hand (had not superannuation regulations, no doubt as sacred to Blackhead as any other official ordinances, precluded any such thing), he could easily have achieved threescore years and ten, with a safe prospect for his century. Emaciated, though obviously immensely strong, he was probably in truth approaching fifty. His hair, which formed an irregular wiry fringe over a furrowed leathery brow, was of a metallic shade that could have been natural to him all his life.

'Glad you've come, Jenkins,' he said, putting his face still closer to the paper on which he was writing. 'Pennistone minuted me . . . Polish Women's Corps . . . terms I haven't been able fully to interpret . . . In short don't at all comprehend . . .'

His hand continued to move at immense speed, with a nervous shaky intensity, backwards and forwards across the page of the file, ending at last in a signature. He blotted the minute, read through what he had written, closed the covers. Then he placed the file on an already overhanging tower of similar dockets, a vast rickety skyscraper of official comment, based on the flimsy foundation of a wire tray. At this final burden, the pyramid began to tremble, at first seemed likely to topple over. Blackhead showed absolute command of the situation. He steadied the pile with scarcely a touch of his practised hand. Then, eyes glinting behind his spectacles, he rose jerkily and began rummaging about among similar foothills of files ranged on a side table.

'Belgian Women's Corps, bicycle for . . . Norwegian military attaché, office furniture . . . Royal Netherlands Artillery, second echelon lorries . . . Czechoslovak Field Security, appointment of cook . . . Distribution of Polish Global Sum in relation to other Allied commitments—now we're getting warm . . . Case of Corporal Altmann, legal costs in alleged rape—that's moving away . . . Luxembourg shoulder flashes —right out . . . Here we are . . . Polish Women's Corps, soap issue for—that's the one I wanted a word about.'

'I really came about the question of restrictions on straw for stuffing hospital palliasses in Scotland.'

Blackhead paused, on the defensive at once.

'You can't be expecting an answer on straw already?'

'We were hoping—'

'But look here . . .'

'It must be a week or ten days.'

'Week or ten days? Cast your eyes over these, Jenkins.'

Blackhead made a gesture with his pen in the direction of the files stacked on the table amongst which he had been excavating.

'Barely had time to glance at the straw,' he said. 'Certainly not think it out properly. It's a tricky subject, straw.'

'Liaison HQ in Scotland hoped for a quick answer.'

'Liaison HQ in Scotland are going to be disappointed.'

'What's so difficult?'

'There's the Ministry of Supply angle.'

'Can't we ignore them for once?'

'Ministry of Agriculture may require notification. Straw interests them . . . We won't talk about that now. What I want you to tell me, Jenkins, is what Pennistone means by this . . .'

Blackhead held—thrust—the file forward in my direction.

'Couldn't we just cast an eye over the straw file too, if you could find it while I try to solve this one?'

Blackhead was unwilling, but in the end, after a certain amount of search, the file about hospital palliasses was found and also extracted.

'Now it's the Women's Corps I want to talk about,' he said. 'Issue of certain items—soap, to be exact, and regulations for same. There's a principle at stake. I pointed that out to Pennistone. Read this . . . where my minute begins . . .'

To define the length of a 'minute'—an official memorandum authorizing or recommending any given course—is, naturally, like trying to lay down the size of a piece of chalk. There can be short minutes or long minutes, as there might be a chalk down or a fragment of chalk scarcely perceptible to the eye. Thus a long minute might be divided into sections and sub-headings, running into pages and signed by an authority of the highest rank. On the other hand, just as a piece of chalk might reasonably be thought of as a length of that limestone convenient for writing on a blackboard, the ordinary run of minutes exchanged between such as Pennistone and Blackhead might be supposed, in general, to take a fairly brief form—say two or three, to perhaps ten or a dozen, lines. Blackhead pointed severely to what he had written. Then he turned the pages several times. It was a real Marathon of a minute, even for Blackhead. When it came to an end at last he tapped his finger sharply on a comment written below his own signature.

'Look at this,' he said.

He spoke indignantly. I leant forward to examine the exhibit, which was in Pennistone's handwriting. Blackhead had written, in all, three and a half pages on the theory and practice of soap issues for military personnel, with especial reference to the Polish Women's Corps. Turning from his spidery scrawl to Pennistone's neat hand, two words only were inscribed. They stood out on the file:

*Please amplify. D. Pennistone. Maj. GS.*

Blackhead stood back.

'What do you think of that?' he asked.

I could find no suitable answer, in fact had nearly laughed, which would have been fatal, an error from which no recovery would have been possible.

'He didn't mention the matter to me.'

'As if I hadn't gone into it carefully,' said Blackhead.

'You'd better have a word with Pennistone.'

'Word with him? Not before I've made sure about the point I've missed. He wouldn't have said that unless he knew. I thought you'd be able to explain, Jenkins. If he thinks I've omitted something, he'd hardly keep it from you.'

'I'm at a loss—but about the palliasse straw—'

'What else can he want to know?' said Blackhead. 'It's me that's asking the questions there, not him.'

'You'll have to speak together.'

'Amplify, indeed,' said Blackhead. 'I spent a couple of hours on that file.'

Blackhead stared down at what Pennistone had written. He was distraught; aghast. Pennistone had gone too far. We should be made to suffer for this frivolity of his. That was, if Blackhead retained his sanity.

'What would you like me to do about it?'

Blackhead took off his spectacles and pointed the shafts at me.

'I'll tell you what,' he said. 'I could send it to F 17 (b) for comments. They're the *only ones*, in my view, who might take exception to not being consulted. They're a touchy lot. Always have been. I may have slipped up in not asking them, but I'd have never guessed Pennistone would have spotted that.'

'The thing we want to get on with is the straw.'

'Get on with?' said Blackhead. 'Get on with? If Pennistone wants to get on with things, why does he minute me in the aforesaid terms? That's what I can't understand.'

'Why not talk to him when he comes back. He's at Polish GHQ at the moment. Can't we just inspect the straw file?'

Blackhead had been put so far off his balance that his usual obstinacy must have become impaired. Quite unexpectedly, he gave way all at once about the straw. We discussed the subject of palliasses fully, Blackhead noting in the file that 'a measure of agreement had been reached'. It was a minor triumph. I also prepared the way for papers about the evacuation, but this Blackhead could hardly take in.

'I can't understand Pennistone writing that,' he said. 'I've never had it written before—*please amplify*—not in all my service, all the years I've worked in this blessed building. It's not right. It suggests a criticism of my method.'

I left him gulping the chill dregs of his tea. Finn would probably be back in his room now, ready to hear the substance of what Q (Ops.) Colonel had said.

Rounding the corner of the passage just beyond the two pictures of George V, I saw Finn's door was open. A tall, stoutish officer, wearing khaki and red tabs, though not for some indefinable reason a British uniform, was taking leave of him. It seemed best to let them finish their conversation, then, when the foreign officer, probably a newly appointed military attaché, had left, catch Finn between interviews. This was never easy, because a steady flow perennially occupied him. He looked up the passage at that moment, and, seeing me, jerked his head as a summons. The red-tabbed officer himself turned. Dark complexioned, hook nose—though that feature was nothing to the size of Finn's—he had something of the air of a famous tenor. More on account of recent photographs in the press, than because of having seen him before, I recognized Prince Theodoric. The story of the escape he had made from his own country at the moment of its invasion (he was said to have shot dead a Gestapo agent) had been given a lot of publicity when he arrived in England.

'Nicholas,' said Finn. 'I want to present you. One of my officers, sir—he will see you to the door, sir.'

Prince Theodoric held out his hand.

'You've been too kind already, Colonel Finn,' he said.

'Allowing me to take up your precious time with our small concerns. I certainly mustn't impose myself further by requisitioning the services of your officers, no doubt as overworked as yourself. I may have shown myself in the past inexperienced in methods of tactical withdrawal—as you know too well from the newspapers, I left the palace without shaving tackle—but at least let me assure you, my dear Colonel, that I can find my way unaided from this building.'

Theodoric talked that precise, rather old-fashioned English, which survives mainly outside the country itself. His manner, very consciously royal, had probably been made more assertive and genial by recent hazards undergone, because he had entirely overcome the self-conscious embarrassment I remembered from former brief contacts with him. Now, he added to that total ease and directness of royalties, who have never doubted for a second the validity of their rank and station, the additional confidence of a man who has made his own way in the world, and a dangerous way at that. Finn began to assure the Prince that we were all at his service at any moment of the day.

'Finn's in many ways an unworldly man,' Pennistone used to say. 'He likes to hobnob with people like Bernhard of the Netherlands, Olaf of Norway, Felix of Luxembourg. Snobbish, if you like, in one sense. On the other hand, he wouldn't for a second allow any such taste to influence an official decision—nor would he walk across the passage to ingratiate himself with anyone, military or civil, for material reasons. In that respect, Finn is quite unlike Farebrother. Farebrother will get right up the arse of anyone he thinks likely to help him on. After all, everyone's got to choose their own approach to life.'

In any case, if Finn were ceremonious in his treatment of Theodoric, the Prince—as Templer had remarked—had always shown himself profoundly anti-Nazi and a friend of this country. There was reason to accord courtesy. At this moment Farebrother himself appeared. He had evidently just made some contact required in our building and was marching along the passage, wearing his cap, a stick tucked under his arm. He came to halt where we stood and saluted, immediately beginning to dispense round him what Stringham used to call 'several million volts of synthetic charm'.

'This is well met, sir,' he said dramatically.

He addressed himself to Theodoric, at the same time putting his hand on Finn's shoulder.

'I was coming to look in on my old friend here, after paying another visit, and now I find Your Royal Highness present too, just when I had made a mental note to telephone your equerry and ask for an interview.'

'Oh, I've nothing so grand as an equerry these days,' said Theodoric. 'But my staff-officer will arrange an appointment, Colonel Farebrother, any time that suits you.'

'There are several things I hoped to discuss, sir.'

'Why, of course, Colonel—'

Finn began to look rather disturbed. However much he might admire Farebrother's 'charm', he was not at all anxious to have some plot hatched on his doorstep. He must now have scented danger of circuitous arrangements being made through himself, because he suddenly assumed the expression of countenance that gave notice his deafness was about to come into play forthwith. At the same time, he twisted round his head and leant forward slightly.

'Can't hear all you say, Sunny, in this passage,' he said. 'Come into my room just for a moment or two. I'd like a word about Belgian arrangements, so far as they affect us both. I can just fit you in before General Asbjørnsen arrives. Don't keep the Prince waiting, Nicholas.'

'Why, Nicholas?' said Farebrother, feigning to recognize me only at that moment. 'You and I must have a talk, too, about yesterday's meeting . . .'

If Farebrother hoped to prolong this interlude with Prince Theodoric by bringing me in, he underrated Finn's capacity for action. The delaying tactic failed entirely. Finn somehow managed to get behind Farebrother, and, with surprising adroitness, propelled him forward into the room, the door of which was immediately closed.

'Then I shall hear from you, Colonel Farebrother?' Theodoric called.

He had shown every sign of being inquisitive about whatever Farebrother had to offer, but now it was clearly too late to go into matters further. He turned and smiled at me a little uncomprehendingly. We set off together in the direction of the front staircase.

'Your car's at the main entrance, sir?'

'Car? Not a bit of it. I walk.'

It seemed wiser not to refer to the party given by Mrs Andriadis more than a dozen years before, where I had in fact first set eyes on Theodoric, but I mentioned my presentation to him when he had been staying with Sir Magnus Donners at Stourwater, and the Walpole-Wilsons had taken me over to luncheon there. According to Penniston, Mrs Andriadis herself was living in one room in Bloomsbury, drinking and drugging heavily. Later, one heard, she occupied herself with making propaganda for the so-called 'Second Front'.

'By Jove, those were the days,' said Theodoric. 'We didn't know how lucky we were. Will you believe me, Captain Jenkins, I had at that time only been shot at twice in my life, on each occasion by certified lunatics? And then, of course, marriage makes one more serious. We have become middle-aged, my dear Captain, we have become middle-aged.'

He sighed.

'I saw Sir Gavin Walpole-Wilson the other day,' he went on. 'Of course he is getting on now, older even than ourselves. We discussed a lot of matters—as you remember, he was formerly your country's minister plenipotentiary to my own. Now he stands well to the left politically. I have certain leanings that way myself, but not as far as Sir Gavin. One must not remain embedded in the past, but Sir Gavin does not always understand our difficulties and the ruthless methods of a certain Ally. There are plenty of good young men in my country who want to get rid of the Germans. There are also men not equally good there who play another part—not all of them our own countrymen.'

Theodoric spoke with great earnestness. It was clear he considered not only people like Finn and Farebrother, but even those of my own rank worth sweeping in as supporters of whatever policy he represented.

'In knowing Sir Magnus Donners,' he said, 'I am particularly fortunate. He is personally conversant with our industrial problems, also—perhaps I should not say this—has the ear of a Very Important Person. If something is to be done, Sir Magnus is the man to do it. I need not tell you that I have had more than one long and interesting talk with him. He says we must wait.'

Theodoric stopped on the way down the marble stairs, where the flights divided, left and right, under the elaborately gilded wall-clock and bronze bust of Kitchener. His tone suggested my views on the matter were scarcely less important than those of Sir Magnus. In terms of propaganda, that was an effective technique. The persuasiveness of the Prince was something to be reckoned with. This characteristic could have direct bearing on the fate of his country.

'I shall continue to put our case,' he said.

By now he had reached the great hall. Vavassor, the

porter, an attendant spirit of some importance in the Section's background, was standing by the door. It was commonly Vavassor's duty to give warning to Finn of the arrival of callers belonging to the higher echelons, some of whom were capable of turning up without previous appointment, and demanding an interview on the spot. Vavassor could hold them in check; in extreme cases, turn them away. He was also, in this office of guarding the door, a key figure in the lives of Pennistone and myself, on account of frequent association with Allied comings and goings, raising no difficulties about our using the main entrance—superstitiously, though uncategorically, apprehended as prerogative of officers of the rank of brigadier and above—when we arrived for duty in the morning. This not only saved several yards of pavement, but, more important, meant avoidance of the teeming mob at the staff entrance. It was a good opening to the day's work. Vavassor saluted Theodoric.

'No fire?' said the Prince.

'Don't let us have any coal when the weather's short of freezing,' said Vavassor. 'That grate takes the best part of a hundredweight a day, it's the truth. Wasn't made for rationing.'

He pointed to the huge fireplace. One supposed that at a certain level of rank—say, lieutenant-general—he called officers 'sir', though I had never heard him do so. In any case it was a formality he always considered inappropriate for foreigners, royal or otherwise.

'When I wait to be summoned by Colonel Finn and warm myself beside the fire,' said Theodoric, 'I always feel like St Peter.'

'I hope you won't cut off any ears, sir, when delay has been intolerably long.'

'How reassuring, Captain Jenkins, that your General Staff are brought up on the Scriptures. They are the foundation of knowledge. Now I must say goodbye. Tell Colonel Finn I will check the figures I gave him—persuade him, something I think he is rather nervous about, that I will not involve him in any matter of which he might disapprove.'

Theodoric laughed. He had evidently summed up Finn correctly. I remembered Sillery (who had recently written a long letter to *The Times* in praise of Stalin's declared war aims) speaking of the shrewdness Theodoric inherited from 'that touch of Coburg blood', adding with characteristic malice, 'though I suppose one should not hint at that.' I saw the Prince down the steps. He waved his hand, and set off at a sharp pace in the direction of Trafalgar Square. I returned under the high portal.

'Prince, is he?' asked Vavassor. 'That's what he calls himself when he arrives.'

'That's what he is.'

'Allied or Neutral?'

'So far as he himself is concerned, Allied.'

'See 'em all down here if you wait long enough.'

'I bet you do.'

'I suppose some of 'em help to win the war.'

'Let's hope so.'

'Not too good in the Far East at the moment of speaking.'

'Ever serve there?'

'Eight years to a day.'

'Things may pick up.'

'I worry too much,' said Vavassor. 'Shakespeare's dying words.'

His attention, my own too, was at that moment unequivocally demanded by the hurricane-like imminence of a thickset general, obviously of high rank, wearing enormous horn-rimmed spectacles. He had just burst from a flagged staff-car almost before it had drawn up by the kerb.

Now he tore up the steps of the building at the charge, exploding through the inner door into the hall. An extraordinary current of physical energy, almost of electricity, suddenly pervaded the place. I could feel it stabbing through me. This was the CIGS. His quite remarkable and palpable extension of personality, in its effect on others, I had noticed not long before, out in the open. Coming down Sackville Street, I had all at once been made aware of something that required attention on the far pavement and saw him pounding along. I saluted at admittedly longish range. The salute was returned. Turning my head to watch his progress, I then had proof of being not alone in acting as a kind of receiving-station for such rays—which had, morally speaking, been observable, on his appointment to the top post, down as low as platoon commander. On this Sackville Street occasion, an officer a hundred yards or more ahead, had his nose glued to the window of a bookshop. As the CIGS passed (whom he might well have missed in his concentration on the contents of the window), this officer suddenly swivelled a complete about-turn, saluting too. No doubt he had seen the reflection in the plate glass. All the same, in its own particular genre, the incident gave the outward appearance of exceptional magnetic impact. That some such impact existed, was confirmed by this closer conjunction in the great hall. Vavassor, momentarily overawed—there could be no doubt of it—came to attention and saluted with much more empressement than usual. Having no cap, I merely came to attention. The CIGS glanced for a split second, as if summarizing all the facts of one's life.

'Good morning.'

It was a terrific volume of sound, an absolute bellow, at the same time quite effortless. A moment later, he was on the landing halfway up the stairs, where Theodoric had paused. Then he disappeared from sight. Vavassor grinned and nodded. He was without comment for once. I left him to his reflections about the Far East, hurrying myself now, again in the hope of catching Finn, quickly passing Kitchener's cold and angry eyes, haunting and haunted, surveying with the deepest disapproval all who came that way. Finn was free. He made no reference to Farebrother.

'You'll have to be quick, Nicholas,' he said. 'Asbjørnsen's due at any moment, but he's sometimes a second or two late. Now what about Q (Ops.)?'

He had quite set aside his deafness. I ran over the points at speed. Finn made some notes, collating the information with whatever material had emerged from his session with our own General. He was now quite recovered from the phase, reported by Pennistone, of feeling the only hope of getting the thing properly done would be to fly to Persia and himself arrange it singlehanded.

'The civilian elements are now definitely coming out, sir?'

'Anders insisted—no doubt rightly—but the women and children will not make the operation any easier.'

There had been controversy about these camp-followers who had managed to exist in the wake of the army, largely on its shared rations. At first it had seemed they might have to stay behind.

'Some of the boys are old enough to be trained as cadets. The CIGS himself noted that point on the paper with approval.'

Finn's telephone bell rang.

'Ask him to come up,' he said. 'It's Asbjørnsen. We'll return to the evacuation later, Nicholas. I shall have to keep Asbjørnsen from talking too much, as Colonel Chu is due in less than twenty minutes. Did I tell you Chu's latest after his six months' course at Sandhurst?'

The Chinese military attaché, well known for the demanding nature of his requests, had just completed an attachment as cadet to the Royal Military College.

'Chu enjoyed the RMC so much he wants to go to Eton.'

'He could see Windsor Castle at the same time, though the state apartments are probably not open.'

'Good God,' said Finn. 'He doesn't just want to visit the place—he hopes to attend the school as a pupil.'

'He's a shade old, sir.'

'I told him thirty-eight is regarded as too mature in this country to be still at school. It was no good. All he said was "I can make myself young." '

Finn sighed.

'I wish I could,' he said.

Sometimes the military attachés dispirited him. Chu's unreasonableness seemed to have achieved that. General Asbjørnsen arrived in the room. Tall, like General Lebedev, not much given to laughter, he always reminded me of Monsieur Ørn, the long craggy Norwegian, who had been at La Grenadière when, as a boy, I had stayed with the Leroys in Touraine. He shook hands with Finn and myself gravely. I withdrew to our room. Corporal Curtis had again increased the pile of stuff on the desk. I was still going through this when Pennistone returned from the Titian.

'What on earth were you about, David, minuting Blackhead *please amplify*?'

'Has it upset him?'

'Beyond description.'

'Good.'

'What were your reasons?'

'Renan says complication is anterior to simplicity. I thought Blackhead would make an interesting experiment for trying out that theory.'

'We can only pray Renan was right.'

'Renan would find prayer charming, but ineffectual. Did you see Q (Ops.)?'

Pennistone went through the points I had cleared with Finn.

'Look, Nick,' he said. 'I shan't be able to collect the Klnisaszewski Report tomorrow afternoon, as there's another meeting about the evacuation. Will you get it? Nothing whatever required, except to receive it from the Polish officer on duty.'

The Klnisaszewski Report was one of those items of Intelligence that fell, as such items sometimes do, in a no-man's-land between normal official channels and those secret services so cautiously handled by Finn. Even Finn saw no harm in our trafficking in this particular exchange of information, which the Operational and 'Country' sections liked to see. For some internal reason, the Polish branch concerned preferred to hand over the report direct, rather than present it, in the normal manner, through the Second Bureau of their GHQ. Pennistone, as it happened, always collected the Klnisaszewski Report, though merely, in the division of our duties, because he had fallen into the habit of doing so.

'Here's the address,' he said. 'It's the north side of the Park. We might discuss some of these evacuation points further at lunch.'

The following day I arranged to collect the report in the afternoon. When I went down to the staff entrance and shouted for our driver, the white-faced girl commended by Borrit again appeared from behind the screen. She was as sulky as ever. The Section's car was just large enough to hold four persons in great discomfort. If you were the only passenger, you could travel at the back or beside the driver, according to whim. I told her the street number and sat in front.

'Can you find your way there?'

'Yes.'

'You know London pretty well?'

She hardly answered. After a few minutes beside her, it was clear this AT possessed in a high degree that power which all women—some men—command to a greater or lesser extent when in the mood, of projecting round them a sense of vast resentment. The girl driving, I noticed, was able to do this with quite superlative effect. Her rankling animosity against the world in general was discharged with adamantine force, comparable with Audrey Maclintick's ill humours when her husband was alive, or Anne Stepney's intimations of rebellion before she had shaken off the trammels of family life. However, those two, although not without their admirers, were hardly in the same class as this girl when it came to looks. Borrit had been right in marking her down. She was very striking. All the same, after another remark received with little or no response, I gave up further talk. Perhaps she had a grievance or the curse. These drivers usually only did duty for a week or two and at the moment inducement was lacking to coax her out of that mood. It occurred to me—one never feels older than in the middle thirties—that she was bored with all but young men or had taken an instantaneous dislike to me. Conversation lapsed. Then, while driving through Hyde Park, she suddenly spoke of her own accord, though even then in a way to suggest that speech was a painful effort to her, every word so far as possible to be conserved.

'You're Captain Jenkins, aren't you?'

'I am.'

'I think you know my mother.'

'What's your mother's name?'

'Flavia Wisebite—but I'm Pamela Flitton. My father was her first husband.'

This was Stringham's niece. I remembered her holding the bride's train at his wedding. She must have been five or six years old then. At one stage of the service there had been a disturbance at the back of the church and someone afterwards said she had been sick in the font. Whoever had remarked that found nothing surprising in unsatisfactory behaviour from her. Someone else had commented: 'That child's a fiend.' I knew little of her father, Cosmo Flitton—not even whether he were still alive—except for the fact that he had lost an arm in the earlier war, drank heavily, and was said to be a professional gambler. Alleged to be not too scrupulous in business dealings, Flitton had been involved in Baby Wentworth's divorce, later rejecting marriage with her. He had left Pamela's mother when this girl was not much more than a baby. Establishing the sequence of inevitable sameness that pursues individual progression through life, Flavia had married another drunk, Harrison F. Wisebite, son of a Minneapolis hardware millionaire, whose jocularity he had inherited with only a minute fragment of a post-depression fortune. I wondered idly whether Flavia owed her name to *The Prisoner of Zenda.* Mrs Foxe would have been quite capable of that. Mrs Foxe was said to have given her daughter a baddish time. Pamela, an only child, must be at least twenty by now. She looked younger.

'Where is your mother at the moment?'

'She's helping with Red Cross libraries. She gets sent all over the place.'

'I suppose you've no news of your Uncle Charles?'

'Charles Stringham?'

'The last I saw of him, he'd been posted overseas. I don't even know where.'

She began driving the little car very fast and we nearly ran into an army truck coming across the Park from the opposite direction. She did not answer. I repeated the question.

'You've heard nothing?'

'He was at Singapore.'

'Oh, God . . .'

With that strange instinct that exists in the ranks for guessing a destination correctly, Stringham had supposed himself on the way to the Far East.

'Nothing's known, I suppose?'

'No.'

'Just reported missing?'

'Yes.'

'He used to be a great friend of mine.'

'We were close when I was quite a child.'

She said that in an odd way, as if almost intending to imply something not to be investigated too far. When I thought the remark over later, it seemed to me unlikely she had seen much of Stringham when she was a child, and he was being cured of drink in the iron grip of Miss Weedon. Later, I understood that the ambiguity might have been deliberate. Girls of Pamela's sort take pleasure in making remarks like that, true or not.

'Will you tell your mother—how dreadfully sorry . . .'

Again she made no answer. Iciness of manner remained complete. She was perhaps not altogether normal, what Borrit called 'a bit off the beam'. There was no denying she was a striking girl to look at. Many men would find this cosmic rage with life, as it seemed to be, an added attraction. Perhaps all these suppositions were wide of the mark, and she was just in poor form because she considered herself crossed in love or something obvious of that sort. All the same, the impression was of an uneasy personality, one to cause a lot of trouble. The news about Stringham made relations even more difficult. Her demeanour suggested only gross indifference on my own part had kept me in ignorance of what had happened, that she did not wish to speak more about a matter specially painful to herself.

'How did you discover I was in the Section?'

'Oh, I don't know. Your name cropped up somewhere

the other night. I was saying what a bloody awful series of jobs I always get, and the next one was to drive for this outfit. Somebody said you were in it.'

'You don't like the ATS?'

'Who wants to be a bloody AT?'

By this time we had entered the confines of Bayswater. Some of the big houses here had been bombed and abandoned, others were still occupied. Several blocks that had formerly housed Victorian judges and merchants now accommodated refugees from Gibraltar, whose tawny skins and brightly coloured shirts and scarves made this once bleak and humdrum quarter of London, with its uncleaned or broken windows and peeling plaster, look like the back streets of a Mediterranean port. Even so, the area was not yet so squalid as it was in due course to become in the period immediately following the end of the war, when squares and crescents over which an aroma of oppressive respectability had gloomily hung, became infested at all hours of day and night by prostitutes of the lowest category.

'What number did you say?'

'It must be the one on the corner.'

She drew up the car in front of a large grey house in the midst of a complex of streets that had on the whole escaped bomb damage. Several steps led up to a sub-palladian porch, the fanlight over the open door daubed with dark paint to comply with black-out regulations. The place had that slightly sinister air common to most of the innumerable buildings hurriedly converted to official use, whether or not they were enclaves of a more or less secret nature.

'Will you wait with the car? I shan't be long.'

After the usual vetting at the door, my arrival being expected, quick admission took place. A guide in civilian clothes led the way to a particular office where the report was to be obtained. We went up some stairs, through a large hall or ante-chamber where several men and women were sitting in front of typewriters, surrounded by walls covered with a faded design of blue and green flowers, enclosed above and below by broad parchment-like embossed surfaces. This was no doubt the double-drawing-room of some old-fashioned family, who had not redecorated their home for decades. I was shown into the office of a Polish lieutenant-colonel in uniform, from whom the report was to be received. We shook hands.

'Good afternoon . . . Please sit down . . . *prosze Pana, prosze Pana* . . . I usually see Major Pennistone, yes.'

He unlocked a drawer and handed over the report. We spoke about its contents for a minute or two, and shook hands again. Then he accompanied me back to where I could find my way out, and, after shaking hands for the third time, we parted. Halfway down the stairs, I grasped that I was in the Ufford, ancient haunt of Uncle Giles. The place of typewriters, so far from being the drawing-room of some banker or tea-broker (perhaps that once), was the combined 'lounge' and 'writing-room', in the former of which my Uncle used to entertain me with fishpaste sandwiches and seed cake. There, Mrs Erdleigh had 'set out the cards', foretold the rows about St John Clarke's book on Isbister, my love affair with Jean Duport. The squat Moorish tables of those days had been replaced by trestles: the engraving of *Bolton Abbey in the Olden Time*, by a poster of characteristically Slavonic design announcing an exhibition of Polish Arts and Crafts. On the ledge of the mantelpiece, on which under a glass dome had stood the clock with hands eternally pointing to twenty minutes past five, were photographs of General Sikorski and Mr Churchill. It struck me the Ufford was in reality the Temple of Janus, the doors between the lounge and the writing-room closed in peace, open in war.

Reaching the entrance, I saw the hotel's name had been obliterated over the front door, as had also that of the De

Tabley opposite, to which Uncle Giles had once, at least, briefly defected; only to return in penitence—had he been capable of that inner state—to the Ufford. The De Tabley was now the local branch of the Food Office. The name always recalled an incident at school. Le Bas used to make a habit of reading from time to time the works of the lesser-known Victorian poets to his pupils. He had been doing this on some occasion, declaiming with his accustomed guttural enunciation and difficulty with the letter 'R':

> 'Sweet are the ways of death to weary feet,
> Calm are the shades of men.
> The phantom fears no tyrant in his seat,
> The slave is master then.'

He asked where the lines came from. Of course no one knew.

'Lord de Tabley's chorus from *Medea.*'

'Never heard of him, sir.'

'A melancholy fellow, but not without merit.'

Stringham, who had previously appeared all but asleep, had asked if he might see the book. Le Bas handed it over. He always rather liked Stringham, although never much at ease with him. Stringham turned the pages for a moment or two, then returned to the poem. Le Bas had read aloud. Stringham himself spoke the second verse:

> 'Love is abolished; well that that is so;
> We know him best as Pain.
> The gods are all cast out, and let them go!
> Who ever found them gain?'

Le Bas was prepared, in moderation, to have Death commended, but he never liked references to Love; probably, for that matter, was unwilling to have the gods so peremptorily dismissed. He had, I suppose, been betrayed into quoting the earlier lines on account of some appositeness they bore to whatever he had been talking about. He must have seen that to allow Stringham to handle the volume itself had been a false step on his own part.

'Love, of course, had a rather different meaning—indeed, two quite separate meanings in Ancient Greece—from what the modern world understands by the term,' he said. 'While railing against the gods was by no means unknown in their mythological stories.'

'Not bad for a peer of the realm, do you think, sir?' said Stringham.

That was rather cheek, but Le Bas had let it pass, probably finding a laugh the easiest channel for moving on to less tricky matters.

As I went down the steps, I saw a uniformed Pole had strolled out of the Ufford—as I now thought of the place—and was chatting with Pamela Flitton. He seemed to be making a better job of it than myself, because, although continuing to look sullen, she was listening with comparative acceptance to what seemed the commonplace of conversation. At first I thought the Pole was an officer, then saw he was an 'other rank', who wore his battledress, as most of them did, with a tough air and some swagger. He was dark, almost Oriental in feature, showing a lot of gold teeth when he smiled and saluted, before withdrawing up the steps. We set off on the return journey. In the far distance sounded the gentle lowing of an Air Raid Warning. They were to be heard intermittently in the daytime. As the car passed once more through the park, the All Clear sounded, equally faint and far.

'Sounds as if they let off the first one by mistake.'

She did not answer. Perhaps she only liked foreigners. In any case, the thought of Stringham put things on an unhappy, uncomfortable basis. I was not sure, in truth, whether she wanted to avoid discussing the subject because she herself felt so deeply, or because she was really scarcely at all interested in anything but her own personality. We reached the staff entrance. I made some further remark about a message to her mother. She nodded, disappearing once more behind the screen. Pennistone had returned from the meeting.

'How did it go?'

'Finn brought off one of his inimitable French phrases—Kielkiewicz is, as you know, more at ease in French. During a moment's silence, Finn suddenly murmured very audibly: "Le Commandant-Chef aime bien les garçons." '

'What provoked this startling revelation?'

'The Polish cadets—a message came down from the top approving of them as potential training material. Thank God, Bobrowski wasn't there. He'd have had a stroke. Even Kielkiewicz went rather red in the face and pretended to blow his nose.'

'You didn't ask Finn to amplify?'

'One was reminded of the French judge comforting the little boy cross-examined in court. "Ne t'inquiètes-pas, mon enfant, les juges aiment les petits garçons"—then remembering himself and adding: "Pourtant les juges aiment les petites filles." '

A day or two later Pamela Flitton drove me again when I was going to Bobrowski's office. This was in the Harley Street neighbourhood (ten years later I used to sit in a dentist's chair where once I had talked with Horaczko), from where I should proceed to the Titian. Horaczko's business was likely to be completed in a few minutes, so she was told to wait with the car. As it happened, Horaczko himself wanted to visit Polish GHQ and asked for a lift. When we came out together from the military attaché's office, Pamela Flitton was standing by the car, surveying the street with her usual look of hatred and despair. Horaczko, seeing her, lightly touched the peak of his cap. For a moment I thought this just another example of well-applied technique in what was generally agreed to be the eminently successful relationship established by the Polish forces with the opposite sex in the country of their exile, but, although her acknowledgment was of the slightest, it was plain they had met before. As there were two of us, Horaczko and I sat at the back of the car. We talked about official matters all the way to the Titian.

Passing through its glass doors, guarded by Military Police wearing red covers, like our own, on their angular ethnic Polish lancer caps, Eastern Europe was instantaneously attained. A similar atmosphere imposed, though in a less powerful form, on the Ufford, no doubt accounted to some extent for the brief exorcism there, on first arrival, of the ghost of Uncle Giles. At the Titian, this Slav ethos was overwhelming. Some Poles, including Horaczko, who prided himself on assimilation with things British, found his own nation's characteristics, so he said, here rather depressingly caricatured. To me, on the other hand, the Titian offered an exotic change from the deadly drabness of the wartime London backcloth. The effect was to some extent odorously created, an aroma that discreetly blended elements of eau-de-cologne and onions, sweat and leather, the hotel's Edwardian past no doubt contributing its own special Art Nouveau pungency to more alien essences.

'I see you know our driver. She's the daughter of a friend of mine, as it happens.'

Horaczko at once became tremendously diplomatic in manner, as if large issues were raised by this remark, which was certainly the product of curiosity.

'Miss Flitton?' he said. 'Oh, yes. She's—well, a rather delicate situation has been raised by her.'

He smiled and looked slightly arch, if that is the right word.

'She is a beautiful girl,' he said.

We shook hands and he went off to whatever duties concerned him. Horaczko was always immensely tactful. For once he had been surprised into giving away more than he was usually prepared to do. It looked as if Pamela Flitton was already quite a famous figure in Polish military circles. I mounted the stairs to General Kielkiewicz's ante-room. One or more of his ADCs was always on duty there, usually in the company of a Polish colonel of uncertain age, probably a good deal older than he looked at first sight, with features resembling those of a death's head, who sat on an upright chair, eternally reading *Dziennik Polski.* This colonel seemed to be awaiting an interview for which the General was never available. Now, he rose, folded his newspaper, shook hands with me and left the room. Michalski was on duty at that moment. We too shook hands.

'I hope the Colonel did not go away on my account?'

'It is to be arranged that he should write a history of cavalry,' said Michalski. 'The General has not yet found time to break the news to him.'

A week or two later, there was trouble about the Section's car. Finn had specially ordered it for an important meeting and it was not at the door when he went down. One of the other ATS drivers said she thought the vehicle was out on duty, but no one could identify a Section officer who was using it, or had sent it on an errand. When Driver Flitton was in due course traced, she said she had been given instructions some weeks before to deliver certain routine papers of a non-secret nature to several of the Neutral military attachés. She had been out by herself doing this. The precise degree of truth in that matter was hard to pinpoint. It was alleged, with apparent conviction, that those particular instructions had later been countermanded, the documents being not at all urgent, though some of them had certainly been sent out. Even if correct that Driver Flitton had misunderstood the instruction, she had taken an unusually long time to make the rounds. Rather a fuss took place about the whole matter. Either on account of that, or simply because, quite by chance, she was given another posting, Driver Flitton was withdrawn from duties with the Section.

## CHAPTER TWO

Like Finn's aching jaw on the line of march, the war throbbed on, punctuated by interludes when more than once the wrong tooth seemed to have been hurriedly extracted. Meanwhile, I inhabited a one-room flat on the eighth floor of a prosaic Chelsea tenement. Private life, apparently at a standstill, as ever formed new patterns. Isobel's brother, George Tolland (by then a lieutenant-colonel serving as 'A & Q' on a Divisional staff in the Middle East), badly wounded in the campaign defeating Rommel, was in hospital in Cairo. Her sister Susan's husband, Roddy Cutts, major of Yeomanry transformed into Reconnaissance Corps, had recently written home to say he had fallen in love with one of the girls decoding cables at GHQ Persia/Iraq Force, and, accepting risk of spoiling a promising political career, wanted a divorce. This eventuality, not at all expected by Susan, nor any of the rest of the family, as Roddy had always been regarded as rather unadventurous in that sort of situation, caused a good deal of dismay.

If not required to stay late in the Whitehall area, I used, as a general routine, to come straight back from duty to a nearby pub, dine there, then retire to bed with a book. At that period the seventeenth-century particularly occupied me, so that works like Wood's *Athenae Oxonienses* or Luttrell's *Brief Relation* opened up vistas of the past, if not necessarily preferable to one's own time, at least appreciably different. These historical readings could be varied with Proust. The flat itself was not wholly unsympathetic. The block's ever-changing population, a mixed bag consisting largely of persons of both sexes working for the ministries, shaded off on the female side from high-grade secretaries, officers of the women's services, organizers of one thing and another, into a nebulous world of divorcées living on their own and transient types even less definable, probably all but unemployable where 'war work' was concerned, yet for one reason or another prepared to stay in London and face the blitz. On warm evenings these unattached ladies were to be met with straying about on the flat roof of the building, watching the bombers fly out, requesting cigarettes or matches and complaining to each other, or anyone else with whom they made contact, about the shortcomings of Miss Wartstone.

On another floor of the block, Hewetson, the Section's officer with the Belgians and Czechs, also rented a flat. For a time he and I used to set out together every morning; then, deciding to share a larger place with a friend in the Admiralty (who had a hold over a woman who could cook) Hewetson moved elsewhere. He was a solicitor in private life, and, although he did not talk much of such things, gave the impression of being more fortunate than Borrit in chance relationships. He did admit to some sort of an adventure, arisen from sunning himself on the roof during a period of convalescence after a bout of 'flu, with one of these sirens of the chimney pots. Another told him she could only achieve emotional intimacy with her own sex, so Hewetson probably knew the roof better than one might think. All the same, he could not get on with Miss Wartstone. She was manageress of the flats. Her outward appearance at once prepared residents for an unusually contentious temperament. Miss Wartstone had, indeed, passed into a middle-age of pathological quarrelsomeness, possibly in part legacy of nervous tensions built up during the earlier years of the blitz. Latterly, nothing worse than an occasional window broken by blast had disturbed the immediate neighbourhood, but, as the war progressed, few tempers remained as steady as at the beginning.

Miss Wartstone used to put up notices, like those at school, and, in the same way, people would draw pictures on them and write comments. '*Disgasting Management*,' somebody scrawled, probably one of the Allied officers, of whom quite a fair number were accommodated at the flats. Hewetson himself would go white if Miss Wartstone's name was mentioned.

'That woman,' he would say.

When the Eighth Army moved into Tripoli, Hewetson was offered promotion in a new branch of the Judge-Advocate-General's department proliferated in North Africa. As things turned out, this resulted in a change of my own position in the Section. It could be dated, more or less, by the fact that, when Hewetson came down from speaking with Finn about his own departure, Colonel Cobb, one of the American assistant military attachés, was in our room at that moment, talking of the capture of the German generals at Stalingrad. Although the Americans had a mission of their own for the bulk of their business, Cobb used to visit Finn from time to time about a few routine matters. He usually dropped in afterwards for a minute or two, chiefly, I think, to satisfy a personal preoccupation with the British army and its unexpected ways, an interest by now past the stage of mere desire for professional enlightenment and become fairly obsessive. He would endlessly question people, if opportunity arose, about their corps, Regular or Territorial, its special peculiarities and customs: when raised: where served: what worn. In the banter that sometimes followed these interrogations, Cobb rather enjoyed a touch of grimness, smiling with grave acquiescence when, in the course of one such scrutiny, it was by chance revealed that my own Regiment had borne among the Battle Honours of its Colours the names of Detroit and Miami.

'Ah, Detroit?' he said, speaking as if it had happened yesterday. 'An unfortunate affair that... Miami... The name reminds me of my great-aunt's grandfather, a man not to be trifled with, who held a commission from King George in the West Florida Provincials.'

To his own anecdotes, of which he possessed an impressive store, Cobb brought a dignified tranquillity of manner that might have earned a high fee in Hollywood, had he ever contemplated acting a military career, rather than living one. He narrated them in a low unemphasized mumble, drawing the words and sentences right back into his mouth, recalling certain old-fashioned types of Paris American. Like Finn, though in a totally different genre, Cobb indulged these dramatic aptitudes in himself, which, one suspected, could even motivate a deliberate visit—for example, the day after Pearl Harbour—should he feel an affirmation required to be made in public.

'What's America's next step, Colonel?' someone had asked on that occasion.

Cobb did not answer at once. Instead, he threw himself into a relatively theatrical pose, one of those attitudes, stylized yet unforced, in which he excelled; this time in the character of a man giving deep attention to a problem of desperate complexity. Then he spoke a considered judgment.

'The US Navy are prohibited alcohol,' he said. 'We'll have to call in their golf-clubs, I guess.'

Years later in New York, I repeated that comment to Harrison F. Wisebite's nephew, Milton, met at a publisher's party at the St Regis. Milton Wisebite, who worked in the *Time-Life* office at that period, had himself served in Europe with his country's expeditionary force.

'Courthouse Cobb?' he said. 'Haven't thought of him in decades.'

'That was his nickname?'

'Throughout the US Army.'

'What did it mean?'

'There was reference to a supposed predilection towards severity in the exercise of discipline.'

That was a side of Colonel Cobb, imaginable, though happily never imperative to encounter. However, Milton Wisebite's words recalled the stern tone in which Cobb had referred to the capitulation of Paulus on that day, endorsing thereby in memory the progress of the war and the moment when Hewetson left the Section. Finn was unwilling to replace him with an officer lacking any previous experience of liaison work. Accordingly the new man, Slade, a schoolmaster by profession, was given to Pennistone as second-string, and I was ordered to take over the Belgians and Czechs.

As it happened, on that evening at the St Regis, when everyone had had a good deal to drink, Milton Wisebite had gone on to ask news of Pamela Flitton, with whom, so it then appeared, he had enjoyed a brief moment of intimacy at some stage of the war. Apparently the episode had been the high peak of romance in his life, more especially as she was a kind of relation of his. Whatever took place between them—he was not explicit—must have been at an appreciably later period than the other surrender at Stalingrad, but, within the year or less that had passed since she had driven for the Section, Pamela Flitton's name had already become fairly notorious for just that sort of adventure.

The stories, as such stories do, came in gradually. For example, the affair of which Horaczko had hinted, when our ways had parted in the hall of the Titian, was confirmed later by Michalski, less reserved in discussing such matters, who said he thought things had ended by a Polish major being brought before one of their army's Courts of Honour. Even if that were an exaggeration, there was much else going round to suggest it might be true. To mention a few of these items: two RAF officers, one from Bomber, the other from Fighter Command, were court-martialled as a consequence of a fight about which was to drive her home after a party. The Naval Police had separated them, and, although a serious view was not taken by the authorities, the episode had made too much disturbance to be disregarded. The Navy was involved again in the person of a paymaster-lieutenant commander, who for some reason received a severe reprimand on her account. He was reported to be a scatterbrained fellow anyway. More ominously, a relatively senior official in the Treasury, a married man with several children, gave her a lift in his car one night at Richmond station—goodness knows what she was doing there in the first instance—starting a trail of indiscretion that led to his transference to a less distinguished ministry. Barker-Shaw, who had been Field Security Officer at my former Division, now at MI 5, hinted there had nearly been an unofficial strike about her down at the docks. These were only some of the tales one heard. No doubt most of them were greatly inflated in the telling, if not positively untrue, but they indicated her range, even if you discounted ones like pouring the wine on the floor when Howard Craggs, the left-wing publisher, now a temporary civil servant of some standing, had given her dinner at an expensive black market restaurant; even less to be believed that—like Barbara Goring discharging the sugar over Widmerpool—she had emptied the bottle over Craggs's head. The latter version was agreed to be untrustworthy if only because he was known still to pursue her.

Even if these highly coloured anecdotes were to be disbelieved, their very existence indicated a troublesome personality. Myth of such pervasive volume does not suddenly arise about a woman entirely without a reason. One thing was certain. She had left the ATS. This was said to be due to bad health, trouble with a lung.

'I never yet met a pretty girl who didn't tell you she had TB,' said Dicky Umfraville. 'Probably the least of the diseases she inherited from Cosmo.'

Umfraville had been unsuccessful in his efforts to find a niche in one of the secret organizations, and was now commanding a transit camp with the rank of major.

'Giving men hell is what Miss Flitton likes,' he said. 'I know the sort. Met plenty of them.'

There was something to be said for accepting that diagnosis, because two discernible features seemed to emerge from a large, often widely diversified, canon of evidence chronicling Pamela Flitton's goings-on: the first, her indifference to the age and status of the men she decided to fascinate; the second, the unvarying technique of silence, followed by violence, with which she persecuted her lovers, or those who hoped to be numbered in that category. She appeared, for example, scarcely at all interested in looks or money, rank or youth, as such; just as happy deranging the modest home life of a middle-aged air-raid warden, as compromising the commission of a rich and handsome Guards ensign recently left school. In fact, she seemed to prefer 'older men' on the whole, possibly because of their potentiality for deeper suffering. Young men might superficially transcend their seniors in this respect, but they probably showed less endurance in sustaining that state, while, once pinioned, the middle-aged could be made to writhe almost indefinitely. In the Section her memory remained with Borrit.

'Wonder what happened to that juicy looking AT,' he said more than once. 'The good-lookers never stay. Wouldn't mind spending a weekend with her.'

'Weekends' took place once a fortnight, most people saving up their weekly one day off to make them up. Once in a way Isobel managed to come to London during the week and we went out for a mild jaunt. This was not often, and, when she rang up one day to say Ted Jeavons had got hold of a couple of bottles of gin and was asking a few people in to share them with him, the invitation presented itself as quite an excitement. After Molly's death, Isobel and her sisters used to keep in closer touch with Jeavons than formerly, making something of a duty to see him at fairly regular intervals, on the grounds that, a widower, he needed more attention than before. I had not seen him myself since suggesting Templer should take a room at the Jeavons' house, but heard Templer had done so. Whether he remained, I did not know. Jeavons, keeping up Molly's tradition of always welcoming any member of the family, had shown surprising resilience in recovering from the unhappy night when he had lost his wife. Certainly he had been greatly upset at the time, but he possessed a kind of innate toughness of spirit that carried him through. Norah Tolland, who did not care for any suggestion of sentimentality that concerned persons of the opposite sex—though she tolerated the loves, hates and regrets of her own exclusively feminine world—insisted that Jeavons's recovery was complete.

'Ted's perfectly capable of looking after himself,' she said. 'In some respects—allowing for the war—the place is better run than when Molly was alive. I get a bit sick of those long disjointed harangues he gives about ARP.'

His duties as an air-raid warden had now become Jeavons's sole interest, the whole background of his life. Apart from his period in the army during the previous war, he must have worked longer and more continuously at air-raid precautions than at any other job. Jeavons, although to be regarded as not much good at jobs, had here found his vocation. No one knew quite how the money situation would resolve itself when Molly died, Jeavons no longer in his first youth, with this admitted lack of handiness at earning a living. It turned out that Molly, with a forethought her noisy manner concealed, had taken steps to compound for her jointure, a financial reconstruction that had included buying the South Kensington house, thereby insuring (air raids unforeseen in that respect) her husband having a roof over his head, if she predeceased him. Although she was older, that possibility seemed unlikely enough in the light of Jeavons's much propagated 'rotten inside', the stomach wound so perpetually reviled by himself. However, the unlikely had come to pass. Chips Lovell, when alive, had never tired of deploring Sleaford stinginess where their widows were concerned, but at least Jeavons had reaped some residue. One felt he deserved that at his age, though what precisely that age was, no one knew. Fifty must be in the offing, if not already attained.

'Norah's bringing a girl-friend with her,' he said. 'Wonder what she's got hold of this time. The last one had a snub nose and freckles with biggish feet.'

Norah Tolland was a driver in one of the several classifications of women's services, a corps which regarded themselves as of rather more consequence than mere ATS, whose officers they were not required to salute. Norah had taken pleasure in explaining that to a very important ATS officer wearing red tabs who had hauled her up for a supposed omission of respect.

'Sorry your friend Templer's gone, Nick,' said Jeavons. 'We got on pretty well. Used to have long talks at odd moments of the night when we'd both come off duty in the small hours. He told me a thing or two. Stories about the ladies, my hat.'

Jeavons's thick dark hair, with its ridges of corkscrew curls, had now turned quite white, the Charlie Chaplin moustache remaining black. This combination of tones for some reason gave him an oddly Italian appearance, enhanced by blue overalls, obscurely suggesting a railway porter at a station in Italy. Jeavons continued to wear these overalls, though by now promoted to an administrative post at the local ARP headquarters. He poured out glasses of gin-and-orange, a drink for ever to recall world war.

'Why did Templer leave?'

'Been fed up for ages. Wanted a more active job. Quite worried him.'

'He told me all that nearly a year ago.'

'There was a woman in the case. Usually is. That's why he wanted to do something more dangerous. London's quite dangerous enough for me. Templer didn't think so.'

'It sounds unlike him.'

'He went off to some training place,' said Jeavons. 'Never know how people will behave. Look at poor Charles Stringham, missing at Singapore. Remember when he lived on the top floor here with Miss Weedon trying to cure him of the booze. He and I used to have one on the sly once in a way. Mrs Conyers, I should call her, not Miss Weedon. Bad luck her husband dropping dead like that, but in your nineties you must be prepared for accidents.'

General Conyers, also an air-raid warden, had collapsed in the street one night, pursuing looters attempting to steal a refrigerator from a bombed house. He died, as he had lived, in active, dramatic, unusual circumstances; such, one felt, as he himself would have preferred.

'Tuffy, as Charles used to call her, is in MI 5 now,' said Jeavons. 'Don't think she has to get into evening dress and jade ear-rings and vamp German agents. Just supervises the girls there. Always looked as if she knew a lot of secrets. Those black dresses and white collars. I expect they want reliable people, and she's reliable all right. This girl of Templer's made him feel he was getting old. He wanted to find out whether that was true or not. Of course, you might argue he oughtn't to have been playing around at all. You've got to remember the circumstances. Wife's in a mental home, as you probably know. Awful thing to happen. It's hard to keep straight, if you're on your own. I remember Smith, that butler of your brother-in-law Erry's, using those very words. Erry used to lend us Smith from time to time, when he was away from Thrubworth. Of course, Smith's wife had been dead for years, luckily for her. I warrant there'd been some high jinks on Smith's part at one time or another. Terrible chap, Smith. Oughtn't to say it, but I'm really glad he's dead. No chance of his ever working here again.'

'Erry said it was a rather ghastly business when Smith pegged out.'

'Ghastly?' said Jeavons. 'Just about. Didn't you know? He was bitten by Maisky, that monkey Molly used to own. It seems Smith tried to take a biscuit away from that tenacious ape. Probably wanted it himself to mop up some of the gin he'd drunk. God, the way that man used to put back our gin. I marked the bottle, but it wasn't a damn bit of use. Silly thing to do, to take issue with Maisky. Of course Smith came off second-best. Perhaps they both reached out for the biscuit at the same moment. Anyway, Maisky wouldn't have any snatching and Smith contracted septicemia with fatal results. Meant the end of Maisky too, which wasn't really just. But then what is just in this life? Still, I suppose some things are, if you think about them. Smith'll be the last butler I'll ever find myself employing—not that there's likely to be many butlers to employ, the way things are going. That fact doesn't break my heart. Taking them all in all, the tall with the short, the fat with the thin, the drunk with the sober, they're not a profession that greatly appeals to me. Of course, I was brought in contact with butlers late in life. Never set eyes on them in the circles I came from. I may have been unlucky in the butlers I've met. There may be the one in a hundred, but it's a long time to wait. Read about butlers in books—see 'em in plays. That's all right. Have 'em in the house—a very different matter. Look what they do to your clothes, apart from anything else. I started without butlers and I'll die without butlers, no less a happy man. There's the bell. No butler, so I'll answer it myself. Probably some of the pals from my ARP dump.'

He went off down the stairs. After the bomb damage, the house had been shored up to prevent collapse, but no interior renovation had taken place. A long, jagged crack still zigzagged across one of the walls, which were in many places covered with large brown patches, like maps showing physical features, or the rather daring ornamental designs of a modernistic decorator. All the pictures, even the Moroccan pastels, had been removed, as well as the Oriental bowls and jars that used to clutter the drawing-room. A snapshot of Molly, wearing a Fair Isle jumper and holding Maisky in her arms like a baby, stood on the mantelpiece, curled and yellowing. Maisky, heedless of mortality, looked infinitely self-satisfied. Jeavons returned, bringing with him several ARP colleagues, male and female.

'Room's not looking very smart for a party,' he said.

A minute or two later Norah Tolland arrived. Her companion—'girl-friend', as Jeavons had termed her—turned out to be Pamela Flitton. Norah was in uniform, which suited her. She was, in general, more settled, more sure of herself than when younger, though on this particular occasion the presence of Pamela seemed to make her both elated and nervous.

'Ted, I felt sure you wouldn't mind my bringing Pam,' she said. 'She's having dinner with me tonight. It seemed so much easier than meeting at the restaurant.'

'Most welcome,' said Jeavons.

He looked Pamela over. Jeavons examining a woman's points was always in itself worth observing. If good-looking, he stared at her as if he had never before seen anything of the kind, though at the same time determined not to be carried away by his own astonishment. Pamela justified this attention. She was wearing a neat black frock, an improvement on her battledress blouse. It was clear she had established over Norah an absolute, even if only temporary, domination. Norah's conciliatory manner showed that.

'Have a drink?' said Jeavons.

'What have you got?'

Pamela glanced aggressively round the room, catching my eye, but making no sign of recognition.

'Gin-and-orange.'

'No whisky?'

'Sorry.'

'I'll have gin-and-water—no, neat gin.'

I went across to her.

'Escaped from the ATS?'

'Got invalided.'

'A lady of leisure?'

'My job's a secret one.'

Jeavons took her lightly by the arm and began to introduce her to the other guests. She shook his hand away with her elbow, but allowed him to tell her the names of two or three persons who worked with him. When introductions were over, she picked up a paper from the table—apparently some not very well printed periodical—and took it, with her glass of gin, to the furthest corner of the room. There she sat on a stool, listlessly turning the pages. Norah, talking to Isobel, gave an anxious glance, but did not take any immediate steps to join Pamela, or try to persuade her to be more sociable. A talkative elderly man with a red face, one of the ARP guests, engaged me in conversation. He said he was a retired indigo planter. Jeavons himself went across the room and spoke to Pamela, but he must have received a rebuff, because he returned a second or two later to the main body of the guests.

'She's reading our ARP bulletin,' he said.

He spoke with more surprise than disapproval; in fact almost with admiration.

'Read the poem in this number?' asked the indigo planter. 'Rather good. It begins "What do you carry, Warden dear?" Gives a schedule of the equipment—you know, helmet, gas-mask, First Aid, all that—but leaves out one item. You have to guess. Quite clever.'

'Jolly good.'

Norah, evidently not happy about Pamela, separated herself from Isobel soon after this, and went across to where her friend was sitting. They talked for a moment, but, if Norah too hoped to make her circulate with the rest, she was defeated. When she returned I asked her what her own life was like.

'I was with Gwen McReith's lot for a time. Quite fun, because Gwen herself is amusing. I first met Pam with her, as a matter of fact.'

'Pam seems quite a famous figure.'

Norah sighed.

'I suppose she is now,' she said.

'Is she all right over there in the corner?'

'No good arguing with her.'

'I mean we both of us might go over and talk to her.'

'For God's sake not.'

Nothing of any note took place during the rest of the party, until Norah and Pamela were leaving. Throughout that time, Pamela had continued to sit in the corner. She accepted another drink from Jeavons, but ceased to read the ARP bulletin, simply looking straight in front of her. However, before she and Norah went off together, an unexpected thing happened. She came across the room and spoke in her accustomed low, almost inaudible tone.

'Are you still working with the Poles?'

'No—I've switched to the Belgians and Czechs.'

'When you were with the Poles, did you ever hear the name Szymanski?'

'It's a very common Polish name, but if you mean the man who used to be with the Free French, and caused endless trouble, then transferred to the Poles, and caused endless trouble there, I know quite a lot about him.'

She laughed.

'I just wondered,' she said.

'What about him?'

'Oh, nothing.'

'Was he the character you were talking to outside that Polish hide-out in Bayswater?'

She shook her head, laughing softly again. Then they went away. The ARP people left too.

'There's enough for one more drink for the three of us,' said Jeavons. 'I hid the last few drops.'

'What do you think of Pamela Flitton?'

'That's the wench that gave Peter Templer such a time,' said Jeavons. 'Couldn't remember the name. It's come back. He said it all started as a joke. Then he got mad about her. That was the way Templer put it. What he didn't like—when she wasn't having any, as I understand it—was the feeling he was no good any more. How I feel all the time. Nothing much you can do about it. Mind you, he was browned off with the job too.'

'Do men really try to get dangerous jobs because they've been disappointed about a woman?'

'Well, I don't,' Jeavons admitted.

The enquiry about Szymanski was odd, even if he were not the Pole outside the Ufford. Neither Pennistone nor I had ever set eyes on this man, though we had been involved in troubles about him, including a question asked in Parliament. There was some uncertainty as to his nationality, even whether the territory where he was stated to have been born was now Polish or Czechoslovak, assuming he had in truth been born there. Most of his life he had lived on his wits as a professional gambler—like Cosmo Flitton—so it appeared, familiar as a dubious character in France, Belgium and the Balkans; in fact all over the place. He had a row of aliases: Kubitsa: Brod: Groza: Dupont: to mention only a few of them. No one—even MI 5 was vague—seemed to know when and how he had first appeared in this country, but at an early stage he was known to have volunteered for the Belgian forces. This offer was prudently declined. Szymanski then tried the Free French, who, with the self-confidence of their race, took him on the strength; later ceding him with relief to the Poles, who may have wanted to make use of him in some special capacity. The general opinion was that he had a reasonable claim to Polish citizenship. The Czechs raised no objection. There were those who insisted his origins were really Balkan.

'It seems fairly clear he's not Norwegian,' said Pennistone, 'but I've learnt to take nothing on trust about Szymanski. You may have him on your hands before we've finished, Dempster.'

Szymanski was one of those professional scourges of authority that appear sporadically in all armies, a type to which the Allied contingents were peculiarly subject owing to the nature of their composition and recruitment. Like Sayce of my former Battalion, Szymanski was always making trouble, but Sayce magnified to a phantasmagoric degree, a kind of super-Sayce of infinitely greater intelligence and disruptive potential. The abiding fear of the Home Office was that individuals of this sort might, after being found stateless, be discharged from the armed forces and have to be coped with as alien civilians.

As it happened, Szymanski's name cropped up again a day or two later in our room. Masham, who was with the British Mission in liaison with the Free French, was waiting to be summoned by Finn, to whom he was to communicate certain points arising out of Giraud taking over from Darlan in North Africa. Masham asked Pennistone how the Poles were getting on with Szymanski, who had caused a lot of trouble to himself in his Free French days.

'Szymanski's gone a bit too far this time,' Pennistone said. 'They've sent him to detention. It was bound to come.'

There was a barracks, under the control of a British commandant, specially to accommodate delinquent Allied personnel.

I asked how recently that had happened.

'A week or so ago.'

'I'm not surprised,' said Masham. 'Though one's got to admit the man was rather a card. It looks as if this North African switch-over will mean a back place for de Gaulle.'

'Has anyone else hanged himself in his braces in that Free French snuggery behind Selfridge's?' asked Borrit.

'Nobody hanged himself in his braces there or in any other Free French establishment,' said Masham, rather irritably. 'You've got the story wrong.'

Like all his Mission, Masham was, as he himself would have expressed it, *plus catholique que le Pape*, far more Francophil than the Free French themselves, who on the whole rather enjoyed a good laugh at less reputable aspects of their own corporate body. When in due course I had direct dealings with them myself, they were always telling stories about some guerrilla of theirs who divided his time between being parachuted into France to make contact with the Resistance, and returning to London to run a couple of girls on Shaftesbury Avenue.

'What did happen then?'

'There was some fuss about an interrogation.'

'De Gaulle was pretty cross when our people enquired about it.'

'He's got to steer his own show, hasn't he?' said Masham. 'Anyway, it looks as if he's on the way out. By the way, Jenkins, the successful candidate for the job you applied to us for caught it at Bir Hakim.'

Kucherman rang up at that moment, and, by the time I had finished with Belgian business, Masham had gone up to see Finn. Transfer to the Belgians and Czechs meant no more physically than ceasing to sit next to Pennistone, though it vitiated a strong alliance in resisting Blackhead. The two Allied contingents with which I was now in liaison were, of course, even in their aggregate, much smaller numerically than the Polish Corps. At first sight, in spite of certain advantages in being one's own master, responsible only to Finn, a loss in other directions seemed threatened by diminution of variety in the general field of activity. A claustrophobic existence offered, in this respect, the consolation of exceptional opportunities for observing people and situations closely in a particular aspect of war. Our Section's viewpoint was no doubt less all embracing than, say, Widmerpool's in his subterranean lair; at the same time could provide keener, more individual savour of things noted at first-hand.

It had been stimulating, for example, to watch the quickly gathering momentum of the apparatus—infinitesimally propelled, among others, by oneself—that reduced to some order the circumstances of the hundred and fifteen thousand Poles permitted to cross the Russian frontier into Iran; assisting, as it were, Pennistone's 'one man and a boy' at the receiving end. Hundreds of thousands were left behind, of course, while those who got out were in poorish shape. All the same, these were the elements to form the Second Polish Army Corps; later so creditably concerned at Monte Cassino and elsewhere. Regarded superficially, the new Belgian and Czech assignments seemed to offer problems less obviously engrossing. However, as matters turned out, plenty of channels for fresh experience were provided by these two. Even the earliest meetings with Major Kucherman and Colonel Hlava promised that.

Precise in manner, serious about detail, Hewetson was judged to perform his duties pretty well, though he possessed no particular qualifications as expert on Belgian affairs, still less those of Czechoslovakia. Before I took over from him, he gave me a briefing about the characteristics of the Allies in question.

'An excellent point about the Belgians,' he said, 'is not caring in the least what they say about each other, or their own national failings. They have none of that painful wish to make a good impression typical of some small nations. It's a great relief. At the same time their standards in certain respects—food and drink, for example—are high ones. They are essentially easy to get on with. Do not believe disobliging propaganda, chiefly French, about them. They are not, it must be admitted, indifferent to social distinction. Their assistant MA, Gauthier de Graef, likes telling a story, no doubt dating from the last war, of an English officer, French officer, and Belgian officer, when a woman rode by on a horse. The Englishman said: "What a fine horse"; the Frenchman, "What a fine woman": the Belgian, "I wonder what she was née". Of course I don't suggest that would happen today.'

'One can't make the classless society retroactive.'

'Another saying of Gauthier's is that when he wakes up in the night in a wagon-lit and hears a frightful row going on in the next compartment, he knows he's back in his own beloved country—though I must say I haven't been subjected to the smallest ill-humour myself on the part of my Belgian charges.'

'They sound all right.'

'One small snag—Lannoo was given promotion the other day, and has already left for his new job. The Belgian authorities still won't make up their minds whom to appoint in his place. I've been dealing with Gauthier de Graef for weeks, who of course can't take the decisions his boss could. I suppose this delay is the sort of thing the Belgians themselves grumble about.'

As it turned out, the official appointment of Kucherman came through only on the day when Hewetson left the Section. There was some misunderstanding about certain customary formalities, one of those departmental awkwardnesses that take place from time to time and can cause coolness. The fact was Kucherman himself was a figure of much more standing at home than the average officer likely to be found in that post. Possibly some of the Belgian Government thought this fact might overweigh the job; others, that more experience was desirable in purely military matters. At least that was the explanation given to Hewetson when things were in the air. As he had said, a particular charm possessed by the Belgians was, in a world everyday increasingly cautious about hazarding in public opinions about public affairs, no Belgian minded in the least criticizing his Government, individually or collectively.

'One of their best points,' Hewetson repeated.

In short, by the time I introduced myself to Kucherman, a faint sense of embarrassment had been infused into the atmosphere by interchanges at a much higher level than Finn's. Kucherman was only a major, because the Belgians were rather justly proud of keeping their ranks low.

'After all the heavy weather that's been made, you'll have to be careful not to get off on the wrong foot,

Nicholas,' said Finn. 'Kucherman's own people may have been to blame for some of that, but we've been rather stiff and unaccommodating ourselves. You'll have to step carefully. Kucherman's a well known international figure.'

I repeated these remarks of Finn's to Pennistone.

'Kucherman's a big shot all right,' said Pennistone. 'I used to hear a lot about him and his products when I was still in business. He's head of probably the largest textile firm. That's just one of his concerns. He's also a coal owner on an extensive scale, not to mention important interests in the Far East—if they still survive. We shall expect your manner to alter after a week or two of putting through deals with Kucherman.'

The picture was a shade disconcerting. One imagined a figure, younger perhaps, but somewhat on the lines of Sir Magnus Donners: tall: schoolmasterish; enigmatic. As it turned out, Kucherman's exterior was quite different from that. Of medium height, neat, brisk, with a high forehead and grey hair, he seemed to belong to the eighteenth-century, the latter half, as if he were wearing a wig of the period tied behind with a black bow. This, I found later, was one of the Belgian physical types, rather an unexpected one, even in a nation rich in physiognomies recalling the past.

On the whole, a march-past of Belgian troops summoned up the Middle Ages or the Renaissance, emaciated, Memling-like men-at-arms on their way to supervise the Crucifixion or some lesser martyrdom, while beside them tramped the clowns of Teniers or Brouwer, round rubicund countenances, hauled away from carousing to be mustered in the ranks. These latter types were even more to be associated with the Netherlands contingent—obviously a hard and fast line was not to be drawn between these Low Country peoples—Colonel Van der Voort himself an almost perfect example. Van der Voort's features seemed to have parted company completely from Walloon admixtures—if, indeed, it was Walloon blood that produced those mediaeval faces. Van der Voort's air had something faintly classical about it too, something belonging not entirely to domestic pot-house or kermesse scenes, a touch of the figures in the train of Bacchus or Silenus; though naturally conceived in Dutch or Flemish terms. Kucherman's high forehead and regular features—the French *abbé* style—was in contrast with all that, a less common, though a fairly consistent Belgian variant that gave the impression, on such occasions as the parade on their National Day, of the sudden influence of a later school of painting.

The first day at Eaton Square—by then almost a preserve of the Belgian ministries—the name of Sir Magnus Donners did indeed crop up. He had been in the headlines that morning on account of some more or less controversial statement made in public on the subject of manpower. Kucherman referred to this item of news, mentioning at the same time that he had once lunched at Stourwater. We talked about the castle. I asked if, since arrival in England, he had seen Sir Magnus. Kucherman laughed.

'A member of your Cabinet does not want to be bothered by a major in one of the smaller Allied contingents.'

'All the same, it might be worth while letting him know you are here.'

'You think so?'

'Sure of it.'

'Certainly he showed great interest in Belgium when we met—knowledge of Belgian affairs. You know Belgium yourself?'

'I've been there once or twice. When my father was at the War Office, I remember him bringing two Belgian officers to our house. It was a great excitement.'

'Your father was *officier de carrière*?'

'He'd come back from Paris, where he'd been on the

staff of the Peace Conference. By the way, several Belgian officers are living at the same block of flats as myself. I don't know any of them.'

Kucherman asked the name of the place.

'Ah, yes,' he said. 'Clanwaert is there. You will be dealing with him about Congo matters. An amusing fellow.'

'I have an appointment with him tomorrow.'

'He was formerly in the Premier Régiment des Guides—like your Life Guards, one might say. I believe he fought his first engagement in 1914 wearing what was almost their parade uniform—green tunic, red breeches, all that. Then a love affair went wrong. He transferred to La Force Publique. A dashing fellow with a romantic outlook. That was why he never married.'

The Force Publique was the Congo army, quite separate from the Belgian army, officered somewhat on the lines, so it seemed, of our own Honourable East India Company's troops in the past.

'Kucherman's going to be all right,' said Finn.

Even Gauthier de Graef, who had all his countrymen's impatience with other people's methods, and would not have hesitated to grumble about his new chief, agreed with that judgment. He was a tall young man with a large moustache, who, after a frantic drive to the coast to catch up the remnant of the Belgian forces embarked for England, had jumped the last yard or so over water, as the boat had already set sail from harbour.

'I needed a drink after that,' he said. 'A long one, let me assure you.'

I was just off to see Kucherman or Hlava one morning, when General Bobrowski was put through on my telephone. Bobrowski, even for himself, was in a tremendous state of excitement. He explained that he had been unable to make contact with Finn, and now he was told that neither Pennistone nor Slade were available. It was a matter of the most urgent importance that he had an appointment with Finn as soon as possible. He appealed to me as Pennistone's former assistant in Polish liaison. Finn was at that moment with one of the brigadiers; Pennistone probably at the Titian—where it was quite likely he would learn of whatever was on Bobrowski's mind—and Slade was no doubt somewhere in the building negotiating with another section. Slade returned at that moment and I handed Bobrowski over to him. I wondered what the trouble was. Bobrowski became easily excited, but this seemed exceptional. Pennistone outlined the enormity on my return.

'Listen to this,' he said. 'Tell me whether you believe it or not.'

He was partly angry himself, partly unable not to laugh.

'Let's go and have lunch. I'll tell you there.'

The story was certainly a strange one.

'Szymanski's out,' said Pennistone.

'Out of where?'

'Jug.'

'He's escaped from the detention barracks?'

'In a rather unusual way.'

'Did he break out?'

'He left by the front door.'

'In disguise?'

'It appears that first of all a certain amount of telephoning took place from the appropriate branches, Polish and British, saying that Szymanski's conviction had been quashed and his case was to be reconsidered. Then two British officers arrived bearing the correct papers to obtain his body. Szymanski was accordingly handed over to their custody.'

'This was bogus?'

'The next thing was, Szymanski himself appeared shortly after at the prison, wearing the uniform of a British second-lieutenant and explaining that he knew the way to get out of anywhere. In fact, the prison hasn't been invented that could keep him inside.'

'Didn't they lock him up again?'

'They couldn't. The documents made him a free man.'

'What had happened?'

'There were those who thought Szymanski's outstanding qualities—not necessarily his most gentlemanly ones—might come in useful for a piece of work required.'

'You mean some of our people?'

'Possibly certain Polish elements were also sympathetic to the scheme. That's not clear yet. It would have been easier to organize, had that been the case. However, one can't be sure. Another country may be in on it too.'

'Was this Sunny Farebrother's crowd?'

'It looks like it.'

'With forged papers?'

'Yes.'

'Won't there be the hell of a row?'

'There will—and is. As liaison officer with the Poles, naturally I can only regard the whole affair as perfectly disgraceful. At the same time, one can't help seeing it has its funny side.'

'Finn must be having a fit.'

'He's beside himself.'

'Is Sunny personally involved?'

'So it's believed—though he did not turn up himself at the prison gates.'

'Is it known who did?'

'One of them was called Stevens. I believe rather a tough nut, quite young, with an MC. He's said to have been wounded in the Middle East, and came back to join Farebrother's show.'

'Odo Stevens?'

'I don't know his first name.'

'Will they re-arrest Szymanski?'

'How can they? He's been disposed of abroad probably. Anyway undergoing training at some secret place.'

'He'll be dropped somewhere?'

'To do something pretty unpleasant, I should imagine.'

'And the Poles are angry?'

'Our ones are livid. Can you blame them? I've never seen Bobrowski in such a state. It's understandable. At one end of the scale, our authorities make a great parade of the letter of the Law. The Home Office, if it possibly can, displays its high-mindedness in hampering the smaller Allies from arresting their deserters—they'd be much too afraid to obstruct the Americans or Russians—then a thing like this happens. All we can do is to grin feebly, and say we hope no offence will be taken.'

Although this incident had its being in the half-light encompassing those under-the-counter activities from which Finn liked to keep his Section so rigorously apart, Finn himself, not to mention Pennistone, had to suffer most of the consequences of what had taken place, so far as the Polish authorities were concerned. They were not at all pleased, saying, not without reason, that a serious blow had been struck against discipline. The episode strongly suggested that the British, when it suited them, could carry disregard of all convention to inordinate lengths; indulge in what might be described as forms of military bohemianism of the most raffish sort. Finn was, of course, entirely on the Polish side in thinking that. It was hard that he himself should have to bear most of the brunt of their complaint. The undertaking was no less remarkable in that Farebrother, outwardly so conventional, was prepared to lend himself to such a plot. It was just another view as to how the war should be won; perhaps the right one.

'A great illusion is that government is carried on by an infallible, incorruptible machine,' Pennistone said. 'Officials

—all officials, of all governments—are just as capable of behaving in an irregular manner as anyone else. In fact they have the additional advantage of being able to assuage their conscience, if they happen to own one, by assuring themselves it's all for the country's good.'

I wondered if Pamela Flitton had known these monkey-tricks were on the way, when she had enquired about Szymanski. Her own exploits continued to be talked about. Clanwaert was the next Ally to mention her. That was a month or two later. We met one evening on the way back to the block of flats. Outwardly, Clanwaert suppressed any indication of the romanticism at which Kucherman had hinted. He had a moustache even larger than Gauthier de Graef's, and an enormous nose to which it seemed attached, as if both were false. The nose was a different shape from Finn's, making one think more of Cyrano de Bergerac. Clanwaert used to tap it, in the old-fashioned traditional gesture, when he knew the answer to some question. Like Kucherman, he talked excellent English, though with a thicker, more guttural accent, a habit of spitting all his words out making most of his remarks sound ironic. Perhaps that was intended. I asked if it were true he had fought his first battle in red breeches.

'Not *red*, my friend—this is important—*amaranthe*. How do you say that in English?'

'Just the same—amaranth.'

'That's the name of a colour?'

'An English writer named St John Clarke called one of his books *Fields of Amaranth*. It was a novel. The flower is supposed to be unfading in legend. The other name for it in English is Love-lies-bleeding. Much play was made about these two meanings in the story.'

'Love-lies-bleeding? That's a strange name. Too good for a pair of breeches.'

'Not if they were unfading.'

'Nothing's unfading, my friend,' said Clanwaert. 'Nothing in Brussels, at least.'

'I've enjoyed visits there before the war.'

'It was a different city after '14-'18. Most places were. That was why I transferred to la Force Publique. I can assure you the Congo was a change from la Porte Louise. For a long time, if you believe me, I was Elephant Officer. Something to hold the attention. I would not mind going back there at the termination of this war. Indeed, one may have no choice—be lucky if one reaches Africa. Nevertheless, there are times when the Blacks get on one's nerves. One must admit that. Perhaps only because they look at the world in a different manner from us—maybe a wiser one. I shall be writing you another letter about those officers in the Congo who want a share in this war of ours. As I told you before, they feel out of it, afraid of people saying afterwards—"As for you, gentlemen, you were safe in the Congo." It is understandable. All the same your High Command say they cannot see their way to employ these Congo officers. I understand that too, but I shall be writing you many letters on the subject. You must forgive me. By the way, I met a young lady last night who told me she knew you.'

'Who was that?'

'Mademoiselle Flitton.'

'How was she?'

Clanwaert laughed, evidently aware of the impression the name would make.

'She told me to remind you of the Pole she mentioned when you last met.'

'She did?'

'That was some joke?'

'Some people thought so. I hope Mademoiselle Flitton is in good Belgian hands now.'

'I think she has higher aspirations than that.'

Clanwaert laughed, but revealed no secrets. As it turned out, the implications of the words were clarified through the agency of the Czechs.

'Colonel Hlava is an excellent man' Hewetson had said. 'More ease of manner than most of his countrymen, some of whom like to emphasize their absolute freedom, as a nation, from the insincere artificialities of social convention. Makes them a bit dour at times. Personally, I find it oils the wheels when there's a drop of Slovak, Hungarian or Jewish blood. Not so deadly serious.'

'Hlava's a flying ace?'

'With innumerable medals for gallantry in the last war—where he served against the Russians, whom he's now very pro—not to mention international awards as a test pilot. He is also rather keen on music, which I know nothing about. For example, he asked me the other day if I didn't get rather tired of Egyptian music. As I'm almost tone deaf, I'd no idea Egypt was in the forefront as a musical country.'

'Tzigane—gipsy.'

'I thought he meant belly-dancing,' said Hewetson. 'By the way, when you're dealing with two Allies at once, it's wiser never to mention one to the other. They can't bear the thought of your being unfaithful to them.'

It was at one of Colonel Hlava's musical occasions that the scene took place which showed what Clanwaert had been talking about. This was a performance of *The Bartered Bride* mounted by the Czechoslovak civil authorities in the interests of some national cause. I was not familiar with the opera, but remembered Maclintick and Gossage having a music critics' argument about Smetana at Mrs Foxe's party for Moreland's symphony. No recollection remained of the motif of their dispute, though no doubt, like all musical differences of opinion, feelings had been bitter when aroused. I was invited, with Isobel, to attend *The Bartered Bride* in a more or less official capacity. We sat with Colonel Hlava, his staff and their wives.

'The heroine is not really a bride, but a fiancée,' explained Hlava. 'The English title being not literal for German *Die Verkaufte Braut.*'

In most respects very different from Kucherman, the Czech colonel possessed the same eighteenth-century appearance. Perhaps it would be truer to say Hlava recalled the nineteenth century, because there was a look of Liszt about his head and thick white hair, together with a certain subdued air of belonging to the Romantic Movement. This physical appearance was possibly due to a drop of Hungarian blood—one of the allegedly lubricating elements mentioned by Hewetson—though Hlava himself claimed entirely Bohemian or Moravian origins. Quiet, almost apologetic in manner, he was also capable of firmness. His appointment dated back to before the war, and, during the uncertainties of the immediately post-Munich period, he had armed his staff, in case an effort was made to take over the military attaché's office by elements that might have British recognition, but were regarded by himself as traitorous. Hlava liked a mild joke and was incomparably easy to work with.

'Smetana's father made beer,' he said. 'Father wanted son to make beer too, but Smetana instead make Czechoslovak national music.'

These wartime social functions had to take place for a variety of reasons: to give employment: raise money: boost morale. They were rarely very enjoyable. Objection was sometimes aimed at them on the grounds that they made people forget the war. Had such oblivion been attainable, they would, indeed, have provided a desirable form of recuperation. In fact, they often risked additionally emphasizing contemporary conditions, the pursuits of peace, especially the arts, elbowed out of life, being hard to re-establish at short notice. Conversations, on such occasions as this opera, were apt to hover round semi-political or semi-official matters, rather than break away into some aesthetic release.

'Your other great national composer is, of course, Dvorák.'

'Dvorák poor man like Smetana. Dvorák's father poor pork butcher.'

'But a musical pork butcher?'

'Played the bagpipes in the mountains,' said Hlava. 'Like in Scotland.'

Most of the theatre was occupied with Allied military or civil elements, members of the Diplomatic Corps and people with some stake in Czech organizations. In one of the boxes, Prince Theodoric sat with the Huntercombes and a grey-haired lady with a distinguished air, probably one of his household, a countrywoman in exile. Lord Huntercombe, now getting on in age, was shown in the programme as on the board staging this performance. He was closely connected with many Allied causes and charities, and looked as shrewd as ever. He and Theodoric were wearing dark suits, the grey-haired lady in black—by this stage of the war not much seen—beside Lady Huntercombe, in rather a different role from that implied by her pre-war Gainsborough hats, was formidable in Red Cross commandant's uniform.

'Who's the big man with the white moustache three rows in front?' asked Isobel.

'General van Strydonck de Burkel, Inspector-General of the Belgian army and air force—rather a figure.'

The overture began. The curtain had already gone up on the scene of the country fair, when a woman came through one of the doors of the auditorium, paused and looked about her for a moment, then, showing no sign of being embarrassed by her own lateness, made her way to an empty seat beside another woman, in the same row as General van Strydonck, but nearer the middle. In doing this she caused a good deal of disturbance. Several men stood up to let her get by, among them Widmerpool, whom I had not before noticed. It was surprising to see him at a show like this, as he was likely to be working late every night at his particular job. When the lights went on again, he was revealed as being in the company of a youngish major-general. Our party went out during the entr'acte.

'How unpunctual Miss Flitton is,' said Isobel.

Pamela Flitton came into the foyer at that moment. She was wearing a bright scarlet coat and skirt, and accompanied by a woman in uniform, Lady McReith, someone I had not seen for the best part of twenty years.

'She must have blown every coupon she's got on that outfit.'

'Or taken them off some poor chap who received a special issue for overseas.'

Apart from hair now iron-grey, very carefully set, Lady McReith remained remarkably unaltered. She was thinner than ever, almost a skeleton, the blue veins more darkly shaded in on her marble skin. She retained her enigmatic air, that disconcerting half-smile that seemed to be laughing at everyone, although at this moment she did not look in the best of humours. Probably she had paid for Pamela's ticket and was cross at her lateness. If Lady McReith were at the head of a detachment of drivers, she would know about discipline. However, annoyance showed only in her eyes, while she and Pamela stood in a corner watching the crowd. Widmerpool and his general, who was of unknown identity, were behaving as if something important was brewing between them, strolling up and down in a preoccupied manner like men talking serious business, rather than a couple of opera-lovers having a night off duty. On the way back to our seats, we found ourselves next to them in the aisle. Widmerpool, who had met Isobel in the past, peered closely to make sure I was out with my wife, and said good evening. Then he muttered a question under his breath.

'Do you happen to know the name of the girl in red who came in late? I've seen her before. With some Americans at one of Biddle's big Allied gatherings.'

'Pamela Flitton.'

'So that's Pamela Flitton?'

'She's a niece of Charles Stringham's. You heard he was at Singapore when the Japs moved in?'

'Yes, yes, poor fellow,' said Widmerpool.

He made no reference to the fact that he had been in some measure responsible for sending Stringham there, indeed, there was no time to do so before he went back to his seat. During the second entr'acte he did not appear, possibly having left the theatre with his companion. The Huntercombes, who had remained in their box on this earlier opportunity for the audience to stretch its legs, now entered the foyer with Theodoric and the foreign lady. Theodoric, always very conscious of the social demands imposed by royal rank, began to look about him for people to whom it was a requirement to make himself agreeable. No doubt feeling the disfavour Czechs, in principle, affected for persons of high degree had first claim on his good manners, he came over to shake hands with Hlava's party.

'How is Colonel Finn? Busy as ever?'

'More than ever, sir.'

'I try not to waste his time with our small problems, but I may have to ask for an interview next week.'

I gave a reassuring reply. Theodoric left the Hlava group, crossing the floor for a word with Van Strydonck de Burkel. Huge, with a white curled moustache, the Belgian general, though now rather old to take an active part in the direction of policy, looked everything he should from his picturesque reputation. In the earlier war, at the head of two squadrons of cavalry, he had led an operationally successful charge against a German machine-gun emplacement; a kind of apotheosis of those last relics of horsed warfare represented by Horaczko and Clanwaert. Having spoken a word or two to Van Strydonck, the Prince was on his way to another sector of the foyer, when Pamela Flitton suddenly detached herself from Lady McReith, and moved swiftly through the crowd. On reaching Theodoric, she slipped her arm through his.

'Don't miss Lola Montez,' said Isobel.

Considering the familiarity of the behaviour, its contrast with Pamela's usually icy demeanour, Theodoric accepted the gesture with composure. If he felt whatever intimacy might exist between them were better left unadvertised in a theatre packed with official personages, he did not encourage gossip by showing any sign of that. On the contrary, he took her hand, pressed it earnestly, as if they scarcely knew each other but he wished to show himself specially grateful for some thoughtful action that had gratified his sense of what was right. Then, having spoken a few words to her, he gave a smile of dismissal, and turned towards General Asbjørnsen who was standing nearby. Pamela was at first not prepared to accept this disengaging movement on the part of the Prince, or at any rate preferred to demonstrate that it was for her rather than Theodoric himself to decide when and how the conversation should be terminated. Accordingly, she constituted herself part of the Theodoric-Asbjørnsen axis for a minute or two; then, giving in her turn a nod to Theodoric, at the same time patting his arm, she coolly returned to Lady McReith, who now made no effort to look anything but cross. The bell sounded. We sat down to the Third Act and the man disguised as a bear.

'British gave Smetana musical degree,' said Hlava.

*The Bartered Bride* was the only occasion, a unique one,

so far as I know, that added any colour to the rumour going round that Pamela Flitton was 'having an affair' with Prince Theodoric. Whether that were true, or whether she merely hoped to create an impression it was true, was never to my knowledge finally cleared up. All that can be said is that later circumstances supplied an odd twist to the possibility. When, subsequently, Jeavons heard the story, he showed interest.

'Sad Molly's gone,' he said. 'She always liked hearing about Theodoric, on account of his having been mixed up years ago with her ex-sister-in-law, Bijou. Looks as if Theodoric falls for an English girl every dozen years or so. Well, his wife's in America and I told you what Smith said. Can't be too cheerful having your country occupied by the Germans either. By all accounts, he's doing what he can to help us get them out. Needs some relaxation. We all do.'

About this time, Jumbo Wilson, in the light-hearted manner of generals, made nonsense of the polite letters Clanwaert and I used to send each other on the subject of the Congo army, by delivering a speech in honour of a visiting Belgian ex-Prime Minister to the effect that the services of La Force Publique would come in very useful in the Middle East. The words were scarcely out of his mouth when they set off with all their vehicles to the field of operation, arriving there very reasonably intact, and, I suppose, justifying Jumbo Wilson's oratory. However, if Clanwaert and I were thereby given something to laugh about, plenty of horrible matters were abroad too.

An announcement was made on the German radio, stating that at a place called Katyn, near the Russian town of Smolensk, an accumulation of communal graves had been found by advancing German troops. These graves were filled with corpses wearing Polish uniform. There were several thousands of bodies. The source of this information was naturally suspect, but, if in any degree to be believed, offered one solution to the mysterious disappearance of the untraced ten or fifteen thousand Polish officers, made prisoners of war by the Soviet army in 1939. 'Rather a large deficiency', as Q (Ops.) Colonel had remarked. The broadcast stated that individual bodies could be identified by papers carried on them, in some cases a tunic still bearing the actual insignia of a decoration, a practice of the Polish army in the case of operation awards. The hands had been tied together and a shot placed in the base of the skull. As a consequence of this radio announcement, the Polish Government in London approached the International Red Cross with a view to instituting an investigation. Exception was at once taken to this step by the USSR, relations with the Polish Government being immediately severed.

'The show-down has come,' said Pennistone.

The day this news was released, I went upstairs to see Finn about a rather complicated minute (to be signed by one of the Brigadiers) on the subject of redundant Czech army doctors being made available for seconding to the Royal Army Medical Corps. There had been difficulty about drafting satisfactory guarantees to make sure the Czechs, should they so require, would be able to recover the services of their MOs. Finn was in one of his unapproachable moods. The Russo-Polish situation had thoroughly upset him.

'It's a bad business,' he kept repeating. 'A bad business. I've got Bobrowski coming to see me this afternoon. What the hell am I to say?'

I tried to get the subject round to Czech medical matters and the views of the RAMC brasshats, but he told me to bring the matter up again that afternoon.

'You've got to go over to the Cabinet Offices now,' he said. 'They've just rung through. Some Belgian papers they want us to see. Something about the King. Nothing of any great importance, I think, but graded "hand of officer", and to be read by those in direct contact with the Belgians.'

The position of the King of the Belgians was delicate. Formally accepted as monarch of their country by the Belgian Government in exile, the royal portrait hanging in Kucherman's office, King Leopold, rightly or wrongly, was not, officially speaking, very well looked on by ourselves. His circumstances had been made no easier by a second marriage disapproved by many of his subjects.

'Have a look at this Belgian file before you bring it up,' said Finn. 'Do a note on it. Then we can discuss it after we've settled the Czech medicos. God, this Polish business.'

I went across to the Ministry of Defence right away. Finn had given the name of a lieutenant-colonel from whom the papers were to be acquired. After some search in the Secretariat, this officer was eventually traced in Widmerpool's room. I arrived there a few minutes before one o'clock, and the morning meeting had begun to adjourn. If they were the same committee as that I had once myself attended, the individual members had all changed, though no doubt they represented the same ministries. The only one known to me was a figure remembered from early London days, Tompsitt, a Foreign Office protégé of Sir Gavin Walpole-Wilson's. Sir Gavin himself had died the previous year. Obituaries, inevitably short in wartime, had none of them mentioned the South American misjudgment that had led to his retirement. His hopes in Tompsitt, untidy as ever and no less pleased with himself, seemed to have been realized, this job being presumably a respectable one for his age, if not particularly glamorous. Widmerpool, again in a good humour, made a facetious gesture of surprise on seeing me.

'Nicholas? Good gracious me. What is it you want, do you say? Belgian papers? Do you know anything about this, Simon? You do? Then we must let him have them.'

Someone was sent to find the papers.

'We finished early this morning,' said Widmerpool. 'An unheard of thing for us to do. I'm going to allow myself the luxury of lunching outside this building for once. So you're looking after the Belgians now, are you, Nicholas? I thought it was the Poles.'

'I've moved over.'

'You must be glad.'

'There were interesting sides.'

'Just at this moment, I mean. You are well out of the Poles. They are rocking the boat in the most deplorable manner. Our own relations with the USSR are never exactly easy—then for the Poles to behave as they have done.'

The attention of the other civilian, who, with Tompsitt, had been attending the meeting, was caught by Widmerpool's reproachful tone. He looked a rather younger version of our former housemaster, Le Bas, distinctly clerical, a thin severe overworked curate or schoolmaster.

'One would really have thought someone at the top of the Polish set-up would have grasped this is not the time to make trouble,' he said. 'Your people must be pretty fed up, aren't they, Tomp?'

Tompsitt shook back his unbrushed hair.

'Fed to the teeth,' he said. 'Probably put everything back to scratch.'

'All the same,' said the sailor, 'it looks a bit as if the Russkis did it.'

He was a heavily built man, with that totally anonymous personality achieved by certain naval officers, sometimes concealing unexpected abilities.

'Not to be ruled out,' said Tompsitt.

'More information's required.'

'Doesn't make it any better to fuss at this moment,' said the curate-schoolmaster.

He stared angrily through his spectacles, his cheeks contorted. The soldier, youngish with a slight stutter, who looked like a Regular, shook his papers together and put them into a briefcase.

'It's quite a crowd,' he said.

'What are the actual figures?' asked the sailor.

'Been put as high as nine or ten thousand,' said the airman.

He was a solid-looking middle-aged man with a lot of decorations, who had not spoken until then.

'How would that compare with our own pre-war army establishment?' asked the sailor. 'Let me see, about . . .'

'Say every third officer,' said the soldier. 'Quite a crowd, as I remarked. Say every third officer in our pre-war army.'

'But it's not pre-war,' said Tompsitt. 'It's war.'

'That's the point,' said Widmerpool. 'It's war. Just because these deaths are very upsetting to the Poles themselves —naturally enough, harrowing, tragic, there isn't a word for it, I don't want to underrate that for a moment—but just because of that, it's no reason to undermine the fabric of our alliances against the Axis. Quarrels among the Allies themselves are not going to defeat the enemy.'

'Even so, you can't exactly blame them for making enquiries through the International Red Cross,' the soldier insisted.

He began to move towards the door.

'But I do blame them,' said Tompsitt. 'I blame them a great deal. Their people did not act at all circumspectly. The Russians were bound to behave as they did under the circumstances.'

'Certainly hard to see what explanation they could give, if they did do it,' said the airman. '"Look here, old boy, we've shot these fellows of yours by accident" . . . Of course, it may turn out the Germans did it after all. They're perfectly capable of it.'

Everyone agreed that fact was undeniable.

'There's quite a chance the Germans did,' said the curate-schoolmaster hopefully.

'In any case,' said Widmerpool, 'whatever materializes, even if it does transpire—which I sincerly trust it will not—that the Russians behaved in such a very regrettable manner, how can this country possibly raise official objection, in the interests of a few thousand Polish exiles, who, however worthy their cause, cannot properly handle their diplomatic relations, even with fellow Slavs? It must be confessed also that the Poles themselves are in a position to offer only a very modest contribution, when it comes to the question of manpower. How, as I say, can we approach our second most powerful Ally about something which, if a fact, cannot be put right, and is almost certainly, from what one knows of them, the consequence of administrative inadequacy, rather than wilful indifference to human life and the dictates of compassion? What we have to do is not to waste time and energy in considering the relative injustices war brings in its train, but to make sure we are going to win it.'

By this time the Belgian file had been found and handed over to me. The others, having settled to their own satisfaction the issues of the Russo-Polish difference, were now talking of luncheon. Tompsitt had begun telling the curate-schoolmaster about some scandal in diplomatic circles when he had been *en poste* in Caracas.

'Going through the park, Michael?' Widmerpool asked the sailor. 'We might set off together if you can be seen walking with a Pongo.'

The sailor had an appointment in the other direction. I wondered whether in the access of self-abasement that seemed to have overcome him, Widmerpool would make a similar suggestion to the airman, referring to himself as a 'brown job'. However, he required instead my own company. Tompsitt came to the climax of the anecdote which made his colleague suck in his thin lips appreciatively.

'Of course he's a Vichy man now,' said Tompsitt.

'Do French diplomats have mistresses?'

'The Italians are worse,' said Tompsitt pontifically.

'Now then, you two, keep off the girls,' said Widmerpool gaily. 'Come on, Nicholas.'

'I've got to take these papers back.'

'You can cut through the Horse Guards.'

We ascended to ground level and set off through St James's Park. The water had been drained from the lake to decrease identification from the air, leaving large dejected basins of clay-like soil. There were no ducks.

'Rather ridiculous the way those two were talking about women,' said Widmerpool. 'You'd hardly believe how unsophisticated some of these Civil Servants are on such subjects, even senior ones, the Foreign Office as much as any, in spite of thinking so much of themselves. They like to behave as if they are a lot of duke's nephews who've got there by aristocratic influence, whereas they're simply a collection of perfectly ordinary middle-class examinees with rather less manners than most. "The Italians are worse!" Did you ever hear such a remark? I've known Tomp for a very long time, and he's not a bad fellow, but lives in a very constricted social sphere.'

'Who was the other?'

'Some fellow from MEW,' said Widmerpool. 'No real experience of the world.'

There was something to be said for Widmerpool's views, though there had been a time when he had argued the other way. This contempt for those uninstructed in moral licence was new too. It was the sort of subject he was inclined to avoid. His own sex life had always been rather a mystery. There was nothing so very unusual about that. Most people's sex life is a mystery, especially that of individuals who seem to make most parade of it. Such is the conclusion one finally arrives at. All the same, Widmerpool had more than once shown himself an exceptional mixture of vehemence and ineptitude; the business of Gypsy Jones, for example, in his early days; then the disastrous engagement to Mrs Haycock or his romantic love for Barbara Goring. Few subjects are more fascinating than other people's sexual habits from the outside; the tangled strands of appetite, tenderness, convenience or some hope of gain. In the light of what he had been saying, a direct question could sound not unreasonably inquisitive.

'How do you organize that side of your own life these days?'

I did not feel absolutely at ease making this unconcealed attempt to satisfy curiosity, but, in supposing Widmerpool might be embarrassed, evasive or annoyed, I was wholly wrong. The enquiry delighted him. He clapped me on the back.

'Plenty of pretty little bits in the black-out.'

'Tarts?'

'Of course.'

The solution was the same as Borrit's. I remembered now that Widmerpool had commented favourably, years before, when I told him my own rooms in Shepherd Market were flanked by a large block of flats housing prostitutes. At the time, I had supposed that remark bombast on his part. Now, such a diagnosis seemed less positive. Perhaps, anyway in the course of the years, his remark, 'How convenient', had acquired a certain authenticity. One wondered what cumbersome burden of desire, satisfied or unsatisfied, possibly charged in its fulfilment with some elaborate order of ritual, Widmerpool carried round with him.

'I suppose you have to be rather careful.'

It was a lame comment, which Widmerpool treated with the contempt it deserved.

'I am careful,' he said. 'Is there anything about my life that would lead you to suppose I should not be careful? I believe in thinking things out. Arranging my life, but arranging it in such a way that I do not fall into a groove. By the way, there is a probability I shall go red in the near future.'

'Go red?'

I had not the least idea what he meant. It seemed possible he might have returned to the subject of sexual habits, planning something in that line embarrassing even to himself.

'Become a full colonel.'

He snapped the words out. Failure to recognize a colloquialism had irritated him. The phrase was peculiar to himself. Usually people spoke of a 'red hat' or 'taking flannel'.

'Only a tanner a day more in pay,' he said, recovering his good humour, 'but it's the real jump in rank.'

It was no doubt specifically to inform me of this imminent promotion that he must have come out of the way across the Horse Guards Parade, I thought. By now we had nearly reached the arch leading into Whitehall. He suddenly lost his high spirits, sinking all at once to the depths of gloom, as I had known him do before, one of those changes of mood that would overcome him without warning.

'You never know about promotion till it's in the bag,' he said. 'There are occupational risks where I work. There are anywhere where you may find yourself in the CIGS's entourage.'

'Why him specially?'

'He's quite ruthless, if he doesn't like the look of you. The other day he said, "I don't want to see that officer again. I don't like his face". Perfectly good man, but they had to get rid of him.'

Widmerpool spoke with infinite dejection. I saw what he meant. Given the CIGS was easily irritated by the faces of staff-officers, Widmerpool's, where survival was in question, was a bad bet, rather than a good one.

'No use worrying,' he said. 'After all, I was not affected by all the trouble Liddament made.'

'His Corps seem to have done well in the desert.'

'No doubt Liddament has his points as a commander in the field. Unfortunately, I was blind to them when serving on the staff of his Division. Tell me—talking of those days made me think of Farebrother—had you left the Poles at the time of the Szymanski scandal?'

'Yes.'

'You heard Farebrother was largely responsible?'

'That was being said.'

'He's been unstuck in consequence. Not without some action on my part.'

'I didn't know you were involved.'

'I made it my business to be involved. Strictly between ourselves, the whole disgraceful affair was not unconnected with Prince Theodoric whom we saw at that musical performance the other night.'

'Where does Theodoric come in?'

'That is naturally secret, but I don't mind telling you that the Prince is bringing a lot of pressure to bear one way and another.'

'You mean from the Resistance point of view.'

'I hold my own views on that subject,' said Widmerpool. 'I hear that young woman in red, whose name I asked, is said to be Theodoric's mistress.'

'That's the gossip.'

'I have little or no time for social life, but one keeps an eye on these things.'

A full colonel, wearing the red tabs with which Widmerpool himself hoped soon to be equipped, came out of a door under the arch and turned into Whitehall. Widmerpool pointed after him and laughed.

'Did you see who that was?' he asked. 'I really strolled with you across here, out of my way, in case we might catch sight of him.'

'Was it Hogbourne-Johnson?'

'Relegated to the Training branch, where, if he's not kicked out from there too, he will remain until the end of the war. The man who thought he was going to get a Division. Do you remember when he was so abominably rude to me?'

'That balls-up about traffic circuits?'

'It won't be long now before I'm his equal in rank. I may find an opportunity to tell him some home truths, should our paths cross, though that's unlikely enough. It's only on the rarest occasions like today that I'm out of my office—and, after all, Hogbourne-Johnson's a very unimportant cog in the machine.'

He nodded and began to move off. I saluted—the uniform, as one was always told, rather than the man—and took the Belgian documents back to our room.

## CHAPTER THREE

One day, several weeks after the Allied Forces had landed in Normandy, I was returning over Westminster Bridge on foot from transacting some minor item of Czechoslovak army business with a ministry housed on the south bank of the river in the former Donners-Brebner Building. It was lovely weather. Even the most pessimistic had begun to concede that the war, on the whole, had taken a turn for the better. Some supposed this might mean the end of raids. Others believed the Germans had a trick or two up their sleeve. Although it was London Bridge to which the poem referred, rather than Westminster, the place from which I had just come, the dark waters of the Thames below, the beauty of the day, brought to mind the lines about Stetson and the ships at Mylae, how death had undone so many. Donners-Brebner—where Howard Craggs, recently knighted, now reigned over one of the branches—had been badly knocked about in the early days of the blitz. The full extent of the damage was not visible, because the main entrance, where Barnby's frescoes had once been, was heaped with sandbags, access by a side door. Barnby was no longer available to repaint his frescoes. Death had undone him. It looked as if death might have undone Stringham too. At Donners-Brebner he had put me off for dinner because he was going to Peggy Stepney's parents. Peggy's second husband was another who had been undone. She was married to Jimmy Klein now, said to have always loved her. These musings were interrupted by a tall officer falling into step with me. It was Sunny Farebrother.

'Hullo, Nicholas. I hope my dear old Finn is not still cross with me about Szymanski?'

'There may still be some disgruntlement, sir.'

'Disgruntlement', one was told, was a word that could be used of all ranks without loss of discipline. As I heard myself utter it, I became immediately aware of the manner in which Farebrother, by some effort of the will, made those with whom he dealt as devious as himself. It was not the first time I had noticed that characteristic in him. The reply, the term, was in truth hopelessly inadequate to express Finn's rage about the whole Szymanski affair.

'Finn's a hard man,' said Farebrother. 'Nobody I admire more. There is not an officer in the entire British army I admire more than Lieutenant-Colonel Lysander Finn, VC.'

'Lysander?'

'Certainly.'

'We never knew.'

'He keeps it quiet.'

Farebrother smiled, not displeased at finding this piece of information so unexpected.

'Who shall blame him?' he said. 'It's modesty, not shame. He thinks the name might sound pretentious in the winner of a VC. Finn's as brave as a lion, as straight as a die, but as hard as nails—especially where he thinks his own honour is concerned.'

Farebrother said the last words in what Pennistone called his religious voice.

'You weren't yourself affected by the Szymanski matter, Nicholas?'

'I'd left the Poles by then.'

'You're no longer in Finn's Section?'

Farebrother made no attempt to conceal his own interest in any change that might take place in employment or status of those known to him, in case these might in some manner, even if unforeseen, react advantageously to himself.

'Ah,' he said. 'The Belgians and Czechs. I should like to have a talk with you one of these days about those two

Allies, but not now. You don't know how sorry I am that poor old Finn was inconvenienced in that way. I hate it when friends think you've let them down. I remember a Frenchman in the last war whom I'd promised to put in for a British decoration that never came through. No use regretting these things, I suppose, but I'm made that way. We all have to do our duty as we see it, Nicholas. Each one of us has to learn that and it's sometimes a hard lesson. In the case of Szymanski, I was made to suffer for being too keen. Disciplined, demoted in rank, shunted off to a bloody awful job. Tell Finn that. Perhaps he will forgive me when he hears I was made to pay for my actions. You know who went out of his way to bring this trouble about—our old friend Kenneth Widmerpool.'

'But you've left that job now?'

'In Civil Affairs, with my old rank and a good chance of promotion.'

The Civil Affairs branch, formed to deal with administration of areas occupied by our enemies, had sprung into being about a year before. In it were already collected together a rich variety of specimens of army life. Farebrother would ornament the collection. Pennistone compared Civil Affairs with 'the head to which all the ends of the world are come, and the eyelids are a little weary.'

'That just describes it,' Pennistone said. '"No crude symbolism disturbs the effect of Civil Affairs' subdued and graceful mystery".'

Among others to find his way into this branch was Dicky Umfraville, who had thereby managed to disengage himself from the transit camp he had been commanding. I asked if Farebrother had any deals with Umfraville, whom I had not seen for some little time. Farebrother nodded. He looked over his shoulder, as if he feared agents were tracking us at that very moment and might overhear his words.

'You know Kenneth pretty well?'

'Yes.'

'Umfraville was talking to one of our people who'd been in Cairo when Kenneth flew out there for a day or two, as member of a high-level conference secretariat. Do you know what happened? Something you'd never guess. He managed to make a fool of himself about some girl employed in a secret outfit there.'

'In what way?'

'Took her out or something. She was absolutely notorious, it seems.'

'What happened?'

'Don't let's talk about it,' said Farebrother. 'If there's one thing I hate, it's a woman who lowers herself in that sort of way. I'm afraid there are quite a few of them about in wartime.'

We had by now turned into Whitehall. Farebrother suddenly raised his arm in a stiff salute. I did the same, taking my time from him, though not immediately conscious of whom we were both saluting. Then I quickly apprehended that Farebrother was paying tribute to the Cenotaph, which we were at that moment passing. The preoccupations of wartime often resulted in this formality—always rather an uncomfortable and precarious one—being allowed to pass unobserved. It was a typical mark of Farebrother's innate regard for ceremoniousness in all its aspects that he brought out his salute as if on a parade ground march-past. However, at that moment, another—and certainly discordant—circumstance clouded the scene. Just as Farebrother had been the first to see and pay homage to the Cenotaph, he was undoubtedly the first of us also to appreciate the necessity of taking another decision, a quick one, in a similar field. This resolve also had important implications, though of a very different sort. The situation was posed by a couple walking briskly towards us from the direction of Trafalgar

Square: a middle-aged civilian—almost certainly a Civil Servant of high standing—wearing a very old hat on the back of his head, beside him an officer in a full colonel's red capband and tabs. Even at this distance the tabs could be seen to be imposed on one of the new 'utility' uniforms, service-dress tunics skimped at the pockets and elsewhere to save cloth. These innovations always gave the wearer, even if a thin man, the air of being too large for his clothes, and this officer, stoutish with spectacles, was bursting from them. I noticed the uniform before appreciating that here was Widmerpool 'gone red'.

'In life—'

Farebrother had just begun to speak. He broke off suddenly. The way in which he did this, obviously abandoning giving expression to some basic rule of human conduct, made me sure, reflecting on the incident afterwards, that he had seen Widmerpool first. There can also be no doubt that he was as ignorant as myself of his old enemy's promotion. That must have been gazetted subsequent to the Cairo tour of duty. For a split second I had time to wonder whether Farebrother would accord Widmerpool as smart an acknowledgment or rank—after all, it was 'the uniform', even if only a 'utility' one—as he had rendered the Cenotaph. It should be explained perhaps that, although in theory majors and upwards had some claim to a salute from those of junior rank, in practice the only officers saluted by other officers in the street were those who wore red. I was therefore once more preparing to take my time from Farebrother, when he suddenly seized my arm. We were just passing 'the Fortress', Combined Operations Headquarters, then more or less underground, after the war covered by a building of many storeys. At first I thought he wanted to draw my attention to something happening on the other side of the road.

'Nicholas?'

'Sir?'

'A moment ago I was telling you I don't like to see a woman making herself cheap. Women's lives should be beautiful, an inspiration. I thought of that the other night. I was taken to a film called *The Song of Bernadette*. Have you seen it?'

'No, sir.'

He looked at me fixedly. He had put on his holy face, as was to be expected from the subject of the movie, and spoke the words in an equally appropriate tone.

'It's about Lourdes.'

I repeated that I had not seen the film.

'You should, Nicholas. I don't often get out in the evenings, much too much to do, but I think that night did me good. Made me a better man.'

I could not imagine what all this was leading up to.

'You really think I ought to make an effort to go, sir?'

Farebrother did not answer. Instead, he gave another of his quick glances over the shoulder. For a moment I remained at a loss to know why *The Song of Bernadette* had so much impressed him that he felt a sudden need to speak of the film so dramatically. Then all at once I grasped that the menace of saluting Widmerpool no longer hung over us. Farebrother, with all his self-control in such matters, all the years he had schooled himself to accept the ways of those set in authority over him, had for one reason or another been unable to face that bitterness in my presence. Inner disciplines, respect for tradition, taste for formality, had none of them been sufficient. The incident showed Farebrother, too, had human weaknesses. Now, he seemed totally to have forgotten about Bernadette. We walked along in silence. Perhaps he was pondering the saintly life. We reached the gates of the Horse Guards. Farebrother paused. His gay blue eyes became a little sad. 'Do your best to make your Colonel forgive me, Nicholas.

You can tell him—without serious breach of security—that Szymanski's already done a first-rate job in one quarter and likely to do as good a one in another. Do you ever see Prince Theodoric in these days? In my present job I no longer have grand contacts like that.'

I told him I had not seen Theodoric since *The Bartered Bride*. We went our separate ways.

That night in bed, reading *Remembrance of Things Past*, I thought again of Theodoric, on account of a passage describing the Princesse de Guermantes' party:

'The Ottoman Ambassadress, now bent on demonstrating to me not only her familiarity with the Royalties present, some of whom I knew our hostess had invited out of sheer kindness of heart and would never have been at home to them if the Prince of Wales or the Queen of Spain were in her drawing-room the afternoon they called, but also her mastery of current appointments under consideration at the Quai d'Orsay or Rue St. Dominique, disregarding my wish to cut short our conversation—additionally so because I saw Professor E—— once more bearing down on us and feared the Ambassadress, whose complexion conveyed unmistakable signs of a recent bout of varicella, might be one of his patients—drew my attention to a young man wearing a cypripeden (the flower Bloch liked to call "sandal of foam-borne Aphrodite") in the buttonhole of his dress coat, whose swarthy appearance required only an astrakhan cap and silver-hilted yataghan to complete evident affinities with the Balkan peninsula. This Apollo of the hospodars was talking vigorously to the Grand Duke Vladimir, who had moved away from the propinquity of the fountain and whose features now showed traces of uneasiness because he thought this distant relative, Prince Odoacer, for that was who I knew the young man of the orchid to be, sought his backing in connexion with a certain secret alliance predicted in Eastern Europe, material to the interests of Prince

Odoacer's country no less than the Muscovite Empire; support which the Grand Duke might be unwilling to afford, either on account of his kinsmen having compromised himself financially, through a childish ignorance of the Bourse, in connexion with a speculation involving Panama Canal shares (making things no better by offering to dispose "on the quiet" of a hunting scene by Wouwerman destined as a birthday present for his mistress), from which he had to be extracted by the good offices of that same Baron Manasch with whom Swann had once fought a duel; or, even more unjustly, because the Grand Duke had heard a rumour of the unfortunate reputation the young Prince had incurred for himself by the innocent employment as valet of a notorious youth whom I had more than once seen visiting Jupien's shop, and, as I learnt much later, was known among his fellow inverts as La Gioconda. "I'm told Gogo —Prince Odoacer—has Dreyfusard leanings!" said the Ambassadress, assuming my ignorance of the Prince's nickname as well as his openly expressed political sympathies, the momentary cruelty of her smile hinting at Janissary blood flowing in her veins. "Albeit a matter that does not concern a foreigner like myself," she went on, "yet, if true that the name of Colonel de Froberville, whom I see standing over there, has been put forward as military attaché designate to the French Legation of Prince Odoacer's country, the fact of such inclinations in one of its Royal House should be made known as soon as possible to any French officer likely to fill the post." '

This description of Prince Odoacer was of special interest because he was a relation—possibly great-uncle—of Theodoric's. I thought about the party for a time, whether there had really been a Turkish Ambassadress, whom Proust found a great bore; then, like the Narrator himself in his childhood days, fell asleep early. This state, left undisturbed by the Warning, was brought to an end by rising hubbub outside. A very noisy attack had started up. Some residents, especially those inhabiting the upper storeys, preferred to descend to the ground floor or basement on these occasions. Rather from lethargy than an indifference to danger, I used in general to remain in my flat during raids, feeling that one's nerve, certainly less steady than at an earlier stage of the war, was unlikely to be improved by exchanging conversational banalities with neighbours equally on edge.

From first beginnings, this particular raid made an unusually obnoxious din and continued to do so. While bombs and flak exploded at the present rate there was little hope of dropping off to sleep again. I lay in the dark, trying to will them to go home, one way, not often an effective one, of passing the time during raids. My interior counter-attack was not successful. An hour went by; then another; and another. So far from decreasing, the noise grew greater in volume. There was a suggestion of more or less regular bursts of detonation launched from the skies, orchestrated against the familiar rise and fall of gunfire. It must have been about two or three in the morning, when, rather illogically, I decided to go downstairs. A move in that direction at least offered something to do. Besides, I could feel myself growing increasingly jumpy. The ground floor at this hour was at worst likely to provide, if nothing else, a certain anthropological interest. The occasion was one for the merest essentials of uniform, pockets filled with stuff from which one did not want to be separated, should damage occur in the room while away. I took a helmet as a matter of principle.

On one of the walls of the lift, incised with a sharp instrument (similar to that used years before to outline the caricature of Widmerpool in the *cabinet* at La Grenadière), someone quite recently—perhaps that very night—had etched at eye-level, in lower case letters suggesting an E. E. Cummings poem, a brief cogent observation about the manageress, one likely to prove ineradicable as long as the life itself remained in existence, for no paint could have obscured it:

*old bitch wartstone*

Quite a few people were below, strolling about talking, or sitting on the benches of the hall. No doubt others were in the basement, a region into which I had never penetrated, where there was said to be some sort of 'shelter'. This crowd was in a perpetual state of change: some, like myself, deciding they needed a spell out of bed; others, too tired or bored to stay longer chatting in the hall, retiring to the basement or simply returning to their own flats. Clanwaert, smoking a cigarette, his hands in the pockets of a rather smart green silk dressing-gown, was present. Living on the ground floor anyway, he had not bothered to dress.

'This raid seems to be going on a long time.'

'Of course it is, my friend. We are getting the famous Secret Weapon we have heard so much about.'

'You think so?'

'Not a doubt of it. We knew it was coming in Eaton Square. Had you not been informed in Whitehall? The interesting thing will be to see how this fine Secret Weapon really turns out.'

It looked as if Clanwaert were right. He began to talk of the Congo army and the difficulties they had encountered in the Sudanese desert. After a while the subject exhausted itself.

'Is there any point in not going back to bed?'

'Hard to say. It may quiet down. I am in any case a bad sleeper. One becomes accustomed to doing without sleep, if one lives a long time in the tropics.'

He put out his cigarette and went to the front door to see

how things were looking in the street. A girl with a helmet set sideways on her head, this headdress assumed for decorative effect rather than as a safety measure, came past. She wore an overcoat over trousers in the manner of Gypsy Jones and Audrey Maclintick. It was Pamela Flitton.

'Hullo.'

She looked angry, as if suspecting an attempted pick-up, then recognized me.

'Hullo.'

She did not smile.

'What a row.'

'Isn't it.'

'Seen anything of Norah?'

'Norah and I haven't been speaking for ages. She's too touchy. That's one of the things wrong with Norah.'

'Still doing your secret job?'

'I've just come back from Cairo.'

'By boat?'

'I got flown back.'

'You were lucky to get an air passage.'

'I travelled on a general's luggage.'

A youngish officer, in uniform but with unbuttoned tunic, came into the hall from the passage leading to the ground floor flats. He was small, powerfully built, with hair growing in regular waves of curls, like Jeavons's, though fair in colour.

'We seem to be out of fags,' he said to Pamela.

'Oh, Christ.'

He turned to me. I registered a crown on his shoulder, MC and bar above the pocket.

'Haven't got a cigarette by any chance, pal?' he said. 'We've smoked our last—why, Nicholas? I'll be buggered. Caught you trying to pick up Pam. What cheek. How are you, old boy. Marvellous to meet again.'

'Pamela and I know each other already. She used to drive

me in her ATS days, not to mention my practically attending her christening.'

'So you live in this dump, too, and suffer from old Wartstone? If I wasn't leaving the place at any moment, I'd carve up that woman with a Commando knife in a way that would make Jack the Ripper look like the vicar cutting sandwiches for a school treat.'

I was not specially pleased to see Odo Stevens, whose conduct, personal and official, could not be approved for a variety of reasons, whatever distinction he might have earned in the field. At the same time, there was small point in attempting to take a high moral line, either about his affair with Priscilla or the part he had played over Szymanski. Priscilla and Chips Lovell were dead: Szymanski too, for all one knew by this time. Besides, to be pompous about such matters was even in a sense to play into the hands of Stevens, to give opportunity for him to justify himself in one of those emotional displays that are always part of the stock-in-trade of persons of his particular sort. With characteristic perspicuity, he guessed at once what was going through my mind. His look changed. It was immediately clear he was going to bring up the subject of Priscilla.

'It was simply awful,' he said. 'What happened after we last met. That bomb on the Madrid killing her husband—then the other where she was staying. I even thought of writing to you. Then I got mixed up with a lot of special duties.'

He had quite changed his tone of voice from the moment before, at the same time assuming an expression reminiscent of Farebrother's 'religious face', the same serious pained contraction of the features. I was determined to endure for as short a time as possible only what was absolutely unavoidable in the exhibition of self-confessed remorse Stevens was obviously proposing to mount for my benefit. He had been, I recalled, unnecessarily public in his carryings-on with Priscilla, had corroded what turned out to be Chips's last year alive. That might be no very particular business of mine, but I had liked Chips, therefore preferred the circumstances should remain unresurrected. That was the long and the short of it.

'Don't let's talk about it. What's the good?'

Stevens was not to be silenced so easily.

'She meant so much to me,' he said.

'Who did?' asked Pamela.

'Someone who was killed in an air-raid.'

He put considerable emotion into his voice when he said that. Perhaps Priscilla had, indeed, 'meant a lot' to him. I did not care. I saw no reason to be dragged in as a kind of prop to his self-esteem, or masochistic pleasure in lacking it. Besides, I wanted to get on to the Szymanski story.

'You're always telling me I mean more to you than any other girl has,' said Pamela. 'At least you do after a couple of drinks. You've the weakest head of any man I've ever met.'

She spoke in that low almost inaudible mutter employed by her most of the time. There was certainly a touch of Audrey Maclintick about her, at least enough to explain why Stevens and Mrs Maclintick had got on so comparatively well together that night in the Café Royal. On the other hand, this girl was not only much better looking, but also much tougher even than Mrs Maclintick. Pamela Flitton gave the impression of being thoroughly vicious, using the word not so much in the moral sense, but as one might speak of a horse—more specifically, a mare.

'I don't claim the capacity for liquor of some of your Slav friends,' said Stevens laughing.

He sounded fairly well able to stand up to her. This seemed a suitable moment to change the subject.

'You were in the news locally not so long ago—where I work, I mean—about one Szymanski.'

'Don't tell me you're with the Poles, Nicholas?'

'I'd left them by the time you got up to your tricks.'

Pamela showed interest at the name Szymanski.

'I sent you a message,' she said. 'Did you get it?'

When she smiled and spoke directly like that, it was possible to guess at some of her powers should she decide to make a victim of a man.

'I got it.'

'Then you were in on the party?' asked Stevens.

'I saw some of the repercussions.'

'God,' he said. 'That was a lark.'

'Not for those engaged in normal liaison duties.'

One's loyalties vary. At that moment I felt wholly on the side of law and order, if only to get some of my own back for his line of talk about the Lovells.

'Oh, bugger normal liaison duties. Even you must admit the operation was beautifully executed. Look here . . .'

He took my arm, and, leaving Pamela sitting sullenly by herself on a bench, walked me away to a deserted corner of the hall. When we reached there, he lowered his voice.

'I'm due for a job in the near future not entirely unconnected with Szymanski himself.'

'Housebreaking?'

Stevens yelled with laughter.

'That'll be the least of our crimes, I'd imagine,' he said. 'That is, the least of his—which might easily not stop at manslaughter, I should guess. Actually, we're doing quite different jobs, but more or less in the same place.'

'Presumably it's a secret where you're conducting these activities.'

'My present situation is being on twenty-four call to

Cairo. I'll release something to you, as an old pal, in addition to that. The plot's not unconnected with one of Pam's conquests. Rather a grand one.'

'You remind me of the man who used to introduce his wife as *ancienne maîtresse de Lord Byron*.'

'This is classier than a lord—besides Pam and I aren't married yet.'

'You don't have to spell the name out.'

I was not impressed by Stevens's regard for 'security,' always a risk in the hands of the vain. All the same, not much damage would be done by my knowing that at last some sort of assistance was to be given to the Resistance in Prince Theodoric's country; and that Stevens and Szymanski were involved. That was certainly interesting.

'I'll be playing for the village boys,' he said. 'Rather than the team the squire is fielding.'

'A tricky situation, I should imagine.'

'You bet.'

'I saw Sunny Farebrother yesterday, who took the rap in the Szymanski business.'

'Cunning old bugger. They pushed him off to a training centre for a bit, but I bet he's back on something good.'

'He thinks so. Was Szymanski a boy-friend of Pamela's?'

I thought I had a right to ask that question after the way Stevens had talked. For once he seemed a shade put out.

'Who can tell?' he said. 'Even if there's still a Szymanski. They may have infiltrated him already and he may have been picked up. I hope not. The great thing is he knows the country like the back of his hand. What are you doing yourself, old boy?'

The change of mood, sudden fear for Szymanski—and by implication for himself—was characteristic. I told him about my job, also explaining how I knew Pamela.

'Won't she be cross if we leave her much longer?'

'She's cross all the time. Bloody cross. Chronic state. Thrives on it. Her chief charm. Makes her wonderful in bed. That is, if you like temper.'

Emphasis expressed as to the high degree of sexual pleasure to be derived from a given person is, for one reason or another, always to be accepted with a certain amount of suspicion, so far as the speaker is concerned, especially if referring to a current situation. Stevens sounded as if he might be bolstering himself up in making the last statement.

'She's the hell of a girl,' he said.

I wondered whether he had run across Pamela with Szymanski in the first instance. In any case, people like that gravitate towards each other at all times, almost more in war than in peace, since war—though perhaps in a more limited sense than might be supposed—offers obvious opportunities for certain sorts of adventure. Stevens, whose self-satisfaction had if anything increased, seemed to have no illusions about Pamela's temperament. He accepted that she was a woman whose sexual disposition was vested in rage and perversity. In fact, if he were to be believed, those were the very qualities he had set out to find. We returned to where she was sitting.

'Where the hell have you two been?'

She spoke through her teeth. There was still a lot of noise going on outside. We all three sat on the bench together. Clanwaert strolled past. He glanced in our direction, slightly inclining his head towards Pamela, who took no perceptible notice of him. He had evidently decided to return to bed and said goodnight to me.

'That was the Belgian officer who gave me your message about Szymanski.'

'Ask him if he's got a cigarette.'

I called after Clanwaert. He turned back and came towards us. I enquired if he had a cigarette for Pamela, saying

I believed they had met. He took a case from his dressing-gown pocket and handed it round. Pamela took one, looking away as she did so. Clanwaert showed himself perfectly at ease under this chilly treatment.

'We could have met at the Belgian Institute,' he said. 'Was it with one of our artillery officers—Wauthier or perhaps Ruys?'

'Perhaps it was,' she said. 'Thanks for the smoke.'

Clanwaert smiled and retired.

'One of your *braves Belges*?' asked Stevens. 'Since you've lived here some time, you've probably come across the old girl standing by the door. She's called Mrs Erdleigh. The other evening, I saw her burning something on the roof. I thought she was sending up smoke signals to the enemy—it wasn't yet dark—but it turned out to be just incense, which seems to play some part in her daily life, as she's a witch. We got on rather well. In the end she told my fortune and said I was going to have all sorts of adventures and get a lot of nice presents from women.'

'Not me,' said Pamela. 'You'll have to go elsewhere if you want to be kept.'

Mrs Erdleigh was, indeed, looking out into the street through the glass doors at the other end of the hall. Her age as indeterminate as ever from her outward appearance, she was smiling slightly to herself. This was the first time I had seen her since living in the flats. A helmet was set very squarely on her head and she wore a long coat or robe, a pushteen or similar garment, woolly inside, skin without, the exterior ornamented with scrolls and patterns of Oriental design in bright colours. She was carrying a small black box under one arm. Now she set this on the ground and removed the helmet, revealing a coiffure of grey-blue curls that had been pressed down by the weight of the tin hat. These she ruffled with her fingers. Then she took the helmet between her hands, and, as if in deep thought, raised it like a basin or sacrificial vessel, a piece of temple equipment for sacred rites. Her quiet smile suggested she was rather enjoying the raid than otherwise. Nothing much seemed to be happening outside, though the row continued unabated.

'She was mixed up with an uncle of mine—in fact he left her his money, such as it was.'

The bequest had caused great annoyance in the family, almost as much on account of Uncle Giles turning out to own a few thousands, as because of the alienation of the capital sum.

'Must have made it quite lately as the result of some very risky speculation,' my father had said at the time. 'Never thought Giles had a penny to bless himself with.'

'Let's go over and talk to her,' said Stevens. 'She's good value.'

He had that taste, peculiar to certain egotists, to collect together close round him everyone he might happen to know in any given area.

'Oh, God,' said Pamela. 'Need we? I suppose she flattered you.'

'Go on, Nicholas,' he said. 'Ask Mrs Erdleigh to join us, if you know her as well.'

I agreed to do this, more from liking the idea of meeting Mrs Erdleigh again than to please Stevens. As I approached, she herself turned towards me.

'I wondered when you would speak,' she said gently.

'You'd already seen me in the hall?'

'Often in this building. But we must not anticipate our destinies. The meeting had to wait until tonight.'

From the way she spoke, it was to be assumed that she was so far above material contacts that the impetus of our reunion must necessarily come from myself. The magical course of events would no doubt have been damaged had she taken the initiative and addressed me first.

'What a night.'

'I could not sleep,' she said, as if that were a matter for surprise. 'The omens have not been good for some days past, though in general better than for many months. I can see at once from your face that you are well situated. The Centaur is friend to strangers and exiles. His arrow defends them.'

'Come and talk to us. There's a young man called Odo Stevens, who has done rather well as a soldier—been very brave, I mean—and a girl called Pamela Flitton. He says he knows you already.'

'I met your young army friend on the roof when I was engaged in certain required exsufflations. He is under Aries, like your poor uncle, but this young man has the Ram in far, far better aspect, the powerful rays of Mars favouring him rather than the reverse, as they might some—your uncle, for example.'

I told her I had seen the Ufford—where we had first met—now in such changed circumstances. She was not at all interested, continuing to speak of Stevens, who had evidently made an impression on her.

'It is the planet Mars that connects him with that very beautiful young woman,' she said. 'The girl herself is under Scorpio—like that unhappy Miss Wartstone, so persecuted by Saturn—and possesses many of the scorpion's cruellest traits. He told me much about her when we talked on the roof. I fear she loves disaster and death—but he will escape her, although not without an appetite for death himself.'

Mrs Erdleigh smiled again, as if she appreciated, even to some extent approved, this taste for death in both of them.

'Lead me to your friends,' she said. 'I am particularly interested in the girl, whom I have not yet met.'

She picked up the black box, which presumably contained spells and jewellery, carrying the helmet in her other hand. We returned to Stevens and Pamela. They were having words about a bar of chocolate, produced from somewhere and alleged to have been unfairly divided. Stevens jumped up and seized Mrs Erdleigh by the hand. It looked as if he were going to kiss her, but he stopped short of that. Pamela put on the helmet that had been lying beside her on the seat. This was evidently a conscious gesture of hostility.

'This is Miss Flitton,' said Stevens.

Pamela made one of her characteristically discouraging acknowledgments of this introduction. I was curious to see whether Mrs Erdleigh would exercise over her the same calming influence she had once exerted on Mona, Peter Templer's first wife, when they had met. Mona, certainly a far less formidable personality than Pamela, had been in a thoroughly bad mood that day—without the excuse of an air-raid being in progress—yet she had been almost immediately tranquillized by Mrs Erdleigh's restorative mixture of flattery, firmness and occultism. For all one knew, air-raids might positively increase Mrs Erdleigh's powers. She took Pamela's hand. Pamela withdrew it at once.

'I'm going to have a walk outside,' she said. 'See what's happening.'

'Don't be a fool,' said Stevens. 'You're not allowed to wander about during raids, especially one like this.'

'My dear,' said Mrs Erdleigh, 'I well discern in your heart that need for bitter things that knows no assuagement, those yearnings for secrecy and tears that pursue without end, wherever you seek to fly them. No harm will come to you, even on this demonic night, that I can tell you. Nevertheless stay for a minute and talk with me. Death, it is true, surrounds your nativity, even though you yourself are not personally threatened—none of us is tonight. There are things I would like to ask you. The dark unfathomable lake over which you glide—you are under a watery sign and yet a fixed one—is sometimes dull and stagnant, sometimes, as now, angry and disturbed.'

Pamela was certainly taken aback by this confident approach, so practised, so self-assured, the tone at once sinister and adulatory, but she did not immediately capitulate, as Mona had done. Instead, she temporized.

'How do you know about me?' she asked. 'Know when I was born, I mean.'

She spoke in a voice of great discontent and truculence. Mrs Erdleigh indicated that Stevens had been her informant. Pamela looked more furious than ever.

'What does he know about me?'

'What do most people know about any of their fellows?' said Mrs Erdleigh quietly. 'Little enough. Only those know, who are aware what is to be revealed. He may have betrayed the day of your birth. I do not remember. The rest I can tell from your beautiful face, my dear. You will not mind if I say that your eyes have something in them of the divine serpent that tempted Eve herself.'

It was impossible not to admire the method of attack. Stevens spoiled its delicacy by blundering in.

'Tell Pam's fortune,' he said. 'She'd love it—and you were wonderful with me.'

'Why should I want my fortune told? Haven't I just said I'm going to have a look round outside?'

'Wiser not, my dear,' said Mrs Erdleigh. 'As I said before, my calculations tell me that we are perfectly safe if we remain here, but one cannot always foresee what may happen to those who ride in the face of destiny. Why not let me look at your hand? It will pass the time.'

'If you really want to. I don't expect it's very interesting.'

I think Mrs Erdleigh was not used to being treated in such an ungracious manner. She did not show this in the smallest degree, but what she went on to say later could be attributed to a well controlled sense of pique. Perhaps that was why she insisted that Pamela's hand should be read by her.

'No human life is uninteresting.'

'Have a look then—but there's not much light here.'

'I have my torch.'

Pamela held out her palm. She was perhaps, in fact, more satisfied than the reverse at finding opposition to her objections overruled. It was likely she would derive at least some gratification in the anodyne process. However farouche, she could scarcely be so entirely different from the rest of the world. On the other hand, some instinct may have warned her against Mrs Erdleigh, capable of operating at as disturbing a level as herself. Mrs Erdleigh examined the lines.

'I would prefer the cards,' she said. 'I have them with me in my box, of course, but this place is really too inconvenient . . . As I guessed, the Mount of Venus highly developed . . . and her Girdle . . . You must be careful, my dear . . . There are things here that surprise even me . . . *les tentations lubriques sont bien prononcées* . . . You have found plenty of people to love you . . . but no marriage at present . . . no . . . but perhaps in about a year . . .'

'Who's it going to be?' asked Stevens. 'What sort of chap?'

'Mind your own business,' said Pamela.

'Perhaps it is my business.'

'Why should it be?'

'A man a little older than yourself,' said Mrs Erdleigh. 'A man in a good position.'

'Pamela's mad about the aged,' said Stevens. 'The balder the better.'

'I see this man as a jealous husband,' said Mrs Erdleigh. 'This older man I spoke of . . . but . . . as I said before, my dear, you must take good care . . . You are not always well governed in yourself . . . your palm makes me think of that passage in Desbarrolles, the terrible words of which always haunt my mind when I see their marks in a hand shown to me . . . *la débauche, l'effronterie, la licence, le dévergondage, la coquetterie, la vanité, l'esprit léger, l'inconstance, la paresse* . . . those are some of the things in your nature you must guard against, my dear.'

Whether or not this catalogue of human frailties was produced mainly in revenge for Pamela's earlier petulance was hard to know. Perhaps not at all. Mrs Erdleigh was probably speaking no more than the truth, voicing an analysis that did not require much occult skill to arrive at. In any case, she never minded what she said to anyone. Whatever her intention, the words had an immediate effect on Pamela herself, who snatched her hand away with a burst of furious laughter. It was the first time I had heard her laugh.

'That's enough to get on with,' she said. 'Now I'm going for my walk.'

She made a move towards the door. Stevens caught her arm.

'I say you're not going.'

She pulled herself away. There was an instant's pause while they faced each other. Then she brought up her arm and gave him a backhand slap in the face, quite a hard one, using the knuckles.

'You don't think I'm going to take orders from a heel like you, do you?' she said. 'You're pathetic as a lover. No good at all. You ought to see a doctor.'

She walked quickly through the glass door of the entrance hall, and, making the concession of putting on her helmet once more, disappeared into the street. Stevens, knocked out for a second or two by the strength of the blow, made no effort to follow. He rubbed his face, but did not seem particularly surprised nor put out by this violence of treatment. Probably he was used to assaults from Pamela. Possibly such incidents were even fairly normal in his relationships with women. There was, indeed, some slight parallel to the moment when Priscilla had suddenly left him in the Café Royal, though events of that night, in some manner telepathically connecting those concerned, had been enough to upset the nerves of everyone present. We might be in the middle of a raid that never seemed to end, but at least personal contacts were less uncomfortable than on the earlier occasion. Mrs Erdleigh, too, accepted with remarkable composure the scene that had just taken place.

'Little bitch,' said Stevens. 'Not the first time she has done that. Nothing I like less than being socked on the jaw. I thought she'd like to have her fortune told.'

He rubbed his face. Mrs Erdleigh smiled one of her slow, sweet, mysterious smiles.

'You do not understand enough her type's love of secrecy, her own unwillingness to give herself.'

'I understand her unwillingness to give herself,' said Stevens. 'I've got hold of that one OK. In fact I'm quite an expert on the subject.'

'To allow me to look longer at her palm would have been to betray too much,' said Mrs Erdleigh. 'I offered to make a reading only because you pressed me. I was not surprised by this result. All the same, you are right not to be unduly disturbed by her behaviour. In that way you show your own candour and courage. She will come to no harm. In any case, I do not see the two of you much longer together.'

'Neither do I, if there are many more of these straight lefts.'

'Besides, you are going overseas.'

'Soon?'

'Very soon.'

'Shall I see things through?'

'There will be danger, but you will survive.'

'What about her. Will she start up with any more Royalties? Perhaps a king this time.'

He said this so seriously that I laughed. Mrs Erdleigh, on the other hand, accepted the question gravely.

'I saw a crown not far away,' she said. 'Her fate lies along a strange road but not a royal one—whatever incident the crown revealed was very brief—but still it is the road of power.'

She picked up her black box again.

'You're going back to your room?'

'As I said before, no danger threatens tonight, but I thoughtlessly allowed myself to run out of a little remedy I have long used against sleeplessness.'

She held out her hand. I took it. Mention of 'little remedies' called to mind Dr Trelawney. I asked if she ever saw him. She made a mysterious sign with her hand.

'He passed over not long after your uncle. Being well instructed in such enlightenments, he knew his own time was appointed—in war conditions some of his innermost needs had become hard to satisfy—so he was ready. Quite ready.'

'Where did he die?'

'There is no death in Nature'—she looked at me with her great misty eyes and I remembered Dr Trelawney himself using much the same words—'only transition, blending, synthesis, mutation. He has re-entered the Vortex of Becoming.'

'I see.'

'But to answer your question in merely terrestrial terms, he re-embarked on his new journey from the little hotel where we last met.'

'And Albert—does he still manage the Bellevue?'

'He too has gone forth in his cerements. His wife, so I

hear, married again—a Pole invalided from the army. They keep a boarding-house together in Weston-super-Mare.'

'Any last words of advice, Mrs Erdleigh?' asked Stevens. He treated her as if he were consulting the Oracle at Delphi.

'Let the palimpsest of your mind absorb the words of Eliphas Lévi—to know, to will, to dare, to be silent.'

'Me, too?' I asked.

'Everyone.'

'The last most of all?'

'Some think so.'

She glided away towards the lift, which seemed hardly needed, with its earthly and mechanical paraphernalia, to bear her up to the higher levels.

'I'm going to kip too,' said Stevens. 'No good wandering all over London on a night like this looking for Pam. She might be anywhere. She usually comes back all right after a tiff like this. Cheers her up. Well, I may or may not see you again, Nicholas. Never know when one may croak at this game.'

'Good luck—and to Szymanski too, if you see him.'

The raid went on, but I managed to get some sleep before morning. When I woke up, it still continued, though in a more desultory manner. This was, indeed, the advent of the Secret Weapon, the inauguration of the V.1's—the so-called 'flying bombs'. They came over at intervals of about twenty minutes or half an hour, all that day and the following night. This attack continued until Monday, a weekend that happened to be my fortnightly leave; spent, as it turned out, on their direct line of route across the Channel on the way to London.

'You see, my friend, I was right,' said Clanwaert.

One of the consequences of the Normandy landings was that the Free French forces became, in due course, merged into their nation's regular army. The British mission formerly in liaison with them was disbanded, a French military attaché in direct contact with Finn's Section coming into being. Accordingly, an additional major was allotted to our establishment, a rank to which I was now promoted, sustaining (with a couple of captains to help) French, Belgians, Czechs and Grand Duchy of Luxembourg. As the course of the war improved, work on the whole increased rather than diminished, so much so that I was unwillingly forced to refuse the offer of two Italian officers, sent over to make certain arrangements, whose problems, among others, included one set of regulations that forbade them in Great Britain to wear uniform; another that forbade them to wear civilian clothes. All routine work with the French was transacted with Kernével, first seen laughing with Masham about *les voies hiérarchiques*, just before my initial interview with Finn.

'They're sending a *général de brigade* from North Africa to take charge,' said Finn. 'A cavalryman called Philidor.'

Since time immemorial, Kernével, a Breton, like so many of the Free French, had worked at the military attaché's office in London as chief clerk. By now he was a captain. At the moment of the fall of France, faced with the alternative of returning to his country or joining the Free French, he had at once decided to remain, his serial number in that organization—if not, like Abou Ben Adhem's, leading all the rest—being very respectably high in order of acceptance. It was tempting to look for characteristics of my old Regiment in these specimens of Romano-Celtic stock emigrated to Gaul under pressure from Teutons, Scandinavians and non-Roman Celts.

'I don't think my mother could speak a word of French,' said Kernével. 'My father could—he spoke very good

French—but I myself learnt the language as I learnt English.'

Under a severe, even priestly exterior, Kernével concealed a persuasive taste for conviviality—on the rare occasions when anything of the sort was to be enjoyed. From their earliest beginnings, the Free French possessed an advantage over the other Allies—and ourselves—of an issue of Algerian wine retailed at their canteens at a shilling a bottle. Everyone else, if lucky enough to find a bottle of Algerian, or any other wine, in a shop, had to pay nearly ten times that amount. So rare was wine, they were glad to give that, when available. This benefaction to the Free French, most acceptable to those in liaison with them, who sometimes lunched or dined at their messes, was no doubt owed to some figure in the higher echelons of our own army administration—almost certainly learned in an adventure story about the Foreign Legion—that French troops could only function on wine. In point of fact, so far as alcohol went, the Free French did not at all mind functioning on spirits, or drinks like *Cap Corse*, relatively exotic in England, of which they consumed a good deal. Their Headquarter mess in Pimlico was decorated with an enormous fresco, the subject of which I always forgot to enquire. Perhaps it was a Free French version of Géricault's *Raft of the Medusa*, brought up to date and depicting themselves as survivors from the wreck of German invasion.

They did not reject, as we sometimes did ourselves, Marshal Lyautey's doctrine, quoted by Dicky Umfraville, that gaiety was the first essential in an officer, that some sort of light relief was required to get an army through a war. Perhaps, indeed, they too liberally interpreted that doctrine. If so, the red-tape they had to endure must have driven them to it; those terrible *bordereaux*—the very name recalling the Dreyfus case whenever they arrived—labyrinthine and ambiguous enough to extort admiration from a Diplock or even a Blackhead.

'All is fixed for General Philidor's interview?' asked Kernével.

'I shall be on duty myself.'

General Philidor, soon after his arrival in London, had to see a personage of very considerable importance, only a degree or so below the CIGS himself. It had taken a lot of arranging. Philidor was a lively little man with a permanently extinguished cigarette-end attached to his lower lip, which, under the peak of his general's khaki képi, gave his face the fierce intensity of a Paris taxi-driver. His rank was that, in practice, held by the commander of a Division. As a former Giraud officer, he was not necessarily an enthusiastic 'Gaullist'. At our first meeting he had asked me how I liked being in liaison with the French, and, after speaking of the purely military aspects of the work, I had mentioned Algerian wine.

'Believe me, mon commandant, before the '14-'18 war many Frenchmen had never tasted wine.'

'You surprise me, sir.'

'It was conscription, serving in the army, that gave them the habit.'

'It is a good one, sir.'

'My father was a *vigneron*.'

'Burgundy or Bordeaux, sir?'

'At Chinon. You have heard of Rabelais, mon commandant?'

'And drunk Chinon, sir—a faint taste of raspberries and to be served cold.'

'The vineyard was not far from our cavalry school at Saumur, convenient when I was on, as you say, a course there.'

I told him about staying at La Grenadière, how the

Leroys had a son instructing at Saumur in those days, but General Philidor did not remember him. It would have been a long shot had he done so. All the same, contacts had been satisfactory, so that by the time he turned up for his interview with the important officer already mentioned, there was no sense of undue formality.

Philidor started in Finn's room, from where I conducted him to a general of highish status—to be regarded, for example, as distinctly pre-eminent to the one in charge of our own Directorate—who was to act as it were as mediator between Philidor and the all but supreme figure. This mediating general was a brusque officer, quickly mounting the rungs of a successful military career and rather given to snapping at his subordinates. After he and Philidor had exchanged conventional army courtesies, all three of us set off down the passage to the great man's room. In the antechamber, the Personal Assistant indicated that his master was momentarily engaged. The British general, lacking small talk, drummed his heels awaiting the summons. I myself should remain in the ante-chamber during the interview. There was a few seconds delay. Then a most unfortunate thing happened. The general acting as midwife to the birth of the parley, misinterpreting a too welcoming gesture or change of facial expression on the part of the PA, guardian of the door, who had up to now been holding us in check, motioned General Philidor to follow him, and advanced boldly into the sanctuary. This reckless incursion produced a really alarming result. Somebody—if it were, indeed, a human being—let out a frightful roar. Whoever it was seemed to have lost all control of himself.

'*I thought I told you to wait outside—get out . . .*'

From where our little group stood, it was not possible to peep within, but the volume of sound almost made one doubt human agency. Even the CIGS saying good-morning was nothing to it. This was the howl of an angry animal, consumed with rage or pain, probably a mixture of both. Considered merely as a rebuke, it would have struck an exceptionally peremptory note addressed to a lance-corporal.

'Sorry, sir . . .'

Diminished greatness is always a painful spectacle. The humility expressed in those muttered words, uttered by so relatively exalted an officer, was disturbing to me. General Philidor, on the other hand, seemed to feel more detachment. Appreciative, like most Frenchmen, of situations to be associated with light comedy—not to say farce—he fixed me with his sharp little eyes, allowing them to glint slightly, though neither of us prejudiced the frontiers of discipline and rank by the smallest modification of expression. Nevertheless, entirely to avoid all danger of doing any such thing, I was forced to look away.

This incident provoked reflections later on the whole question of senior officers, their relations with each other and with those of subordinate rank. There could be no doubt, so I was finally forced to decide, that the longer one dealt with them, the more one developed the habit of treating generals like members of the opposite sex; specifically, like ladies no longer young, who therefore deserve extra courtesy and attention; indeed, whose every whim must be given thought. This was particularly applicable if one were out in the open with a general.

'Come on, sir, *you* have the last sandwich,' one would say, or 'Sit on my mackintosh, sir, the grass is quite wet.'

Perhaps the cumulative effect of such treatment helped to account for the highly strung temperament so many generals developed. They needed constant looking after. I remembered despising Cocksidge, a horrible little captain at the Division Headquarters on which I had served, for behaving so obsequiously to his superiors in rank. In the end, it had to be admitted one was almost equally deferential, though one hoped less slavish.

'They're like a lot of ballerinas,' agreed Pennistone. 'Ballerinas in Borneo, because their behaviour, even as ballerinas, is quite remote from everyday life.'

Meanwhile the V.1's continued to arrive sporadically, their launchers making a habit of sending three of them across Chelsea between seven and eight in the morning, usually a few minutes before one had decided to get up. They would roar towards the flats—so it always sounded—then switch off a second or two before you expected them to pass the window. One would roll over in bed and face the wall, in case the window came in at the explosion. In point of fact it never did. This would happen perhaps two or three times a week. Kucherman described himself as taking cover in just the same way.

'Nevertheless,' he said, 'I must insist that things are taking a very interesting turn from the news in this morning's papers.'

'Insist' was a favourite word of Kucherman's. He used it without the absolute imperative the verb usually implied in English. He was referring to what afterwards became known as the Officers' Plot, the action of the group of German generals and others who had unsuccessfully attempted to assassinate Hitler. They had failed, but even the fact that they had tried was encouraging.

'Colonel von Stauffenberg sounds a brave man.'

'I have met him several times,' said Kucherman.

'The right ideas?'

'I should insist, certainly. We last talked at a shooting party in the Pripet marshes. Prince Theodoric was also staying in the house, as it happened. Our Polish host is now buried in a communal grave not so many miles north of our sport. The Prince is an exile whose chance of getting back to his own country looks very remote. I sit in Eaton Square wondering what is happening to my business affairs.'

'You think Prince Theodoric's situation is hopeless?'

'Your people will have to make a decision soon between his Resistance elements and the Partisans.'

'And we'll come down on the side of the Partisans?'

'That's what it looks increasingly like.'

'Not too pleasant an affair.'

'There's going to be a lot of unpleasantness before we've finished,' said Kucherman. 'Perhaps in my own country too.'

When we had done our business Kucherman came to the top of the stairs. The news had made him restless. Although quiet in manner, he gave the impression at the same time of having bottled up inside him immense reserves of nervous energy. It was, in any case, impossible not to feel excitement about the way events were moving.

'This caving in of the German military caste—that is the significant thing. An attempt to assassinate the Head of the State on the part of a military group is a serious matter in any country—but in Germany how unthinkable. After all, the German army, its officer corps, is almost a family affair.'

Kucherman listened to this conventional enough summary of the situation, then suddenly became very serious.

'That's something you always exaggerate over here,' he said.

'What, Germans and the army? Surely there must be four or five hundred families, the members of which, whatever their individual potentialities, can only adopt the army as a career? Anyway that was true before the Treaty of Versailles. Where they might be successful, say at the Law or in business, they became soldiers. There was no question of the German army not getting the pick. At least that is what one was always told.'

Kucherman remained grave.

'I don't mean what you say isn't true of the Germans,' he said. 'Of course it is—anyway up to a point, even in the last twenty years. What you underestimate is the same element in your own country.'

'Not to any comparable degree.'

Kucherman remained obdurate.

'I speak of something I have thought about and noticed,' he said. 'Your fathers were in the War Office too.'

For the moment—such are the pitfalls of an alien language and alien typifications, however familiar, for Kucherman spoke English and knew England well—it seemed he could only be facetious. I laughed, assuming he was teasing. He had not done so before, but so much optimism in the air may have made him feel a joke was required. He could scarcely be ignorant that nowhere—least of all within the professional army—was the phrase 'War Office' one for anything but raillery. Perhaps he had indeed known that and disregarded the fact, because a joke was certainly not intended. Kucherman was a man to make up his own mind. He did not take his ideas second-hand. Possibly, thinking it over that night on Fire Duty, there was even something to be said for his theory; only our incurable national levity made the remark at that moment sound satirical. A grain of truth, not necessarily derogatory, was to be traced in the opinion.

Fire Duty was something that came round at regular intervals. It meant hanging about the building all night, fully dressed, prepared to go on the roof, if the Warning sounded, with the object of extinguishing incendiary bombs that might fall there. These were said to be easily dealt with by use of sand and an instrument like a garden hoe, both of which were provided as equipment. On previous occasions, up to now, no raid had occurred, the hours passing not too unpleasantly with a book. Feeling I needed a change from the seventeenth century and Proust, I had brought Saltykov-Schredin's *The Golovlyov Family* to read. A more trivial choice would have been humiliating, because Corporal Curtis turned out to be the accompanying NCO that night, and had *Adam Bede* under his arm. We made whatever mutual arrangements were required, then retired to our respective off-duty locations.

Towards midnight I was examining a collection of photographs taken on D-Day, which had not long before this replaced the two Isbister-like oil paintings. Why the pictures had been removed after being allowed to hang throughout the earlier years of the blitz was not apparent. Mime, now a captain, had just hurried past with his telegrams, when the Warning sounded. I found my way to the roof at the same moment as Corporal Curtis.

'I understand, sir, that we ascend into one of the cupolas as an action station.'

'We do.'

'I thought I had better await your arrival and instructions, sir.'

'Tell me the plot of *Adam Bede* as far as you've got. I've never read it.'

Like the muezzin going on duty, we climbed up a steep gangway of iron leading into one of the pepperpot domes constructed at each corner of the building. The particular dome allotted to us, the one nearest the river, was on the far side from that above our own room. The inside was on two floors, rather like an eccentric writer's den for undisturbed work. Curtis and I proceeded to the upper level. These Edwardian belvederes, elaborately pillared and corniced like Temples of Love in a rococo garden, were not in themselves of exceptional beauty, and, when first erected, must have seemed obscure in functional purpose. Now, however, the architect's design showed prophetic aptitude. The exigencies of war had transformed them into true gazebos, not, as it turned out, frequented to observe the 'pleasing prospects' with which such rotundas and follies were commonly associated, but at least to view their antithesis, 'horridly gothick' aspects of the heavens, lit up by fire and rent with thunder.

This extension of purpose was given effect a minute or two later. The moonlit night, now the melancholy strain of the sirens had died away, was surprisingly quiet. All Ack-Ack guns had been sent to the coast, for there was no point in shooting down V.1's over built-up areas. They would come down anyway. Around lay the darkened city, a few solid masses, like the Donners-Brebner Building, recognisable on the far side of the twisting strip of water. Then three rapidly moving lights appeared in the southern sky, two more or less side by side, the third following a short way behind, as if lacking acceleration or will power to keep up. They travelled with that curious shuddering jerky movement characteristic of such bodies, a style of locomotion that seemed to suggest the engine was not working properly, might break down at any moment, which indeed it would. This impression that something was badly wrong with the internal machinery was increased by a shower of sparks emitted from the tail. A more exciting possibility was that dragons were flying through the air in a fabulous tale, and climbing into the turret with Curtis had been done in a dream. The raucous buzz could now be plainly heard. In imagination one smelt brimstone.

'They appear to be heading a few degrees to our right, sir,' said Curtis.

The first two cut-out. It was almost simultaneous. The noisy ticking of the third continued briefly, then also stopped abruptly. This interval between cutting-out and exploding always seemed interminable. At last it came; again two almost at once, the third a few seconds later. All three swooped to the ground, their flaming tails pointing upwards, certainly dragons now, darting earthward to consume their prey of maidens chained to rocks.

'Southwark, do you think?'

'Lambeth, sir—having regard to the incurvations of the river.'

'Sweet Thames run softly . . .'

'I was thinking the same, sir.'

'I'm afraid they've caught it, whichever it was.'

'I'm afraid so, sir.'

The All Clear sounded. We climbed down the iron gangway.

'Do you think that will be all for tonight?'

'I hope so, sir. Just to carry the story on from where we were when we were interrupted: Hetty is then convicted of the murder of her child and transported.'

The rest of the tour of duty was quiet. I read *The Golovlyov Family* and thought what a pity Judushka had not lived at a more recent period and become a commissar. A month later the Allies entered Paris. George Tolland remained too ill to be moved from Cairo.

## CHAPTER FOUR

In due course V.1's went out of fashion, and V.2's, a form of rocket, became the mode. They were apt to come over in the middle of the morning. Finn was talking to me one day about the transference of Luxembourg personnel from the Belgian artillery (where they manned a battery) to the newly raised army of the Grand Duchy (envisaged with a ceiling of three battalions), when his voice was completely drowned. The dull roar blotting out his comments had been preceded by an agonized trembling of the surrounding atmosphere, the window seeming about to cave in, but recovering itself. I just managed not to jump. Finn appeared totally unimpressed by the sound, whether from strength of nerve or deafness was uncertain. He repeated what he had to say without the smallest modification of tone, signed the minute and put down his pen.

'We've been ordered to take the Allied military attachés overseas,' he said. 'Show 'em a few things. Bound to cause trouble, but there it is. Dempster will be in charge while I'm away. David will probably take the Neutrals when their turn comes, so I shall want you to act as an additional Conducting Officer, Nicholas. Just cast your eye over these papers. It's going to be rather a scramble at such short notice.'

He talked about arrangements. I picked up the instructions and was about to go. Finn drummed on the table with his pen.

'By the way,' he said, 'I've made it up with Farebrother. He's in Civil Affairs now and he came in yesterday about some matter he thought might concern us. Of course, he's a fellow of great charm, whatever else one thinks. Told me he was going to get married—a general's widow in MI 5. "Won't be able to conceal anything from her!" he said.'

Finn laughed, as if he thought retribution would now claim Farebrother for any sins committed against law and order in connexion with the Szymanski affair.

'Not a Mrs Conyers?'

'That's her name. Very capable lady, I understand. Don't know whether marriage is a good idea at the age Farebrother's reached, but that's his business. Get to work right away on the details of the tour.'

When the day came, the military attachés assembled outside the staff entrance. We did not move off precisely on time, because General Lebedev was a minute or two late. While we waited, another of those quaverings of the air round about took place, that series of intensely rapid atmospheric tremors, followed by a dull boom. This one seemed to have landed somewhere in the direction of the Strand. The military attachés exchanged polite smiles. Van der Voort made a popping sound with finger and mouth. At that very moment Lebedev appeared at the end of the short street, giving the impression that he had just been physically ejected from a rocket-base on to a pin-pointed target just round the corner from where we stood, a method of arrival deliberately chosen by his superiors to emphasize Soviet technical achievement. He was, in truth, less than a couple of minutes behind time, most of the rest having arrived much too early. Possibly the high-collared blue uniform, with breeches, black top-boots and spurs, had taken longer to adjust than the battledress adopted for the occasion by most of the others. Major Prasad, representative of an independent state in the Indian sub-continent, also wore boots, brown ones without spurs. They were better cut than Lebedev's, as were also his breeches, but that was only noticeable later, as Lebedev wore an overcoat.

He was greeted with a shower of salutes, the formality of Bobrowski's courteously ironical.

Finn was suffering that morning from one of his visitations of administrative anxiety. He counted the party three times before we entered the cars. I opened one of the doors for General Philidor.

'You accompany us to France, Jenkins—*pour les vacances*?'

'I do, sir.'

'You will find a charming country. I lived there some years ago and was very satisfied.'

He was right about *les vacances*. Undoubtedly the buoyancy of a holiday outing was in the air. Only the V.2 had implied a call to order, a reminder that war was not yet done with. We took the Great West Road, passing the illuminated sign of the diving lady, where I had first kissed Jean Duport years before. I idly wondered what had happened to her, if she were involved in the war; what had happened to Duport, too, whether he had managed to 'sweat it out', the words he had used, in South America.

Although there might be a sense of exhilaration in our party, a crowd of officers unconnected by unit, brought together for some exceptional purpose, always tends to evoke a certain tension. The military attachés were no exception, even if on the whole more at ease than the average collection of British officers might prove in similar circumstances. This comparative serenity was, of course, largely due to the nature of the appointment, the fact that they were individuals handpicked for a job that required flexibility of manner. This was no doubt assisted by a tradition of Continental military etiquette in many respects at variance with our own. Officers of most other armies—so one got the impression—though they might be more formal with each other, were taught to be less verbally crisp, less surly, according to how you chose to assess the social bearing of our own officer corps. I had myself been more than once present at inter-Allied military conferences when the manners of our own people left much to be desired—been, in short, abominable by Continental standards—probably more on account of inexperience in dealing with foreign elements than from deliberate rudeness; still less any desire to appear unfriendly—as was apt to be supposed by the foreign officer concerned—for 'political' or 'diplomatic' reasons. However, if individual British officers could at times show themselves unpolished or ill-at-ease with their Allies, other sides of the picture were to be borne in mind. We put up with quite a lot from the Allies too, though usually in the official rather than the personal field.

By the time we entered the Dakota that was to ferry us across the Channel, heavy banter, some of it capable of giving offence among a lot of mixed nationalities, began to take the place of that earlier formality. This change from normal was probably due to nerves being on edge. There was reason for that. It was, indeed, an occasion to stir the least imaginative among those whose country had been involved in the war since the beginning, while he himself, all or most of the time, had been confined in an island awaiting invasion. Such badinage, in fluent but foreign English, was at that moment chiefly on the subject of the imaginary hazards of the flight, some of the party—especially those like Colonel Hlava, with years of flying experience and rows of decorations for bravery in the air—behaving as if they had never entered a plane before. Possibly a hulk like this was indeed a cause for disquiet, if you were used to piloting yourself through the clouds in an equipage of the first order of excellence and modernity. We went up the gangway. Colonel Ramos, the newly appointed Brazilian, swallowed a handful of pills as soon as he reached the top. This precaution was noticed by Van der

Voort, whose round florid clean-shaven face looked more than ever as if it peered out of a Jan Steen canvas. Van der Voort was in his most boisterous form, seeming to belong to some anachronistic genre picture, *Boors at an Airport* or *The Airfield Kermesse*, executed by one of the lesser Netherlands masters. He clapped Ramos on the back.

'Been having a night out, Colonel?' he asked.

Ramos, in spectacles with a woollen scarf round his neck, looked a mild academic figure in spite of his military cap. He was obviously not at all well. The sudden impact of London wartime food—as well it might—had radically disordered his stomach. He had explained his case to me as soon as he arrived that morning, indicating this by gesture rather than words, his English being limited. I promised the aid of such medicaments as I carried, when we could get to them.

'I believe you've been having a party with the girls, Colonel Ramos,' said Van der Voort. 'Staying up too late. Isn't that true, old man?'

Ramos having, as already stated, no great command of the language, understood only that some enquiry, more or less kind, had been made about his health. He delighted Van der Voort by nodding his head vigorously in affirmation.

'You're new to London, but, my God, you haven't taken long to make your way about,' Van der Voort went on. 'How do you find it? Do you like the place?'

'Very good, very good,' said Colonel Ramos.

'Where have you been so far? Burlington Gardens? Have you seen the ladies there? Smeets and I always take a look on the way back from lunch. You ought to recce Burlington Gardens, Colonel.'

'Yes, yes.'

Colonel Ramos nodded and smiled, laughing almost as

much as Van der Voort himself. By this time we were all sitting on the floor of the plane, which was without any sort of interior furnishing. Finn and I had placed ourselves a little way from the rest, because he wanted to run through the programme again. Colonel Chu, who greatly enjoyed all forms of teasing, edged himself across to Ramos and Van der Voort, evidently wanting to join in. He was not in general very popular with his colleagues.

'Like all his race, he's dreadfully conceited,' Kucherman had said. '*Vaniteux*—you never saw anything like them. I have been there more than once and insist they are the vainest people on earth.'

Chu was certainly pleased with himself. He began to finger the scarf Ramos was wearing. The Brazilian, for a man who looked as if he might vomit at any moment, took the broad witticisms of the other two in very good part. He probably understood very little of what was said. Watching the three of them, one saw what Chu had meant by saying he could 'make himself young'. Probably he would have fitted in very tolerably as a boy at Eton, had be been able to persuade the school authorities to accept him for a while. He left his London appointment before the end of the War and returned to China, where he was promoted major-general. About three years later, so I was told, he was killed commanding one of Chiang Kai-Shek's Divisions at Mukden. Chu must have been in his early forties then, no doubt still prepared to pass as a schoolboy. We floated out over a brilliant shining sea.

'They're not to be shown Pluto,' said Finn. 'I bet one and all of them make a bee-line for it. They're as artful as a cartload of monkeys when it comes to breaking the rules.'

Pluto—Pipe Line Under The Ocean, appropriately recalling the Lord of the Underworld—was the system, an ingenious one, by which troops in a state of mobility were supplied with oil.

'Not a hope they won't see Pluto,' repeated Finn gloomily.

That sort of thing sometimes got on his mind. He was still worrying about Pluto when we landed at the army airfield. Once more the military attachés were packed into cars. I was in the last one with Prasad, Al Sharqui and Gauthier de Graef. Kucherman, in his capacity as great industrial magnate, had been recalled to Brussels to confer with the new Government, so Gauthier had come on the tour in his place. The Belgians were heavily burdened with economic problems. They had had no Quisling figure to be taken seriously during the occupation, but their various Resistance movements were, some of them, inclined to be fractious. Gauthier was for taking a firm line with them. Prasad, next door to him, had only come with us owing to his own personal desire to do so. His creed and status at home made it doubtful whether it were permissible for him to take part in an expedition that would inevitably lead to eating in public. I had special instructions to see his requirements in the way of food and accommodation were strictly observed. Al Sharqui, rather shy in this hurly-burly of nationalities and generals, came from one of the Arab states. Like Prasad, he was a major.

'This is like arriving on another planet,' said Gauthier de Graef.

He was right. It was all very strange, incomparably strange. The company one was with certainly did not decrease this sense of fantasy. More personal sensations were harder to define, took time to resolve. I cannot remember whether it was the day we arrived or later that things crystallized. We were bowling along through Normandy and a region of fortified farms. Afterwards, in memory, the apple orchards were all in blossom, like isolated plantations on which snow for some unaccountable reason had fallen, light glinting between the tree trunks.

But it was already November. There can have been no blossom. Blossom was a mirage. Autumnal sunshine, thin, hard, penetrating, must have created that scenic illusion, kindling white and silver sparkles in branches and foliage. What you see conditions feelings, not what is. For me the country was in blossom. At any season the dark ancientness of those massive granges, their stone walls loop-holed with arrow-slits, would have been mesmeric enough. Now, their mysterious aspect was rendered even more enigmatic by a surrounding wrack of armoured vehicles in multiform stages of dissolution. This residue was almost always concentrated within a comparatively small area, in fact whereever, a month or two before, an engagement had been fought out. Then would come stretches of quite different country, fields, woodland, streams, to all intents untouched by war.

In one of these secluded pastoral tracts, a Corot landscape of tall poplars and water meadows executed in light greys, greens and blues, an overturned staff-car, wheels in the air, lay sunk in long grass. The camouflaged bodywork was already eaten away by rust, giving an impression of abandonment by that brook decades before. High up in the branches of one of the poplars, positioned like a cunningly contrived scarcecrow, the tatters of a field-grey tunic, black-and-white collar patches just discernible, fluttered in the faint breeze and hard cold sunlight. The isolation of the two entities, car and uniform, was complete. There seemed no explanation of why either had come to rest where it was.

At that moment, an old and bearded Frenchman appeared plodding along the road. He was wearing a beret, and, like many of the local population, cloaked in the olive green rubber of a British army anti-gas cape. As our convoy passed, he stopped and waved a greeting. He looked absolutely delighted, like a peasant in a fairy story who has found the treasure. For some reason it was all too much. A gigantic release seemed to have taken place. The surroundings had suddenly become overwhelming. I was briefly in tears. The others were sunk in unguessable reflections of their own; Prasad perhaps among Himalayan peaks; Al Sharqui, the sands of the desert; Gauthier, in Clanwaert's magic realm, the Porte de Louise. We sped on down the empty roads.

'This car is like travelling in a coffee-grinding machine,' said Gauthier.

'Or a cement-mixer.'

The convoy halted at last to allow the military attachés to relieve themselves. Out of the corner of my eyes, I saw the worst had happened. We had blundered on a kind of junction of Plutonic equipment. Finn must have instantaneously seen that too. He rushed towards the installation, as if unable to contain himself—perhaps no simulation—taking up his stand in such a place that it would have been doubtful manners to pass in front of him. On the way back to the cars he caught me up.

'I don't think they noticed Pluto,' he whispered.

It was late that night when, after inspecting a mass of things, we reached billets. A clock struck twelve as the cars entered the seaside town where these had been arranged. By the time we arrived I had forgotten the name of the place, evidently a resort in peacetime, because we drew up before the doors of a largish hotel. It was moonlight. We got out. Finn conferred with the Conducting Officer from Army Group, who was still with us. Then he turned to me.

'They can't get us all into the Grand.'

'No room at the inn, sir?'

'Not enough mattresses or something, though it looks big enough. So, Nicholas, you'll attend General Asbjørnsen, General Bobrowski, General Philidor and Major Prasad to La Petite Auberge. Everything's been laid on there for the five of you.'

I never knew, then or later, why that particular quartet was chosen to represent the overflow from the Grand. One would have expected four generals—Lebedev, for example, or Cobb, recently promoted brigadier-general—alternatively, four more junior in rank, Gauthier de Graef, Al Sharqui, a couple of lieutenant-colonels. However, that was how it was. One of the cars took the five of us to La Petite Auberge, which turned out to be a little black-and-white half-timbered building, hotel or pension, in Tudor, or, I suppose, François Premier or Henri Quatre style. Only one of the rooms had a bathroom attached, which was captured by General Asbjørnsen, possibly by being the most senior in rank, more probably because he climbed the stairs first. Obviously I was not in competition for the bath myself, so I did not greatly care who took it, nor by what methods. Prasad, like Asbjørnsen, went straight up to his room, but the other two generals and I had a drink in the bar, presided over by the *patronne*, who seemed prepared to serve Allies all night. Bobrowski and Philidor were talking about shooting wild duck. Then Asbjørnsen came down and had a drink too. He started an argument with Bobrowski about the best sort of skiing boots. Philidor and I left them to it. I had already begun to undress, when there was a knock on the door. It was Prasad.

'Major Jenkins . . .'

'Major Prasad?'

He seemed a little embarrassed about something. I hoped it was nothing like damp sheets, a problem that might spread to the rest of us. Prasad was still wearing breeches and boots and his Sam Browne.

'There's a room with a bath,' he said.

'Yes—General Asbjørnsen's.'

Prasad seemed unhappy. There was a long pause.

'I want it,' he said at last.

That blunt statement surprised me.

'I'm afraid General Asbjørnsen got there first.'

I thought it unnecessary to add that baths were not for mere majors like ourselves, especially when there was only one. Majors were lucky enough to be allowed a basin. I saw how easy it might become to describe the hardness of conditions when one had first joined the army. The declaration was also quite unlike Prasad's apparent appreciation of such things.

'But I need it.'

'I agree it would be nice to have one, but he is a general—a lieutenant-general, at that.'

Prasad was again silent for a few seconds. He was certainly embarrassed, though by no means prepared to give up the struggle.

'Can you ask General Asbjørnsen to let me have it, Major Jenkins?'

He spoke rather firmly. This was totally unlike Prasad, so quiet, easy going, outwardly impregnated with British army 'good form'. I was staggered. Apart from anything else, the request was not a reasonable one. For a major to eject a general from his room in the small hours of the morning was a grotesque conception. It looked as if it might be necessary to embark on an *a priori* disquisition regarding the Rules and Disciplines of War, which certainly laid down that generals had first option where baths were concerned. It was probably Rule One. I indicated that a major—even a military attaché, in a sense representing his own country—could not have a bathroom to himself, if three generals, themselves equally representative, were all of them at least theoretically, in the running. I now saw how lucky I was that neither Bobrowski nor Philidor had shown any sign of considering himself slighted by being allotted a bathless room. In fact Prasad's claim did not merit serious discussion. I tried to put that as tactfully as possible. Prasad listened respectfully. He was not satisfied. I could not understand what had come over him. I changed the ground of argument, abandoning seniority of rank as a reason, pointing out that General Asbjørnsen had won the bath by right of conquest. He had led the way up the stairs, the first man—indeed, the first general—to capture the position. Prasad would not be convinced. There was another long pause. I wondered whether we should stay up all night. Prasad gave the impression of having a secret weapon, a battery he preferred not to unmask unless absolutely necessary. However, it had to come into action at last.

'It's my religion,' he said.

He spoke now apologetically. This was an entirely unexpected aspect.

'Oh, I see.'

I tried to play for time, while I thought up some answer.

'So I must have it,' Prasad said.

He spoke with absolute finality.

'Of course, I appreciate, Major Prasad, that what you have said makes a difference.'

He did not reply. He saw his projectile had landed clean on the target. I was defeated. The case was unanswerable, especially in the light of my instructions. Prasad looked sorry at having been forced to bring matters to this point. He looked more than sorry; terribly upset.

'So can I have the bathroom?'

I buttoned up my battledress blouse again.

'I'll make certain enquiries.'

'I'm sorry to be so much trouble.'

'Wait a moment, Major Prasad.'

By a great piece of good fortune, General Asbjørnsen was still in the bar. He and Bobrowski had not stopped arguing, though the subject had shifted from skiing boots to tactics. Asbjørnsen was perhaps getting the worst of it, because his expression recalled more than ever the craggy features of Monsieur Ørn, the Norwegian at La Grenadière, who had such a row with Monsieur Lundquist, the Swede, for sending 'sneaks' over the net at tennis. I hoped no similar display of short temper was in the offing.

'Sir?'

General Asbjørnsen gave his attention.

'Major Prasad has asked me if you would possibly consider surrendering to him the room with the bath?'

General Asbjørnsen looked absolutely dumbfounded. He did not show the smallest degree of annoyance, merely stark disbelief that he had rightly grasped the meaning of the question.

'But—I have the bath.'

'I know, sir. That was why I was asking.'

'I am there.'

'That's just it, sir. Major Prasad wants it.'

'He wants it?'

'Yes, sir.'

'The bathroom?'

'Yes, sir.'

'But—the bathroom—it is for me.'

'It's a very special request, sir.'

General Asbjørnsen's face by now showed at least that he accepted the request as a special one. It was only too easy to understand his surprise, the fact that the idea took some time to penetrate. This was not at all on account of any language difficulty. General Asbjørnsen spoke English with the greatest fluency. As the conception began to take shape in his mind that Prasad's designs on the bath were perfectly serious, the earlier look of wonder had changed to one of displeasure. His face hardened. Bobrowski, who loved action, especially if it offered conflict, grasping that a superbly comic tussle was promised, now joined in.

'You are trying to take General Asbjørnsen's bath away from him, Major Jenkins?'

'It's for Major Prasad, sir, he—'

'I don't believe it, Major Jenkins, I believe you want it for yourself.'

Bobrowski had begun to laugh a lot.

'It is the particular wish of Major Prasad, sir—'

'Look here,' said Asbjørnsen, 'I have the bath. I keep it.'

That was the crux of the matter. There was no arguing. I had hoped, without much conviction, to achieve General Asbjørnsen's dislodgment without playing Prasad's trump card. Now this would have to be thrown on the table. It had become clear that much more discussion of this sort, to the accompaniment of Bobrowski's determination to treat the matter as a huge joke, would make Asbjørnsen more intractable than ever.

'It's a question of religion, sir.'

'What?'

'Major Prasad requires the room for religious reasons.'

That silenced them both. The statement, at least for the moment, made even more impression than I had hoped.

'Religion?' repeated Bobrowski.

I wished he would keep out of it. The bathroom was no business of his. By now I was entirely on Prasad's side, dedicated to obtaining the bathroom for whatever purpose he needed it.

'But this is a new idea,' said Bobrowski. 'I had not thought that was how baths are allotted on this tour. I am Catholic, what chance have I?'

'Sir—'

'Now I see why General Philidor went off to bed without even asking for the bathroom. Like many Frenchmen, he is perhaps free-thinker. He would have no chance for the bath. You would not let him, Major Jenkins. No religion—no bath. That is what you say. It is not fair.'

Bobrowski thought it all the funniest thing he had ever heard in his life. He laughed and laughed. Perhaps, in the long run, the conclusion of the matter owed something to this laughter of Bobrowski's, because General Asbjørnsen may have suspected that, if much more argument were carried on in this frivolous atmosphere, there was danger of his being made to look silly himself. Grasp of that fact after so comparatively short an interlude of Bobrowski's intervention did Asbjørnsen credit.

'You can really assure me then, Major Jenkins, that this is, as you have reported, a question of religion.'

'I can assure you of that, sir.'

'You are in no doubt?'

'Absolutely none, sir.'

'In that case, I agree to the proposal.'

General Asbjørnsen almost came to attention.

'Thank you, sir. Thank you very much indeed. Major Prasad will be most grateful. I will inform Colonel Finn when I see him.'

'Come upstairs and help me with my valise.'

The gruffness of General Asbjørnsen's tone was fully justified. I followed him to the disputed room, and was relieved to see the valise on the floor still unpacked. The bathroom door was open. It seemed an apartment designed for the ablutions of a very thin dwarf, one of Mime's kind. However, spatial content was neither here nor there. The point was, Prasad must have it. I took one end of the valise, Asbjørnsen the other. Prasad was peeping through the crack of his door. When informed of the way the battle had gone, he came out into the passage. Asbjørnsen was not ungracious about his renunciation. Prasad expressed a lot of thanks, but was unaware, I think, that the victory, like Waterloo, had been 'a damned close run thing'. General Asbjørnsen and I carried his valise into Prasad's former room. I helped Prasad with his valise too, on his taking over of the bathroom. As soon as Prasad and I were out in the passage, General Asbjørnsen shut his bedroom door rather loudly. He could not be blamed. My own relations with him, even when we returned to England, never fully recovered from that night. For the rest of the tour I speculated on what arcane rites Prasad conducted in that minute bathroom.

Next morning I rose early to check transport for the day's journey. The cars were to assemble at the entrance of the Grand Hotel, then pick up baggage of the party at La Petite Auberge on the route out of town. The Grand's main entrance was on the far side from the sea-front. It faced a fairly large, more or less oval open space, ornamented with plots of grass and flower beds long untended. From here the ground sloped away towards a little redbrick seaside town, flanked by green downs along which villas were spreading. The cars, on parade early, were all 'correct'. Finn was not due to appear for some minutes. Wondering what the place was like in peacetime at the height of the season, I strolled to the side of the hotel facing the 'front'. On this façade, a section of the building—evidently the hotel's dining-room, with half-a-dozen or more high arched windows—had been constructed so that it jutted out on to the esplanade. This promenade, running some feet above the beach, was no doubt closed to wheeled traffic in normal times. Now, it was completely deserted. The hotel, in café-au-lait stucco, with turrets and balconies, was about fifty or sixty years old, built at a time when the seaside was coming seriously into fashion. This small resort had a pleasantly out-of-date air. One pictured the visitors as well-to-do, though not at all smart, only insistent on good food and bourgeois comforts; the whole effect rather smug, though at the same time possessing for some reason or other an indefinable, even haunting attraction. Perhaps that was just because one was abroad again; and, for once, away from people. In the early morning light, the paint on the side walls of the hotel had taken on a pinkish tone, very subtle and delicate, blending gently with that marine vaporousness of atmosphere so enthusiastically endorsed by the Impressionists when they painted this luminous northern shore. It was time to find Finn. I returned to the steps of the main entrance. The large hall within was in semi-darkness, because all the windows had been boarded up. Some of the military attachés were already about, polishing their boots in a kind of cloakroom, where the greatcoats had been left the night before. They seemed to be doing no harm, so I went back to the hall. Finn, carrying his valise on his shoulder, was descending the stairs.

'Good morning, sir.'

'Good morning, Nicholas. Couldn't use the lift over there. No lift boys in wartime. Didn't sleep too well. Kept awake by the noise of the sea. Not used to it.'

I reported the matter of the bath. Finn looked grave. 'Awkward situation, damned awkward. I've always tried to keep out of religious controversy. You handled it well, Nicholas. I'll have a word with Asbjørnsen and thank him. Any of them down yet?'

'Some are cleaning their boots in the lobby through there.'

'Cleaning their boots? My God, I believe they must have found my polish. Which way? I must stop this at once. It will be all used up.'

He rushed off. The fleet of cars got under way soon after this. That day I found myself with Cobb, Lebedev and Marinko, the Jugoslav. The seating was altered as a matter of principle from time to time. I was beside the driver. Lebedev—the name always reminded one of the character in *The Idiot* who was good at explaining the Apocalypse, though otherwise unreliable—rarely spoke; nor did he usually attend more than very briefly—so our Mission working with the Russians reported—the occasional parties given by their Soviet opposite numbers, where drinking bouts attained classical proportions, it was alleged. He was, indeed, commonly held to derive his appointment from civil, rather than military, eminence at home, his bearing and methods—despite the top boots and spurs—lacking, in the last resort, the essential stigmata of the *officier de carrière*.

'I tried to talk to Lebedev the other day about Dostoievski's Grand Inquisitor,' Pennistone said. 'He changed the subject at once to Nekrassov, of whom I've never read a line.'

Cobb was making notes in a little book. Marinko gazed out of the window, overcome with Slav melancholy, or, more specifically—being of the party that supported the Resistance groups of Mihailovich—dejection at the course British policy appeared to be taking in that connexion.

'Just spell out the name of that place we stopped over last night, Major Jenkins,' said Cobb.

'C-A-B-O-U-R-G, sir.'

As I uttered the last letter, scales fell from my eyes. Everything was transformed. It all came back—like the tea-soaked madeleine itself—in a torrent of memory . . . Cabourg . . . We had just driven out of Cabourg . . . out of Proust's Balbec. Only a few minutes before, I had been standing on the esplanade along which, wearing her polo cap and accompanied by the little band of girls he had supposed the mistresses of professional bicyclists, Albertine had strolled into Marcel's life. Through the high windows of the Grand Hotel's dining-room—conveying to those without the sensation of staring into an aquarium—was to be seen Saint-Loup, at the same table Bloch, mendaciously claiming acquaintance with the Swanns. A little farther along the promenade was the Casino, its walls still displaying tattered playbills, just like the one Charlus, wearing his black straw hat, had pretended to examine, after an attempt at long range to assess the Narrator's physical attractions and possibilities. Here Elstir had painted; Prince Odoacer played golf. Where was the little railway line that had carried them all to the Verdurins' villa? Perhaps it ran in another direction to that we were taking; more probably it was no more.

'And the name of the brigadier at the Battle Clearance Group?' asked Cobb. 'The tall one who took us round those captured guns?'

He wrote down the name and closed the notebook.

'You told me, Major Jenkins, that at the beginning of the war you yourself saw a Royal Engineer colonel wearing a double-breasted service-dress tunic. You can assure me of that?'

'I can, sir—and, on making enquiries, was told that cut was permitted by regulations, provided no objection was taken by regimental or higher authority.'

Proustian musings still hung in the air when we came down to the edge of the water. It had been a notable adventure. True, an actual night passed in one of the bedrooms of the Grand Hotel itself—especially, like Finn's, an appropriately sleepless one—might have crowned the magic of the happening. At the same time, a faint sense of disappointment superimposed on an otherwise absorbing inner experience was in its way suitably Proustian too: a reminder of the eternal failure of human life to respond a hundred per cent; to rise to the greatest heights without allowing at the same time some suggestion, however slight, to take shape in indication that things could have been even better.

Now, looking north into the light mist that hung over the waves, it was at first difficult to know what we were regarding. In the foreground lay a kind of inland sea, or rather two huge lagoons, the further enclosed by moles and piers that seemed exterior and afloat; the inner and nearer, with fixed breakwaters formed of concrete blocks, from which, here and there, rose tall chimneys, rows of cranes, drawbridges. The faraway floating docks delimited smaller pools and basins. Within the two large and separate surfaces, islands were dotted about supporting similar structures, the outlines of which extended into the misty distances as far as the horizon. What, one wondered, could this great maritime undertaking be? Was it planned to build a new Venice here on the water? Perhaps those were docks constructed on an unusually generous scale to serve some great port—yet no large area of warehouses was at hand to suggest commerce, nor other signs of a big town anywhere along the shore. On the contrary, such houses as were to be seen, near or further inland, were in ruins, their extent in any case not at all resembling the outskirts of a city. The roadstead itself was now all but abandoned, at least the small extent of shipping riding at anchor there altogether disproportionate to the potential accommodation of the harbour—for harbour it must certainly be. There was something unreal, ghostly, even a little horrifying, about these grey marine shapes that seemed to have no present purpose, yet, like battlements of a now ruined castle, implied a violent, bloody history.

'*Tiens*,' said General Philidor. '*C'est bien le Mulberry*.'

The Mulberry it was, vast floating harbour designed for invasion, soon to be dismantled and forgotten, like the Colossus of Rhodes or Hanging Gardens of Babylon. We tramped its causeways out over the sea.

'We'll soon be in Brussels,' said Marinko. 'I hope to get some eau-de-cologne. In London it is unobtainable. Not a drop to be had.'

When we drove into the city's main boulevards, their sedate nineteenth-century self-satisfaction, British troops everywhere, made our cortège somewhat resemble Ensor's *Entry of Christ into Brussels*, with soldiers, bands and workers' delegation. One looked about for the Colman's 'Mustart' advertisement spelt wrong, but it was nowhere to be seen. Our billet was a VIP one, a requisitioned hotel presided over by a brisk little cock-sparrow of a captain, who evidently knew his job.

'We had the hell of a party here the other night,' he said. 'A crowd of senior officers as drunk as monkeys, brigadiers rooting the palms out of the pots.'

His words conjured up the scene in *Antony and Cleopatra*, when arm-in-arm the generals dance on Pompey's galley, a sequence of the play that makes it scarcely possible to disbelieve that Shakespeare himself served for at least a period of his life in the army.

'With thy grapes our hairs be crowned?'

'Took some cleaning up after, I can tell you.'

'Talking of cleanliness, would a cake of soap be any use to yourself?'

'Most acceptable.'

'In return, perhaps you could recommend the best place to buy a bottle of brandy?'

'Leave it to me—a couple, if you feel like spending that amount. I understand your people go to Army Group Main HQ tomorrow.'

'That's it—and we've been promised a visit to the Field-Marshal himself the following day.'

At Army Group Main the atmosphere was taut, the swagger—there was a good deal of swagger—a trifle forced; the court, as it were, of a military Trimalchio. Trimalchio, after all, had been an unusually successful business man; for all that is known, might have proved an unusually successful general. A force of junior staff officers with the demeanour of aggressive schoolboys had to be penetrated.

'You can't park those cars there,' one of them shouted at Finn. 'Get 'em out of the way at once and look sharp about it.'

Finn did as he was told. Indoors, the place was even more like a school, one dominated by specialized, possibly rather cranky theories; efficient, all the same, and encouraging the boys to be independently minded, even self-applauding. Perhaps the last epithet was unfair. This, after all, was a staff that had delivered the goods pretty well so far. They had a right to be pleased with themselves. There was an odd incident while the Chief of Staff, a major-general, addressed the assembled military attachés. In the background a telephone rang. It was answered by a curly haired captain, who looked about fifteen. He began to carry on a long conversation at the top of his voice, accompanied by a lot of laughter. It was on the subject of some more or less official matter, though apparently nothing very weighty. I wondered how long this would be allowed to continue. The Chief of Staff looked up once or twice, but stood it for several minutes.

'Shut down that telephone.'

The captain's chatter was brought to an end. The general had spoken curtly, but most senior officers would have shown far less forbearance, especially in the presence of a relatively distinguished visiting party of Allied officers. Clearly things were run in their own particular way at Army Group Headquarters. I looked forward to seeing whether the same atmosphere would prevail at the Field-Marshal's Tactical HQ.

By this time, the Allied advance into Germany had penetrated about a couple of miles across the frontier at its farthest point. Accordingly, we left Belgium and entered that narrow strip of the Netherlands that runs between the two other countries, travelling towards the town of Roermond, still held by the enemy, against which our artillery was now in action. The long straight roads, leading through minefields, advertised at intervals as 'swept to verges', were lined on either side with wooden crates of ammunition stacked high under the poplars. Armour was moving in a leisurely manner across this dull flat country, designed by

Nature for a battlefield, over which armies had immemorially campaigned. The identification flash of my old Division had appeared more than once on the shoulder of infantrymen passed on the route. When we stopped to inspect the organization of a bridgehead, I asked the local Conducting Officer from Lines of Communication if he knew whether any of my former Regiment were to be found in the neighbourhood.

'Which brigade?'

I told him.

'We should be in the middle of them here. Of course we may not be near your particular battalion. Like to see if we can find some of them? Your funny-wunnies will be happy for a few minutes, won't they?'

The military attachés would be occupied for half an hour or more with what they were inspecting. In any case, Finn as usual well ahead with time schedule, it would be undesirable to arrive unduly early for the Field-Marshal.

'I'd like to see if any of them are about.'

'Come along then.'

The L. of C. captain led the way down a road lined with small houses. Before we had gone far, sure enough, three or four soldiers wearing the Regimental flash were found engaged on some fatigue, piling stuff on to a truck. They were all very young.

'These look like your chaps—right regiment anyway, if not your actual battalion. You'd better have a word with them.'

I made some enquiries. Opportunity to knock off work was, as usual, welcome. They turned out to be my own Battalion, rather than the other one of the same Regiment within the brigade.

'Is an officer named Kedward still with you?'

'Captain Kedward, sir?'

'That's the one.'

'Oh yes, the Company Commander, sir?'

'He actually commands your Company?'

'Why, yes, he does, sir. That's him.'

'You're all in Captain Kedward's Company?'

'We are, sir.'

It seemed astonishing to them that I did not know that already. I could not understand this surprise at first, then remembered that I too was wearing the regimental crest and flash, so that they certainly thought that I belonged to the same brigade as themselves, possibly even newly posted to their own unit. Soldiers often do not know all the officers of their battalion by sight. Indeed, it is not uncommon for the Adjutant to be thought of as the Commanding Officer, because he is the one most often heard giving orders.

'Is Captain Kedward likely to be about?'

'He's in the Company Office just now, sir.'

'Near here?'

'Over there, sir, where the swill tubs are.'

'You stay here, sir,' said one of them. 'I'll get Captain Kedward for you.'

Work was now more or less at a standstill. Cigarettes were handed out. It seemed they had arrived fairly recently in this sector. Earlier, the Battalion had been in action in the Caen area, where casualties had been fairly heavy. I asked about some of the individuals I had known, but they were too young to remember any of them. The L. of C. captain became understandably bored listening to all this.

'Now you're back with your long lost unit, I'll leave you to have a natter,' he said. 'Want to check up on some of my own business round the corner. Be with you again in five minutes.'

He went off. At the same moment Kedward, with the young soldier who had offered to fetch him, appeared from the door of a small farmhouse. It was more than four years since I had set eyes on him. He looked a shade older, though not much; that is to say he had lost that earlier appearance of being merely a schoolboy who had dressed up in uniform for fun, burnt-corking his upper lip to simulate a moustache. The moustache now had a perfectly genuine existence. He saluted, seeming to be rather flustered.

'Idwal.'

'Sir?'

He had not recognized me.

'Don't you remember? I'm Nick Jenkins. We were together in Rowland Gwatkin's Company.'

Even that information did not appear to make any immediate impression on Kedward.

'We last saw each other at Castlemallock.'

'The Castlemallock school of Chemical Warfare, sir?'

On the whole, where duty took one, few captains called a major 'sir', unless they were being very regimental. Everyone below the rank of lieutenant-colonel within the official world in which one moved was regarded as doing much the same sort of job, officers below the rank of captain being in any case rare. Responsibilities might vary, sometimes the lower rank carrying the higher responsibility; for example, the CIGS's ADC, a captain no longer young, being in his way a considerable figure. All the same, this unwonted reminder of having a crown on one's shoulder did not surprise me so much as Kedward's total failure to recall me as a human being. The fragile condition of separate identity, perpetually brought home to one, at the same time remains perpetually incredible.

'Don't you remember the moment when you took over the Company from Rowland—how upset he was at getting the push.'

Kedward's face lighted up at that.

'Why, yes,' he said. 'You were with us then, weren't you, sir? I'm beginning to remember now. Didn't you come from London? . . . Was it Lyn Craddock took over the platoon from you? . . . or Phillpots?'

'Are they still with you?'

'Lyn got it at Caen commanding B Company.'

'Killed?'

'Yes, Lyn caught it. Phillpots? What happened to Phillpots? I believe he went to one of the Regular battalions and was wounded in Crete.'

'What became of Rowland Gwatkin?'

'Fancy you knowing Rowland.'

'But I tell you, we were all in the same Company.'

'So we were, but what a long time ago all that was. Rowland living in my home town makes it seem funny you know him.'

'Is he out here?'

'Rowland?'

Kedward laughed aloud at such an idea. It was apparently unthinkable.

'When I last saw him it looked as if he were due for the Infantry Training Centre.'

'Rowland's been out of the army for years.'

'Out of the army?'

'You never heard?'

Having once established the fact that I knew Gwatkin at all, in itself extraordinary enough, Kedward obviously found it equally extraordinary that I had not kept myself up-to-date about Gwatkin's life history.

'Rowland got invalided,' he said. 'That can't have been long after Castlemallock. I know it was all about the time I married.'

'You got married all right?'

'Father of two kids.'

'What sex?'

'Girls—that's what I wanted. Wouldn't mind a boy next.'

'So Rowland never reached the ITC?'

'I believe he got there, now you mention it, sir, then he went sick.'

'Do, for God's sake, stop calling me "sir", Idwal.'

'Sorry—anyway Rowland was ill about that time. Kidneys, was it? Or something to do with his back? Flat feet, it might have been. Whatever it was, they down-graded his medical category, and then he didn't get any better, and got boarded, and had to leave the army altogether.'

'Rowland must have taken that pretty hard.'

'Oh, he did,' said Kedward cheerfully.

'So what's he doing?'

'Back at the Bank. They're terribly shorthanded. Glad to have him there, you may be sure. I believe somebody here said they had a letter that mentioned Rowland was acting manager at one of the smaller branches. That's quite something for Rowland, who wasn't a great banking brain, I can tell you. Just what a lot of trouble he'll be making for everybody, you bet.'

'And his mother-in-law? Is she still living with them? He told me that was going to happen when we said good-bye to each other. Then, on top of his mother-in-law coming to live with them, having to leave the army himself. Rowland's had the hell of a pasting.'

The thought of Gwatkin and his mother-in-law had sometimes haunted me; the memory of his combined horror and resignation in face of this threatened affliction. To have his dreams of military glory totally shattered as well seemed, as so often in what happens to human beings, out of all proportion to what he had deserved, even if these dreams had, in truth, been impracticable for one of his capacity.

'My God, bloody marvellous what you know about Rowland and his troubles,' said Kedward. 'Mother-in-law and all. Have you come to live in the neighbourhood? I thought you worked in London. Did you hear that Elystan-Edwards got a VC here the other day? That was great, wasn't it?'

'I read about it. He came to the Battalion after I left.'

'It was great for the Regiment, wasn't it?' Kedward repeated.

'Great.'

There was a pause.

'Look here, sir—Nick—I'm afraid I won't be able to talk any more now. Got a lot to do. I thought first when they said a major wanted me, I was going to get a rocket from Brigade. I must make those buggers get a move on with their loading too. They been staging a go-slow since we've been here. Look at them.'

We said goodbye. Kedward saluted and crossed to the truck, where the loading operation had certainly become fairly leisurely. The L. of C. captain reappeared. I waved to Kedward. He saluted again.

'Jaw over?'

'Yes.'

Perhaps as a result of Kedward's exhortations, the fatigue party began to sing. The L. of C. captain and I walked up the road in the direction of the cars, leaving them to move eastward towards the urnfields of their Bronze Age home.

> 'Open now the crystal fountain,
> Whence the healing stream doth flow:
> Let the fire and cloudy pillar
> Lead me all my journey through:
> Strong Deliverer,
> Strong Deliverer
> Be thou still my strength and shield.'

'What a mournful row,' said the L. of C. captain, 'I've heard them chant that one before. It's a hymn.'

Finn was already rounding up the military attachés

when we reached the place where the convoy was parked. In preparation for the visit to the Field-Marshal's Tactical Headquarters, some of our party were already wearing their pullovers in a manner popularized by the Field-Marshal himself—though not generally accepted as correct army turn-out—that is to say showing several inches below the battledress blouse. Among those thus seeking to be in the height of military fashion were Bobrowski and Van der Voort.

'I think I keep mine inside,' said Chu.

There was remarkably little fuss about the approach—no hint of Trimalchio here—security merely kept at its essential minimum. The accommodation for the Headquarters was a medium-sized house, built within the last ten or twelve years, one would guess, dark red brick, set amongst a few trees. The place had little or no character of its own. It might have been a farm, but had none of the farm's picturesque aspects. The fact was, it seemed prophetically built to house a Tactical Headquarters. By an inner wall stood the Field-Marshal's two long motor-caravans, sleeping apartment and office respectively. Here everything seemed quieter, far less exhibitionistic than at Main.

'Will you line up, please, gentlemen,' said Finn, 'in order of seniority of your appointment.'

The prelude to almost all happenings in the army, small and great, is an inspection. This visit was to be no exception. The military attachés were drawn up in a single row facing the caravans. Colonel Hlava, their doyen, was at one end: Gauthier de Graef, the most junior, at the other; with myself rounding off the party. There was a moment's pause, while we stood at ease. Then the Field-Marshal appeared from one of the caravans. He had his hands in his pockets, but removed them as he approached. It was instantaneously clear that he no longer chose to wear his pullover showing under his battledress blouse. Indeed, he had by now, it was revealed, invented a form of battledress peculiar to himself, neatly tailored and of service-dress cloth. There was a moment when we were at attention; then at ease again. The last movement was followed by some rapid fidgeting and tucking up of clothes on the part of Bobrowski, Van der Voort and others with too keen a wish to be in the mode. Finn, out in front, was beaming with excitement. This was the sort of occasion he loved. There was a moment's conference. Then the Field-Marshal proceeded down the line, Finn at his side, presenting the military attachés, one by one. The Field-Marshal said a few words to each. It was quite a long time before he reached Gauthier.

'Captain Gauthier de Graef,' said Finn. 'The Belgian assistant military attaché. Major Kucherman himself was prevented from taking part in the tour. He had to attend a meeting of the new Belgian Government, which he may be joining.'

At the word 'Belgian' the Field-Marshal had begun to look very stern.

'You're the Belgians' man, are you?'

'Yes, sir.'

'Some of your people are showing signs of giving trouble in Brussels.'

'Yes, sir,' said Gauthier.

He and Kucherman had often talked of difficulties with the Resistance elements. Gauthier knew the problem all right.

'If they do give trouble,' said the Field-Marshal. 'I'll shoot 'em up. Is that clear? Shoot 'em up.'

'Yes, sir,' said Gauthier.

'It is?'

'Quite clear, sir.'

Gauthier de Graef replied with the deep agreement he certainly felt in taking firm measures. He had already complained of his own irritation with those of his countrymen whom he judged inadequately to appreciate their luck in having got rid of the Germans. The Field-Marshal moved on. He fixed his eyes on my cap badge.

'Prince of Wales's Volunteers?'

The slip was a very permissible one. The two crests possessed a distinct similarity in design. I named the Regiment. He showed no animus, as some generals might, at such a disavowal, however unavoidable.

'Any of 'em here?'

'Yes, sir—one of them got a VC a few weeks ago.'

The Field-Marshal considered the point, but made no move to develop it. Finn smiled very briefly to himself, almost invisibly to those who did not know him, either contemplating the eternal satisfaction his own bronze Maltese cross gave him; more probably, in the same connexion, appreciating this opportunity of recalling a rumour that the Field-Marshal was said to be not in the least impressed by the mystique of that particular award; indeed, alleged to declare its possession hinted at an undesirable foolhardiness on the part of the wearer. Finn, from his personal viewpoint, may even have seen my statement as a disciplined, if deserved, call to order, should that rumour have any basis in truth.

'Speak all these languages?'

'Only a little French, sir.'

'Don't speak any of 'em.'

'No, sir.'

He laughed, seeming pleased by that.

'Now I thought we'd all be photographed,' he said. 'Good thing on an occasion like this. I'll sign 'em for you.'

Smiling like the Cheshire Cat, a sergeant holding a small camera suddenly came into being. There had been no sign of him a moment before. He seemed risen from the ground or dropped from a tree. We broke ranks and formed up again, this time on either side of the Field-Marshal, who took up a convenient position for this in front of one of the caravans. There was rather a scramble to get next to him, in which Chu and Bobrowski achieved flanking places. Van der Voort, elbowed out of the way by Chu, caught my eye and winked. Photography at an end, we were taken over the caravans, a visit personally conducted by the Field-Marshal, whose manner perfectly fused the feelings of a tenant justly proud of a perfectly equipped luxury flat with those of the lord of an ancient though still inhabited historical monument. Two dogs, not unlike General Liddament's, were making themselves very free of the place, charging about and disregarding the Field-Marshal's shouts. When this was over, the military attachés were led to a spot where a large map hung on a kind of easel.

'You'll want me to put you in the picture.'

With unexpectedly delicate movements of the hands, the Field-Marshal began to explain what had been happening. We were in an area, as I have said, immemorially campaigned over. In fact the map was no less than a great slice of history. As the eye travelled northward, it fell on Zutphen, where Sir Philip Sidney had stopped a bullet in that charge against the Albanian cavalry. One wondered why Albanians should be involved in this part of the world at such a time. Presumably they were some auxiliary unit of the Spanish Command, similar to those exotic corps of which one heard rumours in the current war, anti-Soviet Caucasians enrolled in a German formation, American-Japanese fighting with the Allies. The thought of Sidney, a sympathetic figure, distracted attention from the Field-Marshal's talk. One felt him essentially the kind of soldier Vigny had in mind when writing of the man who, like a monk, submitted himself to the military way of life, because he thought it right, rather than because it appealed to him.

Available evidence, where Sidney was concerned, pointed to quite other than military preoccupations:

> 'Within those woods of Arcadie
> He chief delight and pleasure took,
> And on the mountain Parthenie,
> Upon the crystal liquid brook
> The Muses met him every day
> That taught him sing, to write and say.'

The Field-Marshal pursued his exposition with the greatest clarity, but the place-names of the map continued to stimulate daydreams of forgotten conflicts. Maastricht, for example. It took a moment or two to recall the connexion. Then, oddly enough, another *beau monde* poet was in question, though one of a very different sort to Sidney. Was it Rochester? Certainly a Restoration figure. Something about the moulding of a drinking-cup—boy's limbs entwined, a pederast, and making rather a point of it—with deliberations as to what scenes were to be represented on the vessel? The poet, certainly Rochester, expressed in the strongest terms his disapprobation of army life even in art:

> 'Engrave not battle on his cheek:
> With war I've naught to do.
> I'm none of those that took Maestrich,
> Nor Yarmouth leaguer knew.'

This feeling that war was something to be avoided at all costs for personal reasons was very understandable; more acceptable, indeed, than many of the sometimes rather suspect moral objections put forward. The references, the engagement at Maastricht and 'Yarmouth leaguer' were obscure to me. The latter was presumably a sort of transit camp, the kind of establishment Dicky Umfraville had formerly been in charge of. Then some memory swam to the surface that d'Artagnan's historical prototype had fallen at Maastricht, though details of the particular campaign remained latent. D'Artagnan was, on the whole, rather a non-Vigny figure, anyway on the surface, insomuch as there seemed little or no reason to suppose he was particularly to the fore when it came to disagreeable and unglamorous army jobs. Musing of this sort had reached Marlborough, his taste for being kept by women, remarks made on that subject to Odo Stevens by Pamela Flitton, the connexion between sex and war in this particular aspect, when the Field-Marshal's discourse terminated. By that time the photographs had been developed. They were signed and handed round. Colonel Hlava, as doyen, made a little speech of thanks on behalf of all the military attachés. The Field-Marshal listened gravely. Then he gave a nod of dismissal. Finn and I packed them once more into the cars.

On the way to Brussels we passed a small cart pulled by a muscular-looking dog.

'Once you would have seen that in my country,' said Hlava. 'Now our standards have risen. Dogs no longer work.'

'That one seems positively to like it.'

This particular dog was making a great parade of how well he was accomplishing his task.

'Dogs are so ambitious,' agreed Hlava.

'The Field-Marshal's dogs seemed so. Do you suppose they were pressing for promotion?'

'A great man, I think,' said Hlava.

I tried to reduce to viable terms impressions of this slight, very exterior contact. On the one hand, there had been hardly a trace of the almost overpowering physical impact of the CIGS, that curious electric awareness felt down to the tips of one's fingers of a given presence imparting a sense of stimulation, also the consoling thought that someone of the sort was at the top. On the other hand, the Field-Marshal's outward personality offered what was perhaps even less usual, will-power, not so much natural, as developed to altogether exceptional lengths. No doubt there had been a generous basic endowment, but of not the essentially magnetic quality. In short, the will here might even be more effective from being less dramatic. It was an immense, wiry, calculated, insistent hardness, rather than a force like champagne bursting from the bottle. Observed in tranquillity, the former combination of qualities was not, within the terms of reference, particularly uplifting or agreeable, except again in the manner their synthesis seemed to offer dependability in utter self-reliance and resilience. One felt that a great deal of time and trouble, even intellectual effort of its own sort, had gone into producing this final result.

The eyes were deepset and icy cold. You thought at once of an animal, though a creature not at all in the stylized manner of the two colonels at my Divisional Headquarters, reminiscent respectively of the dog-faced and bird-faced Egyptian deities. No such artificial formality shaped these features, and to say, for example, they resembled those of a fox or ferret would be to imply a disparagement not at all sought. Did the features, in fact, suggest some mythical beast, say one of those encountered in *Alice in Wonderland*, full of awkward questions and downright statements? This sense, that here was perhaps a personage from an imaginary world, was oddly sustained by the voice. It was essentially an army voice, but precise, controlled, almost mincing, when not uttering some awful warning, as to Gauthier de Graef. There was a faint and faraway reminder of the clergy, too; parsonic, yet not in the least numinous, the tone of the incumbent ruthlessly dedicated to his parish, rather than the hierophant celebrating divine mysteries. At the same time, one guessed this parish priest regarded himself as in a high class of hierophancy too, whatever others might think.

From the very beginnings of his fame, the Field-Marshal had never ignored Chips Lovell's often repeated reminder that it was a tailor's war. The new spruceness that had now taken the place of the conscious informality of ready-to-hand garments appropriate to desert warfare—to the confusion of those military attachés obliged hurriedly to tuck up their pullovers—was clearly conceived at the same time to avoid any resemblance to the buttoned-up army officer of caricature. It lacked too, probably also deliberately, the lounging smartness of which, for example, Dicky Umfraville, or even in his own fashion, Sunny Farebrother, knew the secret. The Field-Marshal's turn-out had to be admitted to fall short of any such elegance. Correct: neat: practical: unpompous: all that to perfection. Elegant, he was not. Why should he be? It was wholly unnecessary, probably a positive handicap in terms of personal propaganda. Besides, will-power exercised unrelentingly over a lifetime—as opposed to its display in brilliant flashes—is apt on the whole to be the enemy of elegance. One only had to think of the Dictators to see that. Few of the Great Captains of history, with the possible exception of Wellington, had shown themselves particularly elegant in victory; though there, of course, one moved into the world of moral elegance, and, in any case, victory was not yet finally attained.

The cock-sparrow captain, major-domo to VIPs, handed over the brandy bottles in a neat parcel when we arrived back at billets.

'A chap from Civil Affairs was asking for you. I told him when your party was expected back. He said he'd look in again.'

'What name?'

'Duport—a captain. He talked about getting you out for a drink.'

I was off duty that night. Although I had never much liked Duport, an evening together, if he were free, would be better than one spent alone. If he were in Civil Affairs, it was possible that his branch had received an official notification of our being in Brussels and he wanted to discuss some Belgian matter. It could hardly be mere friendliness, as we scarcely knew each other. I asked where was a good place to go.

'The big brasserie on the corner's not too bad. You'll find all ranks there, but not many senior officers. If you're like me, and see a lot of them, that's a bit of a holiday. What's the food like in England now? Custard on everything when I was last on leave.'

Duport turned up later. I had not seen him since the Bellevue. His reddish hair receded from the forehead, getting grey by the ears. He looked tired, perceptibly older. Like Pennistone, he carried a General Service lion-and-unicorn in his cap, and had changed into service-dress. Uniform did not suit him. Instead of building him up, it diminished the aggressive energy his civilian appearance had always indicated. This lessening of aggression was also signified by a more subdued manner. The war had undoubtedly quieted Duport down.

'I saw your name as Belgian Liaison Officer in London on some document passed to us,' he said. 'Then found you were personally conducting this flight of swans. We run here parallel in a curious way with Army Group, and there are one or two things that could be straightened out if we had a talk. The usual stuff, Leopold's marriage, the Resistance lads. When do you go back?'

'Tomorrow.'

'Then if we had a talk tonight we could straighten out some points about policy. We're very full of work at the moment, as I expect you are too.'

This was a rather different tone from the Duport of former days. We went to the recommended brasserie, as he had no better suggestion. He seemed to have lost some of his old interest in material things. For a time we talked Belgian affairs. Dupont knew all about Kucherman, but had not met him.

'He's one of the ablest blokes they've got,' he said. 'However let's give the subject a rest now. You were cremating your uncle when we last met.'

'How did you come to join the army? At the Bellevue you were talking of sweating it out in South America, if war came.'

'South America wasn't on. As you know I was on my uppers at that moment. Then I got a chance of going to Egypt for a firm that wanted to wind up one of their branches there. Donners had an interest and managed to get me out. Getting back was another matter. The chance of a commission turned up. I took it. Wanted to get into one of the secret shows, but didn't bring it off. I was in the Censorship for a time. Not much to be recommended. Then I had a bad go of Gyppy tummy—with complications. That was what ultimately brought me back to Europe and the mob I now belong to.'

'You haven't seen anything of Peter Templer, have you? Donners was helping to fix him up too—something in the cloak-and-dagger line—but I haven't heard what came of it.'

Duport finished his glass.

'Peter's had it,' he said.

'Do you mean he's been killed?'

'Gone for a Burton.'

'On a secret operation?'

'Yes.'

'I suppose nobody knows more than that?'

Duport hesitated.

'It never struck me you wouldn't have heard about Peter,' he said. 'There was a lot of talk about it all in Cairo —not the best security imaginable, but then Cairo is not a place for the best security. There was certainly a lot of talk.'

'What happened?'

'I daresay Peter's still officially described as missing, but everyone in the know is aware he's dead, even though the details vary. One story was he was murdered by his wireless operator for the money he had on him, but I happen to know that isn't true. We'll go to another place for the next round.'

We left the brasserie and found a café. It was less crowded.

'Does Prince Theodoric mean anything to you?' asked Duport.

'He's done business with our Section once or twice, but not recently—and of course not on the secret operations level.'

'You knew Peter was involved in that quarter?'

'More or less.'

'I always have a fellow feeling for the Prince, though we've never met,' said Duport. 'He and I always seem to be screwing the same ladies. Bijou Ardglas, for example, now, poor girl, in the arms of Jesus. Have you heard of a young woman called Pamela Flitton?'

'Volumes.'

'You know she was the main cause of Peter's trouble?'

'I was told that—but people don't go and get killed because a piece like that won't sleep with them.'

'Well, not exactly, I agree,' said Duport. 'It was more Peter felt he was slowing up, as I see it. The point is that it all builds up round Theodoric. As you know the good Prince's realm is internally divided as to how best repel the invader. One lot wants one thing, the other, another. Peter went in with the Prince's gang.'

'Was someone called Odo Stevens mixed up in all this?'

'I thought you said you didn't deal with the cloak-and-dagger boys?'

'Something Stevens said off the record.'

'You know him? Young Stevens was a bit too fond of making statements off the record.'

'I was on a course with him earlier in the war. Then he was mixed up with a girl I knew, now deceased.'

'Odo the Stoat we used to call him. These boys make me feel my age. That's what got Peter down.'

'Is Stevens missing too?'

'Not he. I met him in Cairo after they'd got him out.'

'Why didn't they get Peter out too?'

Duport gave one of his hard unfriendly laughs.

'There are those in Cairo who allege proper arrangements were never made to get Peter out. At least they were planned, but never put into operation. That's what's said. These things happen sometimes, you know. Little inter-departmental differences. Change of policy at the top. There was a man with an unpronouncable name mixed up with it all too. I don't know which side he was on.'

'Szymanski?'

'Why do you ask about things when you know the whole story already? Are you from MI 5? An agent provocateur, just trying to see what you can get out of me, then shop me for bad security? That's what it sounds like.'

'Was Szymanski with Templer or Stevens?'

'So far as I know, on his own. Not sure it was even ourselves who sent him in. Might have been his own people, whoever they were. He went there in the first instance to knock off someone—the head of the Gestapo or a local traitor. I don't know. It was all lined up, then a signal came down from the top—from the Old Man himself, they say—that war wasn't waged in that manner in his opinion. All that trouble for nothing—but I understand they got Szymanski out. A chap in the Cairo racket told me all this. He was fed up with the way that particular party was run. It came out I'd been Peter's brother-in-law in days gone by, so I suppose he thought, as a former relation, I'd a right to know why he'd kicked the bucket.'

'And you really think Pamela Flitton caused this?'

'I only stuffed her once,' said Duport. 'Against a shed in the back parts of Cairo airport, but even then I could see she might drive you round the bend, if she really decided to. I'll tell you something amusing. You remember that bugger Widmerpool, who'd got me into such a jam about chromite when we last met?'

'He's a full colonel now.'

'He was in Cairo at one moment and took Miss Pamela to a nightclub.'

'Rumours of that even reached England.'

'That girl gets a hold on people,' said Duport. 'Sad about Peter, but there it is. The great thing is he didn't fall into the hands of the Gestapo, as another friend of mine did. Pity you're going back to morrow. We might have gone to the Opera together.'

'Didn't know music was one of your things.'

'Always liked it. One of the reasons my former wife and I never really hit it off was because Jean only knew *God Save the King* because everyone stood up. I was always sneaking off to concerts. They put on *La Muette de Portici* here to celebrate the liberation. Not very polite to the Dutch, as when it was first performed, the Belgians were so excited by it, they kicked the Hollanders out. I'm not all that keen on Auber myself, as it happens, but I've met a lot of dumb girls, so I've been to hear it several times to remind myself of them.'

This revelation of Duport's musical leanings showed how, as ever, people can always produce something unexpected about themselves. In the opposite direction, Kernével was equally unforeseen, on my return, in the lack of interest he showed in Cabourg and its associations with Proust. He knew the name of the novelist, but it aroused no curiosity whatever.

'Doesn't he always write about society people?' was Kernével's chilly comment.

I told Pennistone about Prasad, Asbjørnsen and the bath.

'Prasad merely turned the taps on at the hour of prayer. It was perfectly right that he should have the bathroom. Finn should have arranged that through you in the first instance.'

'I see.'

'Thank God Finn's back, and I shall no longer have to deal directly with that spotty Brigadier who always wants to alter what is brought to him to sign. I have had to point out on three occasions that his emendations contradict himself in a higher unity.'

A day or two after our return, Kucherman telephoned early. It was a Friday.

'Can you come round here at once?'

'Of course. I thought you were still in Brussels.'

'I flew in last night.'

When I reached Eaton Square, Kucherman, unusual for him, was looking a little worried.

'This question I am going to put is rather important,' he said.

'Yes?'

'My Government has come to a decision about the army of the Resistance. As you know, the problem has posed itself since the expulsion of the Germans.'

'So I understand.'

'Were you told what the Field-Marshal threatened to Gauthier de Graef?'

'I was standing beside him when the words were said.'

'They are good young men, but they require something to do.'

'Naturally.'

'The proposal is that they should be brought to this country.'

That was an unexpected proposition.

'You mean to train?'

'Otherwise we shall have trouble. It is certain. These excellent young men have most of them grown up under German occupation, with no means of expressing their hatred for it—the feeling that for years they have not been able to breathe. They must have an outlet of some sort. They want action. A change of scene will to some extent accomplish that.'

'What sort of numbers?'

'Say thirty thousand.'

'A couple of Divisions?'

'But without the equivalent in weapons and services.'

'When do you want them to come?'

'At once.'

'So we've got to move quickly.'

'That is the point.'

I thought about the interminable procedures required to get a project of this sort under way. Blackhead, like a huge bat, seemed already flapping his wings about Eaton Square, bumping blindly against the windows of the room.

'Arrangements for two Divisions will take some time. Are they already cadred?'

'Sufficiently to bring them across.'

'I'll go straight back to Colonel Finn. We'll get a minute out to be signed by the General and go at once to the highest level. There will be all sorts of problems in addition to the actual physical accommodation of two extra Divisions in this country. The Finance people, for one thing. It will take a week or two to get that side fixed.'

'You think so?'

'I know them.'

'Speed is essential.'

'It's no good pretending we're going to get an answer by Monday.'

'You mean it may take quite a long time?'

'You are familiar with ministerial machinery.'

Kucherman got up from his chair.

'What are we going to do?'

'I thought I'd better say all this.'

'I know it already.'

'It's a fact, I'm afraid.'

'But we must do something. What you say is true, I know. How are we going to get round it? I want to speak frankly. This could be a question of avoiding civil war.'

There was a pause. I knew there was only one way out—to cut the Gordian Knot—but could not immediately see how to attain that. Then, perhaps hypnotized by Kucherman's intense need for an answer, I thought of something.

'You said you knew Sir Magnus Donners.'

'Of course.'

'But you have not seen much of him since you've been over here?'

'I have spoken to him a couple of times at official parties. He was very friendly.'

'Ring him up and say you want to see him at once—this very morning.'

'You think so?'

'Tell him what you've just told me.'

'And then—'

'Sir Magnus can tell the Head Man.'

Kucherman thought for a moment.

'I insist you are right,' he said.

'It's worth trying.'

'This is between ourselves.'

'Of course.'

'Not even Colonel Finn.'

'Least of all.'

'Meanwhile you will start things off in the normal manner through *les voies hiérarchiques.*'

'As soon as I get back.'

'So I will get to work,' said Kucherman. 'I am grateful for the suggestion. The next time we meet, I hope I shall have had a word with Sir Magnus.'

I returned to Finn. He listened to the proposal to bring the Belgian Resistance Army to this country.

'It's pretty urgent?'

'Vital, sir.'

'We'll try and move quickly, but I foresee difficulties. Good notion to train those boys over here. Get out a draft right away. Meanwhile I'll consult the Brigadier about the best way of handling the matter. You'd better have a word with Staff Duties. It's not going to be as easy to settle as Kucherman hopes.'

I got out the draft. Finally a tremendous minute was launched on its way that very afternoon. Bureaucratically speaking, grass had not grown under our feet; but this was only a beginning. That weekend was my free one. I told Isobel what I had suggested to Kucherman.

'If the worst comes to the worst we can invoke Matilda.'

Neither of us had seen Matilda since she had married Sir Magnus Donners.

'It's just a long shot.'

On Monday morning a summons came from Finn as soon as he arrived in his room. I went up there.

'This Belgian affair.'

'Yes, sir?'

Finn passed his hands over the smooth ivory surfaces of his skull.

'The most extraordinary thing has happened.'

'Yes, sir?'

'An order has come down from the Highest Level of All to say it is to be treated as top priority. The chaps are to come over the moment their accommodation is decided upon. Things like financial details can be worked out later. All other minor matters too. Tell Blackhead he can talk to the PM about it, if he isn't satisfied.'

'This is splendid, sir.'

Finn put on the face he usually assumed when about to go deaf, but did not do so.

'Providential,' he said. 'Can't understand it. It just shows how the Old Man's got his finger on every pulse. I don't know whether Kucherman did—well, a bit of intriguing. He's a very able fellow, and in the circumstances it would have been almost justified. You will attend a conference on the subject under the DSD at eleven o'clock this morning, all branches concerned being represented.'

The Director of Staff Duties was the general responsible for planning matters. When I next saw Kucherman, we agreed things had gone through with remarkable smoothness. The name of Sir Magnus Donners was not mentioned when we discussed certain administrative details. Thinking over the incident after, it was easy to see how a taste for intrigue, as Finn called it, could develop in people.

## CHAPTER FIVE

During the period between the Potsdam Conference and the dropping of the first atomic bomb, I read in the paper one morning that Widmerpool was engaged to Pamela Flitton. This piece of news was undramatically announced in the column dedicated to such items. It was not even top of the list. Pamela was described as daughter of Captain Cosmo Flitton and Mrs Flavia Wisebite; an address in Montana (suggesting a ranch) showed her father was still alive and living in America. Her mother, whose style indicated divorce from Harrison Wisebite (sunk, so far as I knew, without a trace), had come to rest in the country round Glimber, possibly a cottage on the estate. Widmerpool—'Colonel K. G. Widmerpool, OBE'— was based on a block of flats in Victoria Street. Apart from stories already vaguely propagated by Farebrother and Duport, there was no clue to how this engagement had come about. Surprising as it was, the immediate implications seemed no more than that a piece of colossal folly on both their parts would soon be readjusted by another announcement saying the marriage was 'off'. The world was in such a state of flux that such inanities were only to be expected in one quarter or another. Only later, considered in cold blood, did the arrangement appear credible; even then for less than obvious reasons.

'Drove for the Section, did she?' said Pennistone. 'I never remember those girls' faces. I haven't heard anything of Widmerpool for some time. I suppose he's now passed into a world beyond good and evil.'

I had not set eyes on Widmerpool myself since the day Farebrother had recoiled from saluting him in Whitehall.

Although, as an archetypal figure, one of those fabulous monsters that haunt the recesses of the individual imagination, he held an immutable place in my own private mythology, with the passing of Stringham and Templer, I no longer knew anyone to whom he might present quite the same absorbing spectacle, accordingly with whom the present conjunction could be at all adequately discussed. By this time, in any case, changes both inside and outside the Section were so many it was hard to keep pace with them. Allied relationships had become more complex with the defeat of the enemy, especially in the comportment of new political régimes that had emerged in formerly occupied countries—Poland's, for example—some of which were making difficulties about such matters as the 'Victory march'; in general the manner in which Peace was to be celebrated in London. In other merely administrative respects the Section's position was becoming less pivotal than formerly, some of the Allies—France, the Netherlands, Czechoslovakia—sending over special military missions. These were naturally less familiar with the routines of liaison than colleagues long worked with, while the new entities, unlike the old ones, were sometimes authorized to deal directly with whatever branch of the Services specially concerned them.

'Not all the fruits of Victory are appetising to the palate,' said Pennistone. 'An issue of gall and wormwood has been laid on.'

By that time he was himself on the point of demobilization. He had dealt with the Poles up to the end. Dempster and others had gone already. The Old Guard, like the soldiers in the song, were fading away, leaving me as final residue, Finn's second-in-command. In a month or two I should also enter that intermediate state of grace, technically 'on leave', through which in due course civilian life was once more attained. Finn, for reasons best known to himself—he could certainly have claimed early release had he so wished—remained on in his old appointment, where there was still plenty of work to do. Other branches round about were, of course, dwindling in the same manner. All sorts of unexpected individuals, barely remembered, or at best remembered only for acrimonious interchanges in the course of doing business with them, would from time to time turn up in our room to say goodbye, hearty or sheepish, according to temperament. Quite often they behaved as if these farewells were addressed to the only friends they had ever known.

'My Dad's taking me away from this school,' said Borrit, when he shook my hand. 'I'm going into his office. He's got some jolly pretty typists.'

'Wish mine would buck up and remove me too.'

'He says the boys don't learn anything here, just get up to nasty tricks,' said Borrit. 'I'm going to have a room to myself, he says. What do you think of that? Hope my secretary looks like that AT with black hair and a white face who once drove us for a week or two, can't remember her name.'

'Going back to the same job?'

'You bet—the old oranges and lemons/bells of St Clement's.'

As always, after making a joke, Borrit began to look sad again.

'We'll have to meet.'

'Course we will.'

'When I want to buy a banana.'

'Anything up to twenty-thousand bunches, say the word and I'll fix a discount.'

'Will Sydney Stebbings be one of your customers now?'

About eighteen months before, Stebbings, suffering another nervous breakdown, had been invalided out of the army. He was presumed to have returned to the retail side of the fruit business. Borrit shook his head.

'Didn't you hear about poor old Syd? Gassed himself. Felt as browned off out of the army as in it. I used to think it was those Latin-Americans got him down, but it was just Syd's moody nature.'

Borrit and I never did manage to meet again. Some years after the war I ran into Slade in Jermyn Street, by the hat shop with the stuffed cat in the window smoking a cigarette. He had a brown paper bag in his hand and said he had been buying cheese. We had a word together. He was teaching languages at a school in the Midlands and by then a headmastership in the offing. I asked if he had any news, among others, of Borrit.

'Borrit died a few months ago,' said Slade. 'Sad. Bad luck too, because he was going to marry a widow with a little money. She'd been the wife of a man in his business.'

I wondered whether on this final confrontation Borrit had brought off the never realized 'free poke', before the grave claimed him. The war drawing to a close must have something to do with this readiness for marriage on the part of those like Borrit, Widmerpool, Farebrother, no longer in their first youth. These were only a few of them among the dozens who had never tried it before, or tried it without much success. Norah Tolland spoke with great disapproval of Pamela Flitton's engagement.

'Pam must need a Father-Figure,' she said. 'I think it's a tragic mistake. Like Titania and Bottom.'

Not long before the Victory Service, announced to take place at St Paul's, Prasad's Embassy gave a party on their National Day. It was a bigger affair than usual on account of the advent of Peace, primarily a civilian gathering, though a strong military element was included among the guests. The huge saloons, built at the turn of the century, were done up in sage green, the style of decoration displaying a nostalgic leaning towards Art Nouveau, a period always sympathetic to Asian taste. Gauthier de Graef, ethnically confused, had been anxious to know whether there were eunuchs in the ladies' apartments above the rooms where we were being entertained. Accordingly, to settle the point, on which he was very insistent, Madame Philidor and Isobel arranged to be conducted to their hostess in purdah, promising to report on this matter, though without much hope of returning with an affirmative answer. They had just set out on this visit of exploration, when I saw Farebrother moving purposefully through the crowd. I went over to congratulate him on his marriage. He was immensely cordial.

'I hear Geraldine's an old friend of yours, Nicholas. You knew her in her "Tuffy" days.'

I said I did not think I had ever quite had the courage to address her by that nickname when she had still been Miss Weedon.

'I mean when she was Mrs Foxe's secretary,' said Farebrother. 'Then you knew the old General too. Splendid old fellow, he must have been. Wish I'd met him. Both he and Mrs Foxe opened up a lot of very useful contacts for Geraldine, which she's never lost sight of. They're going to stand me in good stead too. A wonderful woman. Couldn't believe my ears when she said she'd be mine.'

He seemed very pleased about it all.

'She's not here tonight.'

'Too busy.'

'Catching spies?'

'Ah, so you know where she's working? We try to keep that a secret. No, Geraldine's getting our new flat straight. We've actually found somewhere to live. Not too easy these days. Quite a reasonable rent for the neighbourhood, which is a good one. Now I must go and have a word with old

Lord Perkins over there. He married poor Peter Templer's elder sister, Babs, as I expect you know.'

'I didn't know.'

'One of the creations of the first Labour Government. Of course he's getting on now—but, with Labour in again, we all need friends at court.'

'Did anything more ever come out as to what happened to Peter?'

'Nothing, so far as I know. He was absolutely set on doing that job. As soon as he heard I was going to work with those people he got on to me to try and get him something of the sort. You ought to meet Lord Perkins. I think Babs found him a change for the better after that rather dreadful fellow Stripling. I ran into Stripling in Aldershot about eighteen months ago. He was lecturing to the troops. Just come from the Glasshouse, where he'd given a talk on the early days of motor-racing. Someone told me Babs had been a great help to her present husband when he was writing his last book on industrial relations.'

He smiled and moved off. Widmerpool arrived in the room at that moment. He stood looking round, evidently deciding where best to launch an attack. Farebrother must have seen him, because he suddenly swerved into a new direction to avoid contact. This seemed a good opportunity to congratulate Widmerpool too. I went over to him. He seemed very pleased with himself.

'Thank you very much, Nicholas. Some people have expressed the opinion, without much delicacy, that Pamela is too young for me. That is not my own view at all. A man is as young as he feels. I had quite a scene with my mother, I'm afraid. My mother is getting an old lady now, of course, and does not always know what she is talking about. As a matter of fact I am making arrangements for her to live, anyway temporarily, with some distant relations of ours in the Lowlands. It's not too far from Glasgow. I think she will be happier with them than on her own, after I am married. She is in touch with one or two nice families on the Borders.'

This was a very different tone from that Widmerpool was in the habit of using about his mother in the old days. It seemed likely the engagement represented one of his conscious decisions to put life on a new footing. He embarked on these from time to time, with consequent rearrangements all round. It looked as if sending Mrs Widmerpool into exile was going to be one such. It was hard to feel wholly condemnatory. I enquired about the circumstances in which he had met Pamela, a matter about which I was curious.

'In Cairo. An extraordinary chance. As you know, my work throughout the war has never given me a second for social life. Even tonight I am here only because Pamela herself wanted to come—she is arriving at any moment—and I shall leave as soon as I have introduced her. I requested the Ambassador as a personal favour that I might bring my fiancée. He was charming about it. To tell the truth, I have to dine with the Minister tonight. A lot to talk about. Questions of policy. Adjustment to new régimes. But I was telling you how Pamela and I met. In Cairo there was trouble about my returning plane. One had been shot down, resulting in my having to kick my heels in the place for twenty-four hours. You know how vexatious that sort of situation is to me. I was taken to a place called Groppi's. Someone introduced us. Before I knew where I was, we were dining together and on our way to a night-club. I had not been to a place of that sort for years. Had, indeed, quite forgotten what they were like. The fact was we had a most enjoyable evening.'

He laughed quite hysterically.

'Then, as luck would have it, Pam was posted back to England. I should have added that she was working as secretary in one of the secret organizations there. I was glad about her return, because I don't think she moved in a very good set in Cairo. When she arrived in London, she sent me a postcard—and what a postcard.'

Widmerpool giggled violently, then recovered himself.

'It arrived one morning in that basement where I work night and day,' he said. 'You can imagine how pleased I was. It seems extraordinary that we hardly knew each other then, and now I've got a great big photograph of her on my desk.'

He was almost gasping. The words vividly conjured up his subterranean life. Photographs on a desk were never without interest. People who placed them there belonged to a special category in their human relationships. There was, for example, that peculiarly tortured-looking midshipman in a leather-and-talc frame in the room of a Section with which ours was often in contact. Some lines of John Davidson suddenly came into my head:

> And so they wait, while empires sprung
> Of hatred thunder past above,
> Deep in the earth for ever young
> Tannhäuser and the Queen of Love.'

On reflection, the situation was not a very close parallel, because it was most unlikely Pamela had ever visited Widmerpool's underground office. On the other hand, she herself could easily be envisaged as one of the myriad incarnations of Venus, even if Widmerpool were not much of a Tannhäuser. At least he seemed in a similar way to have stumbled on the secret entrance to the court of the Paphian goddess in the Hollow Hill where his own duties were diurnally enacted. That was some qualification.

'You know she's Charles Stringham's niece?'

'Naturally I am aware of that.'

The question had not pleased him.

'No news of Stringham, I suppose?'

'There has been, as a matter of fact.'

Widmerpool seemed half angry, half desirous of making some statement about this.

'He was captured,' he said. 'He didn't survive.'

Scarcely anything was known still about individual prisoners in Japanese POW camps, except that the lives of many of them had certainly been saved by the Bomb. News came through slowly from the Far East. I asked how Widmerpool could speak so definitely.

'At the end of last year the Americans sank a Jap transport on the way from Singapore. They rescued some British prisoners on board. They had been in the same camp. One of them got in touch with Stringham's mother when repatriated. It was only just in time, because Mrs Foxe herself died soon after that, as you probably saw.'

'I hadn't.'

He seemed to want to make some further confession.

'As I expect you know, Mrs Foxe was a very extravagant woman. At the end, she found it not only impossible to live in anything like the way she used, but was even quite short of money.'

'Stringham himself said something about that when I last saw him.'

'The irony of the situation is that his mother's South African money was tied up on Stringham,' said Widmerpool. 'Owing to bad management, she never got much out of those securities herself, but a lot of South African stock has recently made a very good recovery.'

'I suppose Flavia will benefit.'

'No, she doesn't, as it turns out,' said Widmerpool. 'Rather an odd thing happened. Stringham left a will bequeathing all he had to Pam. He'd always been fond of her as a child. He obviously thought it would be just a few personal odds and ends. As it turns out, there could be a good deal more than that. With the right attention, Stringham's estate in due course might be nursed into something quite respectable.'

He looked rather guilty, not without reason. We abandoned the subject of Stringham.

'I don't pretend Pamela's an easy girl,' he said. 'We fairly often have rows—in fact are not on speaking terms for twenty-four hours or more. Never mind. Rows often clear the air. We shall see it through, whatever my position when I leave the army.'

'You'll go back to the City, I suppose?'

'I'm not so sure.'

'Other plans?'

'I have come to the conclusion that I enjoy power,' said Widmerpool. 'That is something the war has taught me. In this connexion, it has more than once occurred to me that I might like governing . . .'

He brought his lips together, then parted them. This contortion formed a phrase, but, the words inaudible, its sense escaped me.

'Governing whom?'

Leaning forward and smiling, Widmerpool repeated the movement of his lips. This time, although he spoke only in a whisper, the two words were intelligible.

'*Black men . . .*'

'Abroad?'

'Naturally.'

'That's feasible?'

'My reputation among those who matter could scarcely be higher.'

'You mean you could easily get an appointment of that sort?'

'Nothing in life is ever easy, my boy. Not in the sense you use the term. It is one of the mistakes you always make. The point is, we are going to see great changes. As you know, my leanings have always been leftwards. From what I see round me, I have no reason to suppose such sympathies were mistaken. Men like myself will be needed.'

'If they are to be found.'

He clapped me on the back.

'No flattery,' he said. 'No flattery, but I sometimes wonder whether you're not right.'

He looked at his watch and sighed.

'Being engaged accustoms one to unpunctuality,' he went on in rather another tone, a less exuberant one. 'I think I'll have a word with that old stalwart, Lord Perkins, whom I see over there.'

'I didn't know till a moment ago that Perkins was married to Peter Templer's sister.'

'Oh, yes. So I believe. I don't see them as having much in common as brothers-in-law, but one never knows. Unfortunate Templer getting killed like that. He was too old for that sort of business, of course. Stringham, too. I fear the war has taken a sad toll of our friends. I notice Donners over there talking to the Portuguese Ambassador. I must say a word to him too.'

In the seven years or so that had passed since I had last seen him, Sir Magnus Donners had grown not so much older in appearance, as less like a human being. He now resembled an animated tailor's dummy, one designed to recommend second-hand, though immensely discreet, clothes (if the suit he was wearing could be regarded as a sample) adapted to the taste of distinguished men no longer young. Jerky movements, like those of a marionette—perhaps indicating all was not absolutely well with his physical system—added to the impression of an outsize puppet that had somehow escaped from its box and begun to mix with real people, who were momentarily taken in by the extraordinary conviction of its mechanism. The set of Sir Magnus's mouth, always a trifle uncomfortable to contemplate, had become very slightly less under control, increasing the vaguely warning note the rest of his appearance implied. On the whole he had lost that former air of desperately seeking to seem more ordinary than everyone else round him; or, if he still hoped for that, its consolations had certainly escaped him. A lifetime of weighty negotiation in the worlds of politics and business had left their mark. One would now guess at once he was an unusual person, who, even within his own terms of reference, had lived an unusual life. He looked less parsonic than in the days when he had suggested a clerical headmaster. Perhaps that was because he had not, so to speak, inwardly progressed to the archiepiscopal level in that calling; at least his face had not developed the fleshy, theatrical accentuations so often attendant on the features of the higher grades of the clergy. At some moment, conscious or not, he had probably branched off from this interior priestly strain in his make-up. That would be the logical explanation. Matilda, looking decidedly smart in a dress of blue and black stripes, was standing beside her husband, talking with the Portuguese Ambassador. I had not seen her since their marriage. She caught sight of me and waved, then separated herself from the others and made her way through the ever thickening crowd.

'Nick.'

'How are you, Matty?'

'Don't you admire my frock? An unsolicited gift from New York.'

'Too smart for words. I couldn't imagine where it had come from.'

To be rather older suited her; that or being married to a member of the Cabinet. She had dyed her hair a reddish tint that suited her, too, set off the large green eyes, which were always her most striking feature.

'Do you ever see anything of Hugh the Drover?'

She used sometimes to call Moreland that while they had been married, usually when not best pleased with him. I told her we had not met since the night of the bomb on the Café de Madrid: that, so far as I knew, Moreland was still touring the country, putting on musical performances of one sort or another, under more or less official control; whatever happened in the war to make mounting such entertainments possible.

'What's his health been like?'

'I don't know at all.'

'Extraordinary about Audrey Maclintick. Are they married?'

'I don't know that either.'

'Does she look after him all right?'

'I think she does.'

Obviously Matilda still took quite a keen interest in Moreland and his condition. That was natural enough. All the same, one felt instinctively that she had entirely given up Moreland's world, everything to do with it. She had taken on Sir Magnus, lock, stock and barrel. The metaphor made one think of his alleged sexual oddities. Presumably she had taken them on too, though as a former mistress they would be relatively familiar. Perhaps she guessed the train of thought, because she smiled.

'Donners has to be looked after too,' she said. 'I'm rather worried about him at the moment as a matter of fact.'

'His job must be a great strain.'

Matilda brushed such a banal comment aside.

'Will you come and see me?' she said. 'We're going to Washington next week—but when we're back.'

'My Release Group comes up reasonably soon. We'll probably go away for a bit when I get out of the army.'

'Later then. Is Isobel here?'

'Last seen on her way to the harem upstairs.'

Sir Magnus had now begun to make signs indicating

that he wanted Matilda to return to him and be introduced to someone. She left me, repeating that we must meet when they came back from America. I had always liked Matilda and felt glad to see her again and hear that her life seemed endurable. Widmerpool reappeared at my side. He seemed agitated.

'I wish Pamela would turn up,' he said. 'I shall be late if she doesn't arrive soon. I can't very well leave until she comes—ah, thank God, there she is.'

Pamela Flitton came towards us. Unlike the night at *The Bartered Bride*, she had this evening taken no trouble whatever about her clothes. Perhaps that was untrue, and she had gone out of her way to find the oldest, most filthy garments she possessed. She was almost in rags. By this time the party had advanced too far for it to be obvious to a newcomer whom to greet as host. She had in any case obviously not bothered about any such formalities.

'Hullo, my dear,' said Widmerpool. 'I didn't guess you'd be so late.'

He spoke in a conciliatory voice, making as if to kiss her. She allowed the merest peck.

'I'll just introduce you to His Excellency,' he said. 'Then I'll have to fly.'

Pamela, who was looking very pretty in spite of her disarray, was having none of that.

'I don't want to be introduced,' she said. 'I just came to have a look round.'

She gave me a nod. I made some conventional remark about their engagement. She listened to this rather more graciously than usual.

'I think you ought to meet the Ambassador, dearest.'

'Stuff the Ambassador.'

The phrase recalled Duport. Widmerpool laughed nervously.

'You really oughtn't to say things like that, darling,' he said. 'Not when you're at a party like this. Nicholas and I think it very amusing, but someone else might overhear and not understand. If you really don't feel like being introduced at the moment, I shall have to leave you. Nicholas or someone can do the honours, if you decide you want to meet your host later. Personally, I think you should. If you do, make my apologies. I shall have to go now. I am late already.'

'Late for what?'

'I told you—I'm dining with the Minister.'

'You're giving me dinner.'

'I only wish I was. Much as I'd love to, I can't. I did explain all this before. You said you'd like to come to the party, even though we couldn't have dinner together after. Besides, I'm sure you told me you were dining with Lady McReith.'

'I'm going to dine with you.'

I was about to move away and leave them to it, feeling an engaged couple should settle such matters so far as possible in private, but Widmerpool, either believing himself safer with a witness, or because he foresaw some method of disposing of Pamela in which I might play a part, took me by the arm, while he continued to speak persuasively to her.

'Be reasonable, darling,' he said. 'I can't cut a dinner I've gone out of my way to arrange—least of all with the Minister.'

'Stand him up. I couldn't care less. That's what you'd do if you really wanted to dine with me.'

She was in a sudden rage. Her usually dead white face now had some colour in it. Widmerpool must have thought that a change of subject would cool her down, also give him a chance of escape.

'I'm going to leave you with Nicholas,' he said. 'Let me

tell you first, what you probably don't know, that Nicholas used to be a friend of your uncle, Charles Stringham, whom you were so fond of.'

If he hoped that information would calm her, Widmerpool made a big mistake. She went absolutely rigid.

'Yes,' she said, 'and Charles isn't the only one he knew. He knew Peter Templer too—the man you murdered.'

Widmerpool, not surprisingly, was apparently stupefied by this onslaught; myself scarcely less so. She spoke the words in a quiet voice. We were in a corner of the room behind some pillars, a little away from the rest of the party. Even so, plenty of people were close enough. It was no place to allow a scene to develop. Pamela turned to me.

'Do you know what happened?'

'About what?'

'About Peter Templer. This man persuaded them to leave Peter to die. The nicest man I ever knew. He just had him killed.'

Tears appeared in her eyes. She was in a state of near hysteria. It was clearly an occasion when rational argument was going to do no good. The only thing would be to get her away quietly on any terms. Widmerpool did not grasp that. He could perhaps not be blamed for being unable to consider matters coolly. He had now recovered sufficiently from his earlier astonishment to rebut the charges made against him and was even showing signs of himself losing his temper.

'How could you utter such rubbish?' he said. 'I see now that I ought never to have mentioned to you I had any hand at all in that affair, even at long range. It was a breach of security for which I deserve to be punished. Please stop talking in such an absurd way.'

Pamela was not in the least calmed by this remonstrance.

Quite the contrary. She did not raise her voice, but spoke if possible with more intensity. Now it was me she addressed.

'He put up a paper. That was the word he used—put up a paper. He wanted them to stop supporting the people Peter was with. We didn't send them any more arms. We didn't even bother to get Peter out. Why should we? We didn't want his side to win any more.'

Widmerpool was himself pretty angry by now.

'Because my duties happen to include the promulgation of matters appropriate for general consideration by our committee—perhaps ultimately by the Chiefs of Staff, perhaps even the Cabinet—because, as I say, this happens to be my function, that does not mean the decisions are mine, nor, for that matter, even the recommendations. Matters are discussed as fully as possible at every level. The paper is finalized. The decision is made. I may tell you this particular decision was taken at the highest level. As for not getting Templer out, as you call it, how could I possibly have anything to do with the action, right or wrong, for which the Operational people on the spot are responsible? These are just the sort of disgraceful stories that get disseminated, probably at the direct instance of the enemy.'

'You were in favour of withdrawing support. You said so. You told me.'

'Perhaps I was. Anyway, I was a fool to say so to you.'

His own rage made him able to stand up to her.

'Therefore you represented Peter's people in as bad a light as possible. No doubt you carried the meeting.'

She had absorbed the jargon of Widmerpool's employment in a remarkable manner. I remembered noticing, on occasions when Matilda differed with Moreland about some musical matter, how dexterously women can take in the ideas of a man with whom they are connected, then outmanoeuvre him with his own arguments. Widmerpool made a despairing gesture, but spoke now with less violence.

'I am only a member of the Secretariat, darling. I am the servant, very humble servant, of whatever committees it is my duty to attend.'

'You said yourself it was a rare meeting when you didn't get what you wanted into the finalized version.'

This roused Widmerpool again.

'So it is,' he said. 'So it is. And, as it happens, what I thought went into the paper you're talking about. I admit it. That doesn't mean I was in the smallest degree responsible for Templer's death. We don't know for certain even if he is dead.'

'Yes, we do.'

'All right. I concede that.'

'You're a murderer,' she said.

There was a pause. They glared at each other. Then Widmerpool looked down at his watch.

'Good God,' he said. 'What will the Minister think?'

Without another word, he pushed his way through the crowd towards the door. He disappeared hurriedly through it. I was wondering what on earth to say to Pamela, when she too turned away, and began to stroll through the party in the opposite direction. I saw her smile at the Swiss military attaché, who had rather a reputation as a lady-killer, then she too was lost to sight. Isobel and Madame Philidor reappeared from their visit to our hostess in purdah.

'The first wife looked kind, did you not think?' said Madame Philidor. 'The other perhaps not so kind.'

After this extraordinary incident, it seemed more certain than ever that an announcement would be made stating the engagement had been broken off. However, there were other things to think about, chiefly one's own demobilization; more immediately, arrangements regarding the

Victory Day Service, which took place some weeks later at St Paul's. I was to be on duty there with Finn, superintending the foreign military attachés invited. Among these were many gaps in the ranks of those known earlier. The several new Allied missions were not accommodated in the Cathedral under the Section's arrangements, nor were the dispossessed—Bobrowski and Kielkiewicz, for example—individuals amongst our Allies who had played a relatively prominent part in the war, but now found themselves deprived of their birthright for no reason except an unlucky turn of the wheel of international politics manipulated by the inexorable hand of Fate.

This day of General Thanksgiving had been fixed on a Sunday in the second half of August. Its weather seemed designed to emphasize complexities and low temperatures of Allied relationships. Summer, like one of the new régimes abroad, offered no warmth, but chilly, draughty, unwelcoming perspectives, under a grey and threatening sky. The London streets by this time were, in any case, far from cheerful: windows broken: paint peeling: jagged, ruined brickwork enclosing the shells of roofless houses. Acres of desolated buildings, the burnt and battered City lay about St Paul's on all sides. Finn and I arrived early, entering by the south door. Within the vast cool interior, traces of war were as evident as outside, though on a less wholesale, less utterly ruthless scale. The Allied military attachés, as such, were to be segregated in the south transept, in a recess lined with huge marble monuments in pseudo-classical style. I had been put in charge of the Allied group, because Finn decided the Neutrals, some of whom could be unreliable in matters of discipline and procedure, required his undivided attention. The Neutrals were to occupy a block of seats nearer the choir, the wooden carving of its stalls still showing signs of bomb damage.

'I'm glad to say no difficulties have been made about

Theodoric,' said Finn. 'He's been asked to the Service in a perfectly correct manner. It's not a large return for a lifetime of being pro-British—and accepting exile—but that's all they can do, I suppose. He'd be even worse off if he'd plumped for the other side. By the way, an ambulance party has been provided in the crypt, should any of your boys come over faint. I shall probably need medical attention myself before the day is over.'

I checked the Allied military attachés as they arrived. They were punctual, on the whole well behaved, whispering together with the air of children at a village Sunday school, a little overawed at the promised visit of the bishop of the diocese, glancing uneasily at the enigmatic sculptural scenes looming above them on the tombs. Among them, as I have said, were many absences and new faces. One regretted Van der Voort. A churchly background would have enhanced his pristine Netherlandish countenance. Colonel Hlava had returned to Prague. 'Russia is our Big Brother,' (the phrase had not yet developed Orwellian overtones) he had remarked to me some weeks before he left; even so, when the moment came to shake hands for the last time, he said: 'We can only hope.' Hlava was promoted major-general when he got home. Then, a year or two later, he was put under house arrest. He was still under house arrest when he died of heart failure; a flying ace and man one greatly liked.

Kucherman had gone back to a ministerial portfolio in the Belgian Government, his place taken by Bruylant, a quiet professional soldier, with musical leanings, though less marked than Hlava's and not of the sort to be expressed actively by playing duets with Dempster, had Dempster still been with the Section, not returned to his Norwegian timber. In place of Marinko—out of a job like the rest of his countrymen who had supported Mihailovich's Resistance Movement, rather than Tito's—was a newly arrived, long haired, jack-booted young 'Partisan' colonel, who talked a little French and, although possessing a Polish-sounding name, designated himself as 'Macédoin'. Macedonia was perhaps where Szymanski had come from too. One wondered what had happened to him.

Examining the neighbouring monuments more closely, I was delighted to find among them more than one of those celebrated in *The Ingoldsby Legends*, a favourite book of mine about the time when we lived at Stonehurst. There, for example, only a few feet away from where the military attachés sat, several figures far larger than life were enacting a battle scene in which a general had been struck from the saddle by a cannon ball, as his charger bore him at a furious gallop across the path of a kilted private from some Highland regiment. There could be no doubt whatever this was:

'... Sir Ralph Abercrombie going to tumble
With a thump that alone were enough to dispatch him
If the Scotchman in front shouldn't happen to catch him.'

Stendhal had seen these monuments when he visited London.

'Style lourd,' he noted. 'Celui d'Abercromby bien ridicule.'

Nevertheless, one felt glad it remained there. It put on record what was then officially felt about death in battle, begging all that large question of why the depiction of action in the graphic arts had fallen in our own day almost entirely into the hands of the Surrealists.

'La jolie figure de Moore rend son tombeau meilleur,' Stendhal thought.

This was against the wall by the side door through which we had entered the Cathedral, at right angles to the Abercrombie memorial. Less enormously vehement, this group too had its own exuberance of style, though in quite another mood. Here a sinister charade was being enacted by several figures not so gigantic in size. What they were doing was not immediately clear, until Barham's lines threw light on them too:

> 'Where the man and the Angel have got Sir John Moore,
> And are quietly letting him down through the floor.

I looked about for 'that queer-looking horse that is rolling on Ponsonby', but disappointingly failed to identify either man or beast in the immediate vicinity of the recess. The field of vision was too limited, only a short length of the nave to be viewed, where it joined the more or less circular area under the dome. However, recognition of these other episodes, so often pictured imaginatively in the past when the book had been read aloud by my mother—yet never for some reason appraised by a deliberate visit to St Paul's to verify the facts—mitigated an atmosphere in other respects oddly frigid, even downright depressing. With a fashionably egalitarian ideal in view, those responsible for such things had decided no mere skimming of the cream from the top echelons, civil and military, should be assembled together to give symbolic thanks for Victory. Everyone was to be represented. The congregation—except for those who had a job to do—had been handpicked from the highest official levels to the lowest.

For some reason this principle, fair enough in theory, had in practice resulted in an extension of that atmosphere of restraint, uneasy nervous tension, common enough in a larger or smaller degree to all such ceremonies. The sense of being present at a Great Occasion—for, if this was not a Great Occasion, then what was?—had somehow failed to take adequate shape, to catch on the wing those inner perceptions of a more exalted sort, evasive by their very nature, at best transient enough, but not altogether unknown. They were, in fact, so it seemed to me—unlike that morning in Normandy—entirely absent. Perhaps that was because everyone was by now so tired. The country, there could be no doubt, was absolutely worn out. That was the truth of the matter. One felt it in St Paul's. It was interesting to speculate who, among the less obvious, had been invited to the Service. Vavassor, for example? If so, was he wearing his blue frockcoat and gold-banded top hat? One of the ordinary security guards could look after the front-door for an hour or two. Had Blackhead been torn from his files to attend this Thanksgiving? If so, it was hard to believe he would not bring a file or two with him to mull over during the prayers. Q. (Ops.) Colonel? Mime? Widmerpool?

Meanwhile, the band of the Welsh Guards strummed away at Holst, Elgar, Grieg, finally Handel's 'Water Music'. Bruylant almost imperceptibly beat time with his forefinger, while he listened to these diversions, of which I felt Moreland would have only partially approved. The Jugoslav Colonel, rather a morose young man, did not seem altogether at ease in these surroundings. Possibly to reassure himself, he produced a pocket-comb and began to smooth his hair. General Cobb, contemplating the verdict on life's court-martial, was frowning darkly. I had all my charges in their seats by now, with a place to spare at the end of the row on which the Partisan could leave his cap. Someone might have failed to turn up because he was ill; possibly Colonel Ramos indisposed again. Then I saw Ramos in the back row, anxiously studying the service paper. I checked the list. They all seemed to be there. The Neutrals, in their position further east of the transept, had some of them shown inferior mastery of the drill; at least, not all were in their places in such good time as the Allies. Finn had rightly estimated them a more tricky crowd to manipulate.

He appeared to be finding difficulty in fitting his party into the available seats. It was too far to see for certain, but looked as if some flaw had been revealed in the organization. Finn came across the transept.

'Look here, Nicholas. I seem to have a South American too many.'

He clenched his teeth as if some appalling consequence were likely to overtake us as a result of that.

'Which one, sir?'

'Colonel Flores.'

'Can't place his country for the moment, sir.'

'You probably haven't heard of him. His predecessor, Hernandez, was recalled in a hurry for political reasons. It was thought Flores would not be in London in time for this show. There was a misunderstanding. The fact is things have never been the same with Latin America since we lost Borrit. You haven't a spare place?'

'As a matter of fact, I have, sir. I don't know why, because I've checked the list and no one seems ill or late.'

'They must have allowed for the Grand Duchy, whose military representative is in the Diplomatic block. The situation's saved. I'll bring Flores across.'

He returned a moment later with an officer wearing a heavy gold aiguilette, though without the sword that had survived the war in some South American ceremonial turnouts. Finn, evidently suffering stress at this last minute rearrangement, had taken Colonel Flores firmly by the arm—rather in the manner of General Conyers, with whom perhaps he had, after all, something in common—as if he were making an arrest and a dangerous customer at that. Flores, obviously appreciating the humour of this manhandling, was smiling. Dark, blue-chinned, with regular features, rather a handsome Mediterranean type, his age was hard to assess. He gave a quick heel-click and handshake on introduction.

'Major Jenkins will look after you, Colonel,' said Finn.

'Must leave you now or your colleagues will get out of hand.'

Flores laughed, and turned to me.

'I'm really frightfully sorry to be the cause of all this muddle,' he said. 'Especially as a bloody Neutral. Can you indeed accommodate me with your boys over here?'

This speech showed a rather surprising mastery of the English language, not to say unexpected psychological grasp of the British approach in such matters. One never knew what to expect from the South Americans. Sometimes they would speak perfect English like Colonel Flores, were sophisticated to a degree; alternatively, they would know not a word of any language but their own, seemed to find any ways but their own incomprehensible. Neutral military attachés were required to give notification of journeys made further than a given distance from London. The Latin Americans did not always observe this regulation. We would receive official reports from MI 5 chronicling jaunts with tarts to Maidenhead and elsewhere. Colonel Flores, one saw in a moment, was much too spry to be caught out in anything like that. He had only the smallest trace of an accent, that hard Spanish drawl that can be so attractive on the lips of a woman. The Flores manner was not unlike Theodoric's, short of Theodoric's ever present sense of his own royalty. In fact, anglicization was if anything almost too perfect, suggesting a smoothness comparable almost with Farebrother's. All the same, I immediately liked him. I caused the Jugoslav to take his cap from the spare seat and put it under his own chair, fitting in Flores next to him. If the Jugoslav came from Macedonia, he must be used to rubbing shoulders with all sorts of merging races, ought to have learnt early in life to be a good mixer. Perhaps in Macedonia things did not work that way. If he had not acquired the art, he would have to do so pretty soon, or give up hope of getting the best out of his

London appointment. Flores, smiling and apologizing, edged his way along the row, like a member of the audience arriving late for his stall at the opera. He safely reached the place at the end only a minute or two before the fanfare from Household Cavalry trumpets announced the arrival of the Royal Party on the steps of the Cathedral.

There was an impression of copes and mitres, vestments of cream and gold, streaks of ruby-coloured velvet, the Lord Mayor bearing the City Sword point upward, khaki uniforms and blue, a train of royal personages—the phrase always recalled Mr Deacon speaking of Mrs Andriadis's past—the King and Queen, the Princesses, King of the Hellenes, Regent of Iraq, King and Queen of Jugoslavia, Prince Theodoric. Colonel Budd, as it happened, was in attendance. The years seemed to have made no impression on him. White-moustached, spruce, very upright, he glanced about him with an air of total informality, as if prepared for any eventuality from assassination to imperfect acoustics. When the Royal Party reached their seats, all knelt. Prayers followed. We rose for a hymn.

> 'Angels in the height, adore him;
> Ye behold him face to face;
> Saints triumphant, bow before him,
> Gather'd in from every race.'

Under the great dome, saints or not, they were undoubtedly gathered in from every race. Colonel Flores and the Partisan Colonel were sharing a service paper. General Asbjørnsen, legitimately proud of his powerful baritone, sang out with full lungs. Hymns always made me think of Stringham, addicted to quoting their imagery within the context of his own life.

'Hymns describe people and places so well,' he used to

say. 'Nothing else quite like them. What could be better, for example, on the subject of one's friends and relations than:

> Some are sick and some are sad,
> And some have never loved one well,
> And some have lost the love they had.

The explicitness of the categories is marvellous. Then that wonderful statement: "fading is the world's best pleasure". One sees very clearly which particular pleasure its writer considered the best.'

Thoughts about Singapore: the conditions of a Japanese POW camp. Cheesman must have been there too, the middle-aged subaltern in charge of the Mobile Laundry Unit, that bespectacled accountant who had a waistcoat made to fit under his army tunic, and renounced the Pay Corps because he wanted to 'command men'. Had he survived? In any case there were no limits to the sheer improbability of individual fate. Templer, for instance, even as a boy innately opposed to the romantic approach, dying in the service of what he himself would certainly regard as a Musical Comedy country, on account of a Musical Comedy love affair. On the subject of death, it looked as if George Tolland was not going to pull through. An ecclesiastic began to read from Isaiah.

'The wilderness and the solitary place shall be glad for them; and the desert shall rejoice, and blossom as the rose . . . Strengthen ye the weak hands, and confirm the feeble knees . . . And the parched ground shall become a pool, and the thirsty land springs of water: in the habitation of dragons, where each lay, shall be grass with reeds and rushes. And an highway shall be there, and a way, and it shall be called The way of holiness; the unclean shall not pass over it; but it shall be for those: the wayfaring men, though fools, shall not err therein . . .'

The habitation of dragons. Looking back on the V.1's flying through the night, one thought of dragons as, physically speaking, less remote than formerly. Probably they lived in caves and came down from time to time to the banks of a river or lake to drink. The ground 'where each lay' would, of course, be scorched by fiery breath, their tails too, no doubt, giving out fire that made the water hiss and steam, the sedge become charred. Not all the later promises of the prophecy were easily comprehensible. An intense, mysterious beauty pervaded the obscurity of the text, its assurances all the more magical for being enigmatic. Who, for example, were the wayfaring men? Were they themselves all fools, or only some of them? Perhaps, on the contrary, the wayfaring men were contrasted with the fools, as persons of entirely different sort. One thing was fairly clear, the fools, whoever they were, must keep off the highway; 'absolutely *verboten*', as Biggs, Staff Officer Physical Training, used to say. Brief thoughts of Biggs, hanging by the neck until he was dead in that poky little cricket pavilion; another war casualty, so far as it went. The problem of biblical exegesis remained. Perhaps it was merely a warning: wayfaring men should not make fools of themselves. Taking the war period, limiting the field to the army, one had met quite a few wayfaring men. Biggs himself was essentially not of that category: Bithel, perhaps: Odo Stevens, certainly. Borrit? It was fascinating that Borrit should have remembered Pamela Flitton's face after three years or more.

'I've been in Spain on business sometimes,' Borrit said. 'A honeymoon couple would arrive at the hotel. Be shown up to their bedroom. Last you'd see of them. They wouldn't leave that room for a fortnight—not for three weeks. You'd just get an occasional sight of a brassed-off chambermaid once in a way lugging off a slop-pail. They've got their own ways, the Spaniards. "With a beard, St Joseph; without, the Virgin Mary." That's a Spanish proverb. Never quite know what it means, but it makes you see what the Spaniards are like somehow.'

There were more prayers. A psalm. The Archbishop unenthrallingly preached. We rose to sing *Jerusalem*.

> 'Bring me my Bow of burning gold;
> Bring me my Arrows of desire;
> Bring me my spear; O Clouds unfold!
> Bring me my chariot of fire!'

Was all that about sex too? If so, why were we singing it at the Victory Service? Blake was as impenetrable as Isaiah; in his way, more so. It was not quite such wonderful stuff as the Prophet rendered into Elizabethan English, yet wonderful enough. At the same time, so I always felt, never quite for me. Blake was a genius, but not one for the classical taste. He was too cranky. No doubt that was being ungrateful for undoubted marvels offered and accepted. One often felt ungrateful in literary matters, as in so many others. It would be interesting to know what the military attachés made of the poem. General Asbjørnsen certainly enjoyed singing the words. He was quite flushed in the face, like a suddenly converted Viking, joining in with the monks instead of massacring them.

Reflections about poetry, its changes in form and fashion, persisted throughout further prayers. 'Arrows of desire', for example, made one think of Cowley. Cowley had been an outstanding success in his own time. He had been buried in Westminster Abbey. That was something which would never have happened to Blake. However, it was Blake who had come out on top in the end. Pope was characteristically direct on the subject.

'Who now reads Cowley? If he pleases yet,
His moral pleases, not his pointed wit;
Forgot his epic, nay Pindaric art,
But still I love the language of his heart.'

But, admitting nobody read the *Pindarique Odes*, surely the pointed wit was just what did survive? In Cowley's quite peculiar grasp of the contrasted tenderness and brutality of love, wit was just the quality he brought to bear with such remarkable effect:

'Thou with strange adultery
Doest in each breast a brothel keep;
Awake, all men do lust for thee,
And some enjoy thee when they sleep.'

No poet deserved to be forgotten who could face facts like that, the blending of conscious and unconscious, Love's free-for-all in dreams. You only had to compare the dream situation with that adumbrated by poor old Edgar Allan Poe—for whom, for some reason, I always had a weakness—when he trafficked in a similar vein:

'Now all my days are trances
And all my nightly dreams
Are where thy grey eye glances,
And where thy footstep gleams—
In what ethereal dances
By what eternal streams.'

Ethereal dances would have been no good to Cowley, by eternal streams or anywhere else. He wanted substance. That verse used to run in my head when in love with Jean Duport—her grey eyes—though she laid no claims to being a dancer, and Poe's open-air interpretive choreography sounded unimpressive. However, there were no limits when one was in that state. We rose once more for another hymn, 'Now thank we all our God', which was, I felt pretty sure, of German origin. Whoever was responsible for choosing had either forgotten that, or judged it peculiarly apposite for this reason. We had just prayed for the 'United Nations' and 'our enemies in defeat'. In the same mood, deliberate selection of a German hymn might be intended to indicate public forgiveness and reconciliation. Quite soon, of course, people would, in any case, begin to say the war was pointless, particularly those, and their associates, moral and actual, who had chalked on walls, 'Strike now in the West' or 'Bomb Rome'. Political activities of that kind might by now have brought together Mrs Andriadis and Gypsy Jones. The Te Deum. Then the National Anthem, all three verses:

'God save our gracious King!
Long live our noble King!
God save the King!
Send him victorious,
Happy and glorious
Long to reign over us;
God save the King!

O Lord our God arise
Scatter his enemies,
And make them fall.
Confound their politics,
Frustrate their knavish tricks,
On thee our hopes we fix;
God save us all.

Thy choicest gift in store
On him be pleased to pour;
Long may he reign!
May he defend our laws,
And ever give us cause
To sing with heart and voice,
God save the King!'

Repetitive, jerky, subjective in feeling, not much ornamented by imagination nor subtlety of thought and phraseology, the words possessed at the same time a kind of depth, an unpretentious expression of sentiments suited somehow to the moment. It would be interesting to know whether, at the period they were written, 'reign' had been considered an adequate rhyme to 'king'; or whether the poet had simply not bothered to achieve identity of sound in the termination of the last verse. Language, pronunciation, sentiment, were always changing. There must have been advantages, moral and otherwise, in living at an outwardly less squeamish period, when the verbiage of high-thinking had not yet cloaked such petitions as those put forward in the second verse, incidentally much the best; when, in certain respects at least, hypocrisy had established less of a stranglehold on the public mind. Such a mental picture of the past was no doubt largely unhistorical, indeed totally illusory, freedom from one sort of humbug merely implying, with human beings of any epoch, thraldom to another. The past, just as the present, had to be accepted for what it thought and what it was.

The Royal Party withdrew. There was a long pause while photographs were taken outside on the steps. The Welsh Guards turned their attention to something in Moreland's line, Walton's 'Grand March'. Orders had been issued that the congregation was to leave by the south portico, the door just behind us. It was now thrown open.

Finn and I drove the military attachés like sheep before us in that direction. Once in the street, they would have to find their own cars. The last of them disappeared into the crowd. Finn drew a deep breath.

'That appeared to go off all right.'

'I think so, sir.'

'Might have been trouble when we couldn't fit that fellow in.'

'He was quite happy with my lot.'

'Nice chap.'

'He seemed to be.'

'Going back now?'

'I was, sir. Shall I get the car?'

Something was troubling Finn.

'Look here, Nicholas, will you operate under your own steam—leave me the car?'

'Of course, sir.'

Finn paused again. He lowered his voice.

'I'll make a confession to you, Nicholas.'

'Yes, sir?'

'A friend of mine has sent me a salmon from Scotland.'

That was certainly a matter for envy in the current food situation, though hardly basis for the sense of guilt that seemed to be troubling Finn. There was no obvious reason why he should make such a to-do about the gift. His voice became a whisper.

'I've got to collect the fish.'

'Yes, sir?'

'At Euston Station.'

'Yes?'

'I'm going to take the Section's car,' said Finn. 'Risk court-martial if I'm caught. Be stripped of my VC. It's the only way to get the salmon.'

'I won't betray you, sir.'

'Good boy.'

Finn nodded his head several times, laughing to himself, looking even more than usual like a Punchinello.

'After all, we've won the war,' he said. 'We've just celebrated the fact.'

He thought for a moment.

'Another thing about Flores,' he said. 'Just while I think of it. The Foreign Office are very anxious to keep in with his country. They want us to give him a decoration. He's going to get a CBE.'

'But he's only just arrived.'

'I know, I know. It's just to improve relations between the two countries.'

'But we were frightfully stingy in what we handed out to the Allies in the way of decorations after six years. Hlava told me he didn't know how he was going to face his people when he reported what we offered. Foreigners expect something after they've worked with you for ages.'

'The argument is that we like to make our decorations rare.'

'And then we hand one out to a chap who's just got off the plane.'

'It's all a shambles,' said Finn. 'You get somebody like myself who does something and gets a VC. Then my son-in-law's dropped in France and killed, and no one ever hears about him at all, or what he's done. It's just a toss-up.'

'I didn't know about your son-in-law.'

'Long time ago now,' said Finn. 'Anyway, Flores is going to get a CBE. Don't breathe a word about the car.'

He turned away and stumped off towards the car park. It had evidently been a heavy decision for him to transgress in this manner; use a War Department vehicle for a private purpose, even over so short a distance. This was an unexpected piece of luck so far as I was concerned. Just what I wanted. There had seemed no avoiding going back with

Finn to duty, when in fact some sort of a break was badly required. Now it would be possible to walk, achieve adjustment, after the loaded atmosphere of the Cathedral. One was more aware of this need outside in the open air than within, when the ceremony was just at an end. After all, one did not every day of the week attend a Thanksgiving Service in St Paul's for Victory after six years of war. It was not unreasonable to experience a need to mull things over for half an hour or so. The ritual itself might not have been exactly moving, too impersonal for that, too well thought out, too forward-looking in the fashionable sense (except for the invocation to confound their politics and frustrate their knavish tricks), but I was aware of some sort of inner disturbance, though its form was hard to define. There were still large crowds round the Cathedral. I hung about for a while by the west door, waiting for them to disperse.

'So you were lucky enough to be invited to the Service?'

It was Widmerpool.

'I've been superintending the military attachés.'

'Ah, I wondered how you got here—though of course I knew they selected at all levels.'

'Including yours.'

'I did not have much trouble in arranging matters. What a splendid ceremony. I was carried away. I should like to be buried in St Paul's—would prefer it really to the Abbey.'

'Make that clear in your will.'

Widmerpool laughed heartily.

'Look, Nicholas,' he said. 'I'm glad we met. You were present at a rather silly incident when Pam and I had a tiff. At that embassy. I hope you did not attribute too much seriousness to the words that passed.'

'It was no business of mine.'

'Of course not—but people do not always understand her moods. I flatter myself I do. Pamela is undoubtedly *difficile* at times. I did not wish you to form a wrong impression.'

'All's made up?'

'Perfectly. I am glad to have this opportunity of putting you right, if you ever supposed the contrary. The very reckless way she was talking about official matters was, of course, the sheerest nonsense. Perhaps you hardly took in how absurd she was being. One can forgive a lot to a little person who looks so decorative, however. Now I must hurry off.'

'The Minister again?'

'The Minister showed the utmost good humour about my lateness on that occasion. I knew he would, but I thought it was right for Pam to be apprised that official life must take precedence.'

He went off, infinitely pleased with himself, bringing back forcibly the opinion once expressed by General Conyers:

'I can see that fellow has a touch of exaggerated narcissism.'

The scene with Pamela had been altogether dismissed from Widmerpool's mind, as he had risen above failure with Mrs Haycock. Just then I had other things to ponder: Isaiah: Blake: Cowley: the wayfaring men: matters of that sort that seemed to claim attention.

A lot of people were still about the streets, making progress slow, so at the foot of Ludgate Hill I turned into New Bridge Street in the direction of the river. There was no need to hurry. A stroll along the Embankment might be what was required. Then my mind was suddenly recalled to duty. Colonel Flores was walking in front of me. Seeing a foreign military attaché, even a Neutral one, was at once to experience the conditioned reflex, by now second-nature, that is to say instant awareness that he must be looked after to the best of my ability, although not one of my own particular charges. I caught him up and saluted.

'I think you're going the wrong way for the official car park, Colonel, it's—'

Flores seized my hand and smiled.

'None of my arrangements have been official today,' he said. 'In fact none of them have been properly conducted at all. My car had another job to do after dropping me at the Cathedral, so I arranged to meet it, when all was over, in one of the turnings off the Embankment. I thought there would be no parking difficulties there, whatever happened elsewhere. Was not that a brilliant idea? You must admire my knowledge of London topography.'

'I do, sir.'

'Come with me. I'll give you a lift to wherever you want to go.'

It was no use explaining that I only wanted to walk by the river for a while, to be left alone briefly, to think of other things for a time, before returning to our room to complete whatever remained to be done. There was a fair amount of that too.

'You know London well, Colonel?'

'Not really. It was all done with a map, this great plan for the car. Am I not a credit to our Staff College?'

'It's your first visit?'

'I was here—what—fifteen years ago, it must be. With all my family, an absolute tribe of us. We stayed at the Ritz, I remember. Now we will cross the road and advance west along the line of the Thames.'

He led the way to a side turning.

'The car should be somewhere near this spot. Ah, here they are. It had to go and pick up my wife and step-daughter.'

An oldish Rolls, displaying a CD number plate, was drawn up by the pavement in one of the streets running north and south. It was a little way ahead. As we approached, two ladies stepped out and walked towards us. They both looked incredibly elegant. In fact their elegance appalled one. Nobody in England had been able to get hold of any smart clothes for a long time now—except for the occasional 'unsolicited gift' like Matilda's—and the sight of these two gave the impression that they had walked off the stage, or from some display of exotic fashions, into the street. Colonel Flores shouted something in Spanish. We came up with them.

'This is Major—'

'Jenkins.'

'Major Jenkins was incredibly kind to me in St Paul's.'

Madame Flores took my hand. In spite of the sunlessness of the day, she was wearing spectacles with dark lenses. When I turned to the younger one, her charming figure immediately renewed those thoughts of Jean Duport the atmosphere of the Cathedral had somehow generated. This girl had the same leggy, coltish look, untaught, yet hinting at the same time of captivating sophistications and artifices. She was much tidier than Jean had been when I first set eyes on her, tennis racquet against her hip.

'But why was it necessary to be so kind to Carlos?' asked her mother.

She spoke English as well as her husband, the accent even less perceptible.

'Major Jenkins allowed me to sit in his own special seats.'

'How very grand of him to have special seats.'

'Otherwise there would have been nowhere but the steps of the altar.'

'A most unsuitable place for you, Carlos.'

'We are going to take Major Jenkins as far as Whitehall.'

The tone of Colonel Flores with his wife was that of a man in complete control. She seemed to accept this. All the same, she began to laugh a lot.

'Nick,' she said. 'You look so different in uniform.'

'You know each other already?' asked Flores.

'Of course we do,' said Jean.

'But we haven't met for a long time.'

'This is perfectly splendid,' said Colonel Flores. 'Come along. Let's jump into the car.'

It was not only the dark lenses and changed hair-do. Jean had altered her whole style. Even the first impression, that she had contracted the faint suggestion of a foreign accent, was not wholly imaginary. The accent was there, though whether result of years in foreign parts, or adopted as a small affectation on return to her own country as a wife of a foreigner, was uncertain. Oddly enough, the fact of having noticed at once that Polly Duport looked so like her mother when younger, made the presence of Jean herself less, rather than more, to be expected. It was as if the mother was someone different; the daughter, the remembered Jean. About seventeen or eighteen, Polly Duport was certainly a very pretty girl; prettier, so far as that went, than her mother at the same age. Jean's attraction in those days had been something other than mere prettiness. Polly had a certain look of her father, said to be very devoted to her. She seemed quite at ease, obviously brought up in a rather old-fashioned tradition, Spanish or exported English, that made her seem older than her age. Relations with her step-father appeared cordial. The whole story began to come back. Duport himself had spoken of the South American army officer his wife had married after her affair with Brent.

'He looks like Rudolph Valentino on an off day,' Duport had said.

Colonel Flores did not fall short of that description; if anything, he rose above it. He seemed not at all surprised that his wife and I knew each other. I wondered what sort of a picture, if any, Jean had given him of her life before their marriage. Probably reminiscence played no part whatever in their relationship. It does with few people. For that matter, one did not know what the former life of Flores himself had been. We exchanged conversational banalities. Formal and smiling, Jean too was perfectly at ease. More so than myself. I suddenly remembered about Peter. She had always been fond of her brother, without anything at all obsessive about that affection. His death must have upset her.

'Poor Peter, yes. I suppose you heard over here before we did. He didn't write often. We were rather out of touch in a way. Babs was sent the official thing, being rather in with that sort of world, and as . . .'

She meant that, in the circumstances, her elder sister had been informed of Templer's death, rather than his wife.

'Used you to see anything of him?' she asked.

'Once or twice at the beginning of the war. Not after he went into that secret show.'

'I don't even know where it was.'

'Nor me—for certain.'

One suddenly remembered that she was the wife of a Neutral military attaché, with whom secret matters must even now not be discussed.

'It's all too sad. Why did he do it?'

This was not really a question. In any case, to speak of Pamela Flitton would be too complicated. Bob Duport was better unmentioned too. The car was not an ideal place for conversations of that sort, especially with her husband present.

'You must come and see us,' she said. 'We're really not properly moved in yet. I expect you know we've only just arrived. The appointment was quite a surprise—due to a change of Government.'

She mentioned an address in Knightsbridge, as it happened not far from the flat at the back of Rutland Gate, where once, quite naked, she had opened the door when we were lovers. Like so many things that have actually taken place, the incident was now wholly unbelievable. How could this chic South American lady have shared with me embraces, passionate and polymorphous as those depicted on the tapestry of Luxuria that we had discussed together when we had met at Stourwater? Had she really used those words, those very unexpected expressions, she was accustomed to cry out aloud at the moment of achievement? Once I had thought life unthinkable without her. How could that have been, when she was now only just short of a perfect stranger? An absurd incident suddenly came into my head to put things in proportion. Representatives of the Section had to attend an official party the Greeks were giving at the Ritz. In the hall, a page-boy had said to another: 'General de Gaulle's in that room over there'. The second boy had been withering. He had simply replied: 'Give me news, not history.' Jean, I remembered, had become history. Perhaps not so much history as legend, the story true only in a symbolical sense; because, although its outlines might have general application to ourselves, or even to other people, Jean and I were no longer the persons we then had been.

'Where would you like the chauffeur to drop you?' asked Colonel Flores.

'Just on this corner would be perfect.'

There were a lot more assurances, endless ones, that we must meet again, in spite of difficulties about getting the flat straight in the midst of such shortage of labour, and the imminence of demobilization, which would be followed by absence from London. I got out. The car drove off. Jean turned and waved, making that particular gesture of the hand, the palm inwards, the movement rather hesitating, that I well remembered. Vavassor had not been at the Service. He was on duty in the hall when I came through the door. We had a word together.

'Big crowd?'

'Pretty big.'

'Dull day for an affair like that.'

'Very dull.'

'How did the King look.'

'I was too far away to see.'

'All your foreigners?'

'Yes.'

Later in the afternoon I took some letters up to Finn for signature. He was sitting in his chair looking straight ahead of him.

'I got that fish.'

'You did, sir?'

'Home and dry.'

'A great relief?'

Finn nodded.

'Did I tell you David Pennistone is going to join our Paris firm?' he said.

Pennistone, though he would not reveal before he left what his post-war plans were, had said they would make me laugh when I heard them.

'I think the work will appeal to him,' said Finn. 'He wants a change. Tired of all that . . .'

He paused, searching for the right word.

'Liaison?'

'No, no,' said Finn. 'I don't mean his work here. All that . . . philosophy.'

He smiled at the absurdity of the concept.

'Any idea what you're going to do yourself when you get out of uniform, Nicholas?'

I outlined a few possibilities. Even on my own ears, they sounded grotesque figments of a fevered imagination. Finn accepted them apparently; anyway for what they were worth. I excused myself by adding that the whole idea of starting up all that sort of thing again after six years seemed strange enough.

'Remember Borrit?' asked Finn.

It already seemed a hundred years since Borrit had been with the Section, but I admitted his image faintly lingered on. Finn pushed back his chair. He spoke slowly.

'Borrit told me when he was serving on the Gold Coast, one of the Africans said to him: "What is it white men write at their desks all day?"'

Finn nodded his head several times.

'It's a question I've often asked myself,' he said. 'Ah, well. Let's see those files, Nicholas.'

Just before my own release was due, I went to take formal leave of General Philidor, whose staff by this time lived in one of the streets off Grosvenor Square. I looked in on Kernével's room on the way out, but he was not at home. Then, when I reached the pavement outside, someone shouted from a top storey window. It was Kernével himself.

'Wait a moment—I'm coming down.'

I returned to the hall. Kernével came clattering down the stairs. Travelling at high speed, he was red in the face.

'Some wine's arrived from France. Come and have a glass. We're in one of the upper rooms.'

We climbed the stairs. I told him this was probably the last time we should meet officially.

'You know that French writer you spoke about? Something to do with a *plage*—in *Normandie*?'

'Proust?'

'That's the one. I've been into it about him. He's not taught in the schools.'

Kernével looked severe. He implied that the standards of literature must be kept high. We reached a room on the top floor with which I was not familiar. Borda, Kernével's assistant—who came from Roussillon and afterwards married an English girl—was there, with a French captain called Montsaldy, who seemed responsible for the wine. There were several bottles. It was a red Bordeaux, soft and fruity after the Algerian years. We talked about demobilization.

'It is true your army gives you a suit of clothes when you retire?' asked Borda.

'More than just a suit—shirt, tie, vest, pants, socks, shoes, hat, mackintosh.'

'Some of the uniform I wore in North Africa will do for civilian life, I think,' said Borda. 'In the hot weather.'

'I carried tropical uniform in the other war,' said Montsaldy, who looked a grizzled fifty. 'It wears out quickly.'

'Me, too,' said Kernével. 'Tropical uniform always makes me think of Leprince. He was a big fellow in our platoon. Ah, Leprince, *c'était un lapin*. What a fellow. We used to call him *le prince des cons*. That man was what you call well provided. I remember we were being inspected one day by a new officer. As I say, we were in tropical uniform. The major came to the end of the line where Leprince stood. He pointed to Leprince. "A quoi, cet homme?" '

Kernével jumped to attention and saluted, as if he were the platoon sergeant.

' "C'est son sexe, mon commandant."

"C'est dégoûtant!" '

Kernével made as if to march on, now acting the outraged major.

'He was an old fellow,' he said, 'white haired and very religious.'

We all laughed.

'Borda's blushing,' said Kernével. 'He's going to be married quite soon.'

That was the last time Kernével and I met in uniform,

but we used to see each other occasionally afterwards, because he continued to work in London. Indeed, we shared a rather absurd incident together a few years after the war was over. Kernével had been awarded an MBE for his work with us, but for some reason, the delay probably due to French rather than British red tape, this decoration did not 'come through' for a long time. Kernével, at last told by his own authorities he could accept the order, was informed by ours that it would be presented by the CIGS; not, of course, the same one who had held the post during the war. Kernével, also notified that he might bring a friend to witness the ceremony, invited me to attend. We were taken to the Army Council Room—Vasassor, too, seemed by now to have faded away—where it turned out the investiture consisted of only half-a-dozen recipients, of whom Kernével was the only Frenchman. When the citations were read out, it appeared the rest had performed prodigies of bravery. There were two Poles, an American, an Australian and a New Zealander, perhaps one or two more, all equally distinguished operationally, but whose awards had for one reason or another been deferred. The Field-Marshal now CIGS—again not the one whose Tactical HQ we had visited—was a very distinguished officer, but without much small talk. Huge, impressive, *sérieux* to a degree, he was not, so it appeared, greatly at ease in making the appropriate individual remark when the actual medal was handed out. Before this was done, an officer from the Military Secretary's branch read aloud each individual citation:

'In the face of heavy enemy fire . . . total disregard for danger . . . although already twice wounded . . . managed to reach the objective . . . got through with the message . . . brought up the relief in spite of . . . silenced the machine-gun nest . . .'

Kernével came last.

'Captain Kernével,' announced the MS officer.

He paused for a second, then slightly changed his tone of voice.

'Citation withheld for security reasons.'

For a moment I was taken by surprise, almost immediately grasping that a technicality of procedure was involved. Liaison duties came under 'Intelligence', which included all sorts of secret activities; accordingly, 'I' awards were automatically conferred without citation. It was one of those characteristic regulations to which the routine of official life accustoms one. However, the CIGS heard the words with quite other reactions to these. Hitherto, as I have said, although perfectly correct and dignified in his demeanour, his cordiality had been essentially formal, erring if anything on emphasis of the doctrine that nothing short of unconditional courage is to be expected of a soldier. These chronicles of the brave had not galvanized him into being in the least garrulous. Now, at last, his face changed and softened. He was deeply moved. He took a step forward. A giant of a man, towering above Kernével, he put his hand round his shoulder.

'You people were the real heroes of that war,' he said.

Afterwards, when we walked back across the Horse Guards, Kernével insisted I had arranged the whole incident on purpose to rag him.

'It was a good leg-pull,' he said. 'How did you manage it?'

'I promise you.'

'That's just what you pretend.'

'I suppose it would be true to say that there were moments when the Vichy people might have taken disagreeable measures if they had been able to lay their hands on you.'

'You never know,' said Kernével.

The final rites were performed the day after I took wine with the Frenchmen in Upper Grosvenor Street. Forms were signed, equipment handed in, the arcane processes of entering the army enacted, like one of Dr Trelawney's Black Masses, in reverse continuity with an unbelievable symmetry of rhythm. I almost expected the greatcoat, six years before seeming to symbolize induction into this world through the Looking Glass, would be ceremonially lifted from my shoulders. That did not take place. Nevertheless, observances similarly sartorial in character were to close the chapter. This time the *mise-en-scène* was Olympia, rather than the theatrical costumier's, a shop once more, yet at the same time not a shop.

Olympia, London's equivalent of colosseum or bull-ring, had been metamorphosed into a vast emporium for men's wear. Here, how often as a child had one watched the Royal Tournament, horse and rider deftly clearing the posts-and-rails, sweating ratings dragging screw-guns over dummy fortifications, marines and airmen executing inconceivably elaborate configurations of drill. Here, in the tan, these shows had ended in a grand finale of historical conflict, Ancient Britons and Romans, Saxons and Normans, the Spanish Armada, Malplaquet, Minden, Waterloo, the Light Brigade. Now all memory of such stirring moments had been swept away. Rank on rank, as far as the eye could scan, hung flannel trousers and tweed coats, drab macintoshes and grey suits with a white line running through the material. If this were not a shop, what was it? Perhaps the last scene of the play in which one had been performing, set in an outfitter's, where you 'acted' buying the clothes, put them on, then left the theatre to give up the Stage and find something else to do. Or were those weird unnerving shapes on the coat-hangers anonymous cohorts of that 'exceeding great army', who would need no demob suits, but had come to watch the lucky ones?

'Ropey togs,' said a quartermaster-captain.

'The hats are a bit *outré*,' agreed a Coldstreamer with a

limp. 'But one of those sports jackets, as I believe they're called, will come in useful in the country.'

Assistants round about were urbane and attentive. They too seemed to be acting the part with almost passionate dedication, recommending the garments available with the greatest enthusiasm. Was this promise of a better world? Perhaps one had reached that already and this was a celestial haberdasher's. The place was not even at all crowded. Most of the customers, if that was what they ought to be called, looked about forty, demobilization groups taking precedence on points gained by age, length of service, period overseas and so on. We wandered round like men in a dream. As one moved from suits to shoes, shoes to socks, socks back again to suits, the face of a Gunner captain seemed familiar. In due course we found ourselves side by side examining ties.

'This pink one with a criss-cross pattern might not look too bad for occasions,' he said thoughtfully. 'We used to meet sometimes, didn't we?'

'Aren't you called Gilbert?'

'At dances years ago.'

Archie Gilbert had been the 'spare man' *par excellence* for every hostess in need, perfectly dressed, invariably punctual, prepared to deal with mothers or daughters without prejudice regarding looks or age, quietly conversational, unthinkable as taking a glass too much or making unwelcome advances in a taxi. His work had been believed to be in a firm concerned with non-ferrous metals, whatever they might be, though it had never been easy to imagine him in day clothes doing an ordinary job. However, in spite of that outward appearance, he had somehow or other taken on a world war. His fair moustache was a shade thicker, he himself had filled out, indeed become almost portly. Otherwise, more closely examined, he had not greatly changed. His appearance, always discreetly military, had, as it were, camouflaged him from instant recognition at first sight. His uniform—he wore very neat battledress, of normal cloth, otherwise cut rather like the Field-Marshal's—was as spick and span as his evening clothes had always been. We talked of our respective war careers. He had been in an anti-aircraft battery stationed in one of the northern suburbs of London. One pictured a lot of hard, rather dreary work, sometimes fairly dangerous, sometimes demanding endurance in unexciting circumstances. Perhaps experience in the London ballrooms had stood him in good stead in the latter respect. It was impossible to remain incurious about the question of marriage; which of the scores of girls with whom he used to dance he had finally chosen. Perhaps his bachelor gifts were still too overwhelming to be extinguished in matrimony. I crudely asked the question. Archie Gilbert nodded, smiling gently.

'Used I to meet your wife in those days?'

He shook his head, smiling again.

'We ran across each other when I was with the battery,' he said. 'Her family lived just over the road.'

There the matter rested. He divulged no more. We talked of some of the girls we had known in the past.

'Haven't seen any of them for ages,' he said. 'One hears their names occasionally. Usen't you to know Barbara Goring, who married Johnny Pardoe? He was rather odd for a time—melancholia or something—then he went back to the army and did well in Burma, I believe. Rosie Manasch had a lot of ups-and-downs, they say, with Jock Udall. Of course, he was shot by the Germans after that mass attempt to escape from a POW camp. Rosie was a great character. I used to like her a lot.'

He unfolded an evening paper.

'If you were doing liaison work with the Poles, you may know the one who's just married Margaret Budd. Do you remember her? What a beauty. I don't know what happened to her husband, whether he was killed or whether it didn't work. He was quite a bit older than her and distilled whisky.'

He held out the paper. Margaret Budd's bridegroom was Horaczko; the marriage celebrated at a registry office. The paragraph below recorded another wedding at the same place. It was that of Widmerpool and Pamela Flitton. Archie Gilbert pointed a finger towards this additional item.

'That name always sticks in my mind,' he said. 'Barbara Goring once poured sugar over his head at a ball of the Huntercombes'. It was really too bad. Made an awful mess too. Have you decided what you're going to take from the stuff here? It might be much worse. I think everything myself.'

'Except the underclothes.'

# André Brink

One of South Africa's
leading Afrikaner Writers

**An Instant in the Wind** **£2.50**

'It is difficult to see how any South African novelist will be able to surpass the honesty of this novel' *World Literature Today*

**A Dry White Season** **£2.50**

Winner of the Martin Luther King Memorial Prize, 1980. 'The revolt of the reasonable . . . far more deadly than any amount of shouting from the housetops' *Guardian*

**A Chain of Voices** **£2 95**

This novel transforms a political statement into a compelling and moving artistic achievement. 'A triumph' *The Times*

# SIMONE DE BEAUVOIR

**She Came to Stay** £3.50
The passionately eloquent and ironic novel she wrote as an act of revenge against the woman who so nearly destroyed her life with the philosopher Sartre. 'A writer whose tears for her characters freeze as they drop.' *Sunday Times*

**The Mandarins** £3.95
'A magnificent satire by the author of *The Second Sex. The Mandarins* gives us a brilliant survey of the post-war French intellectual . . . a dazzling panorama.' *New Statesman*. 'A superb document . . . a remarkable novel.' *Sunday Times*

**When Things of the Spirit Come First** £1.95
The five women at the centre of this novel are all enmeshed in the moral and social demands of middle-class society. Even those among them who try to be rebels themselves are hobbled by their upbringing and their self-deception.

'It is because of women like Simone de Beauvoir that the prejudice and repression of which she writes no longer has such effect.' *Over 21*